Note:
Sale of this book without a front cover may be unauthorized. If this book was purchased without a cover, it may have been reported to the publisher as "unsold or destroyed". Neither the author nor the publisher may have received payment for the sale of this book.

Published by
La' Femme Fatale' Productions
9900 Greenbelt Road
Suite E-333
Greenbelt, MD 20706
www.LaFemmeFataleProductions.com

For Information regarding special discounts or bulk purchases, please contact La' Femme Fatale' Productions at (866) 50- femme and info@lafemmefataleproductions.com

Library of Congress Catalog Card No: In publication data
ISBN: 978-0-9792656-0-0

Charge it to the Game Credits:
Written by: Michele A. Fletcher
Edited by: L.A. Smith & BE'N ORIGINAL
Publicist: Andrea Ferguson
Text Formation: BE'N ORIGINAL for UMA Marketing
Cover Graphics: BE'N ORIGINAL for iDesignFlyers.com
Concept Design and Layout by: UMA & Dream Relations
Project Consultant: Dawn Michelle for Dream Relations
Photography by: Reggie Anderson

Manufactured in Canada at Transcontinental

LA FEMME

CHARGE IT TO THE GAME

AN URBAN NOVEL BASED ON A TRUE STORY

Dedication

I dedicate this book to my three daughter's Mone', Jade & Nyya whom I adored more then life itself.

To my husband Francis E. Fletcher who has always been there for me.

To my mother Vivian A. Mason-Lewis who was my mother and father, who gave me life and continues to be there for me unconditionally wrong or right.

To my dear friend Loretta Williams we share a sister hood unlike any other which stems from whom we both are.

A Note From The Author

I wrote this book with plenty of time to reflect on my life and my actions. While serving a 48 month sentence in Federal Prison for illegal credit card manufacturing , I decided to start jotting down some thoughts on paper about things that have transpired in my lifetime. After compiling several pads of my writing together, I sat back and realized damn, all this drama would make a great novel. After adding some embellishments, Charge It To the Game was the end result.

Being incarcerated was very trying and difficult at times. Being away from my children and family seemed unbearable. In the beginning I felt as if I didn't deserve to be in my situation, but as time allowed me to reflect, I realized that my situation was a result of the choices I had made. After coming to terms with facing the responsibility of my actions, I wanted my time to be as well spent as possible … so I wrote a lot.

I would like to apologize to my children and my family for having to take them through this roller coaster ride. The time that was taken away from me being a mother to my children can never be repaid. Those years can never be relived. I can only make use of the lessons I've learned and make the most of the time I have now.

I never chose to look at myself as a victim of my circumstances or feel like I was just dealt a bad hand in life. There are plenty of people far more successful than I could imagine who were brought up in similar surroundings if not worse. I did make a series of bad choices however that led me to the federal penitentiary. I now realize that if I had applied as much energy to lawful endeavors as I did to the illegal ones, I would be better off.

Since my release, I have had to overcome several obstacles associated with being in the life I chose to live. I am picking up the pieces and spend everyday thankful for my kids. My activity in their lives is my number one priority. I have also started a publishing company La Femme Fatale Productions and will release Charge It To the Game as the first novel. Although it is fictional, I have pulled some personal experiences from my own life. I hope that Charge It To the game is found to be entertaining as well as intriguing. I thank you for reading Charge It To the Game and look forward to further entertaining you with more great books to follow.

Thanks again and God Bless.
Michele A. Fletcher

Acknowledgements

First in foremost I would like to thank God. Without you I couldn't have made it this far. Without your blessing it wouldn't have been possible.

Megan Cameron- my one and my only niece auntie love's you always. Dance your heart away Dancing Diva!

Monique Cameron- To my big sister! Thank you for being you. I love you with all my heart.

Scott Greene- Thank you for one of the most precious gift of them all, Our Daughter Mone'.

Robert Lewis- In appreciation for all you have done.

Concetta Mason-Wyatt- Thank you for being there through the struggles. Everybody should have an aunt like you.

Alicia Brown- For all the endless nights of pushing me to get this project done. I thank you.

To my Publishing Company La'Femme Fatale who don't know what that name means better ask somebody.

Edgar Gamory- Real recognize real at all times. Much love!

Dexter Williams- Who don't know better ask somebody, because he the player of the SOUTH!

Lester Simpson- It's been a long struggle and I can't say anything but thank you.

BE'N ORIGINAL - To my Marketing Manger, we been grinding together through this project from the beginning, you never let me down, much love!

Andrea Ferguson- To my Publicist, I wouldn't have made it without you.

Dawn Michelle Hardy- To my literary agent, I love when a plan comes together.

To all my family thanks for being there every step of the way.

I would like to give a shout out to all my friends that have been there for me. Keep your head up!

To all my Sister's and Brother's on lockdown, never stop believing because you will make it through in life.

Now for all my hater's all I can do is laugh at you because ya'll thought I wouldn't make it but look at me now!!!! HAHAHAHAHA-HAHAHAHAHAHAHAHAHAHAHAHAHAHAHAHAHAHAHAHA-HAHAHAHAHAHAHAHAHAHAHAHAHAHAHAHAHAHAHAHA-HAHAHAHAHAHA

Praise For Charge It To The Game

"Charge it the Game is a remarkable story, had me fiending for more. Writers better step their game up." — K. Elliott Essence Bestselling Author & Coauthor of The Ski Mask Way on G-Unit Books

"Michele Fletcher's debut novel is clearly in a class by itself. By far, Charge It to The Game is the most honest and heart wrenching urban tale since Black Girl Lost. She clearly succeeds Teri Woods as genre's best female author of all time."
— Urban Magazine

"Charge it to the Game is a lively tale surely to rile readers who imagine what it's like to be the boss" —Bone Crusher, Gold Selling Atlanta Rapper

"Interesting read. A page turner from cover to cover!" —Young B, Recording Artist

"Michele is not trying to get paid she is trying to stay paid by penning this awesome page turner for the streets. —Rio CEO, Stay Paid Records

"Don't keep this great read on the hush... spread the word Charge it to the Game is fire." —Edgar Gamory, CEO Hush Records

"Michele Fletcher puts her pen game down and stays true to the streets with Charge it the Game her debut novel." —Star, Fearless Artist Entertainment.

"Michele Fletcher is one to watch in 2007... In addition to the drama, sizzling sex, and crafty money making schemes Charge it to the Game is a gutsy tale starring a provocative and brazen main character. " —XPOZ Magazine

Like a well crafted song, it build in intensity until its explosive ending. -Scott D. Greene, CEO 4 Real Doe Entertainment

Prelude

BOOM! I was awakened by a loud, yet distant crashing sound. As I tried my best to maintain my composure, I found myself overcome by single thought … what the hell is going on. It was then; I heard the weighted footsteps of several people aggressively into my home. Reaching for Victor, I felt only the warm empty space of where he should have been laying. He was gone.

Moments later, I heard Victor's booming voice rising from the bottom of the stairs, followed by a series of distorted incoherent shouts and the unmistakable sound of what could only be weapon discharge. From my experiences of being in the streets, I could tell it was a 9mm. In a blind panic, I jumped from the bed shouting, "No!"

Carefully opening the door to the bedroom, I looked toward the stairway. I could only see shadowy figures moving around on the lower level of my home. They call themselves peace officers. What kind of keepers of the peace storms your home at the midnight hour, firing semi-automatics? Peace my ass, I know gang bangers who would have made less commotion. The term under these kinds of circumstances is completely absurd. There was nothing peaceful or tranquil about their actions that night. But what should I have expected, my life had been many things, but peaceful was not one of them. It was never a part of my world. It was only an illusion from time to time that left me for the most part unprepared for the forthcoming violence and chaos.

Flashlights beamed through every window illuminating the hallways of my house, detailing every wall, staircase and entryway.

While some whispered, others just didn't give a fuck. I could hear their adrenaline charged voices elevated outside in the hallway. The static from the chirps of the communication devices was distinct. I realized the loud crash was the sound of the reinforced front door being taken off its hinges. I listened intently to see what else I could hear and heard another loud crash, which could only have been my antique vase falling to the floor and breaking into a million pieces. Damn that shit cost a lot of money! Probably more than any one of those pricks made in a year! No kind of respect for people's shit! At this point any attempt of discretion was long gone. These sorry bastards were tearing my damn house apart.

Looking toward the area where my front door used to be, I saw Victor lying spread out on the floor. Already unable to stand, one of the so called "peace officers" continued to shock him with a taser gun. I clutched my abdomen and fell to the floor on my knees, struggling to breathe. As I got up and rushed back to the bed, I wanted to lie down and pretend that this had all been a bad dream, but I knew it was not. As I sat on the edge of the bed waiting for someone to enter, my heart continued to pound. I felt the cold painful rush of adrenaline coursing through my veins. We were trapped. "Damn it", I muttered to myself.

I could not say that I was completely caught off-guard. I took in the situation that I had pictured in my mind a thousand times. I thought I knew what to do. I was to grab the bag in my closet, get the girls and escape through the window, but they had us outnumbered. I felt like I was envisioning my soon to be eminent death. How am I going to play this out? It can't end like this. Not here and damn sure not now.

I darted around panicking like a chicken with its head cut off trying to think of something to do. Think Erica, think. I had to get my children out of here fast. I wasn't sure how deep the home invaders were numbered or if they would try to shoot me if they saw me sneaking through the hallways. My mind started calculating as it often did. I knew there was no way I could reach the girls' room without being seen. I had to figure something out. Think! Think! There was no way we could make it out. Even if I could slip out undetected, leaving my angels behind was not an option.

"Shit," I whispered to myself, as I heard the loud footsteps coming up the stairs. Slowly… one by one I heard them approaching my bedroom door. They were coming in…

Chapter 1

Erica Payne was born the younger sister of two children. Although it may have appeared that she was born with somewhat of a silver spoon in her mouth, her life was always filled with turmoil. Her father, Gregory Payne, also known in the streets as Big G, was a well respected confidence man. His scams and pitches were as legendary as the fear and respect he gained in the Fort Greene section of Brooklyn. He was the Tony Montana of his time.

Although most people from the neighborhood knew exactly where to find him, none would ever divulge his whereabouts to the countless number of detectives that often came searching for him for fear of any reprisals. A fear that was well-deserved. He had learned early on that he had to make extreme examples of those that crossed him. An occasional torture or floater in the nearby beaches was nothing to Big G. What had to be done was done with no questions asked. But of course there was always your hustler that thought he could outdo Big G and be naïve enough to violate. He would quickly meet his demise and make the front page of the Daily News as "another victim of urban street life".

Now don't get things twisted, G never took a man's life unless it was absolutely necessary. He enjoyed breaking people down. Death was too easy. He'd rather a hustler give up his spots voluntarily rather than having to take them by force. He got more respect from disabling someone, not only physically, but emotionally as well. The bottom line was he was ruthless.

Erica's mother, Dorothy, was the complete opposite of Gregory. She was absolutely beautiful and her family and close friends always said she was the spitting image of Vanessa Williams, from her creamy light brown complexion, to her long wavy hair and hazel eyes. Dorothy had something about her that just commanded the attention of everyone when she entered a room. All the women were jealous of her and all the men wanted to be her one and only true love. She was often told that she could have been anything in life if not under the controlling thumb of Gregory. She was beauty and brains all mixed into one. Her parents had hopes that she would graduate high school and go straight to college to become some high executive or even a business owner one day. But after getting together with Gregory, what followed was the birth of her children and a life of physical and emotional abuse. Her only hope was that her daughters would go much further in life and she could live vicariously through them.

At the start of Dorothy and Gregory's relationship, she thought things couldn't get any better. Their relationship was the epitome of the saying "good girls love bad boys." Gregory was everything that Dorothy fantasized about. At 18, Gregory had the three most important things: money, power and respect. Gregory was handsome and cunning. He was six feet tall, with a rich chocolate complexion. His deep set brown eyes were said to be his best attribute. When he looked into your eyes, it was almost as if he was looking through to your soul. To top it off he had a beautiful smile with one dimple in the left cheek and the body of a Greek god, and was always dressed to impress. Every girl in the neighborhood wanted to be with him, even if they were afraid to say so.

Although Dorothy knew of Gregory's ill habits, she couldn't resist his charm, sex appeal, and most of all, his power. The day that Gregory caught the eye of this quiet and shy girl from a well-respected family, he knew he had to have her. She was different from all the other women who lusted after him and from day one he knew that Dorothy would be his and his only.

Things were great between Dorothy and Gregory, but Dorothy's parents weren't fooled by his charm and pretty-boy looks. They saw Gregory for what he was, a street hustler and a womanizer who equaled bad news for their oldest daughter. But it seemed like the more they tried to keep her away from Gregory, the closer the two became until things were at the point of no return. Gregory had Dorothy wrapped around his finger and he knew that he could get her to do whatever he wanted, when he wanted.

Not long after Dorothy and Gregory had been together, she got pregnant. She was distraught and afraid, and had no idea how Gregory would react. Keeping it from him for the first two months of her pregnancy, Dorothy had become an Oscar worthy actress. She hid her morning sickness and her gaining of weight by blaming it on this or that while G ran the streets unknowing of her true condition. It wasn't until Gregory got arrested that Dorothy was forced to reveal her secret. She was afraid that she would end up alone and pregnant. Although she was working a nine-to-five at a local bank, she knew that it wasn't enough to take care of herself and her child. She had to tell Gregory so that he could make sure everything was taken care of even if he was incarcerated. When Gregory got released on a technicality,

Dorothy was happy that she had come clean, especially when she saw how excited G was. He catered to her every need and told her that he would be there for her and do everything he could do for his unborn child, who he had obsessively hoped would be a boy.

During Dorothy's second trimester, the couple found out that they would be having a baby girl and Gregory was outraged. He started throwing a fit blaming the sex of the child on Dorothy. This was a side of Gregory that she had never seen and grew very afraid of him and his sudden outburst. She threatened to leave and stay with her younger sister, Kat, but Big G quickly regained his composure apologizing for his behavior and telling Dorothy he would love his child no matter what.

Eight months pregnant now, Dorothy was awakened in the middle of the night to find out that Gregory had been arrested again, this time on a drug and gun possession charge. Once again she found herself afraid and alone. While in custody, Big G told her that he had everything taken care of. He pointed her in the direction of his most trusted men on his team who would make sure that her bills were paid and that she had someone to accompany her on her doctor's visits, as well as anything else she needed. All she had to do was be in charge of all his money, which meant overseeing transactions. Dorothy was afraid at first because although she was with Gregory, she was never directly involved in his business. But Gregory used his charm once again, telling her that her handling his money was no different than handling the money at the bank. Dorothy trusted Gregory's words and did what he asked.

Gregory had a few months before his trial and used this time to set up his family. Dorothy gave birth to a healthy baby girl that she named Monica Christina Payne, and the couple married not long after Monica's arrival. Gregory made sure to leave Dorothy a nice amount of money to keep the family secure. Gregory's trial came, and he was sentenced to three years in prison.

After Gregory went away, there were times when Dorothy cried herself to sleep thinking about all the horrible things that could have been happening to him while in prison. She also thought about the fact that she was now alone and a single mother. But as the days and nights got shorter, Dorothy learned to miss Gregory less and less. Although she was able to get along better without him, she visited him twice a month and made sure that their little Monica Christina knew who her father was. Dorothy juggled her nine-to-five at the bank. And with the help of her sister who cared for Monica during the day Dorothy worked Gregory's business during free hours.

As time went on, Dorothy noticed a change in Gregory. He had always been a hard ass in the streets, but he was sweet to her aside from when he found out his first child was going to be a girl. He now had become cold towards her and by year two, he had even asked her not to visit as much, blaming it on the fact that he couldn't handle not being able to be with his family. Dorothy was heartbroken, for she had been standing by her husband and wanted so hard for their marriage to stand the final year of G's prison term, but he was making things unbearable for her. Dorothy realized that all she could do was move on and the only person she could trust was herself.

* * *

She had to be the best mother that she could be for Monica, and that's exactly what she did.

Dorothy had put her all into her job and had been promoted to manager at the bank. She also took pride in managing G's business and had become very well respected in the game. She made very wise business decisions and made sure that G got the best product for his money. When Gregory was finally released from prison, he returned to their apartment in the Fort Greene projects. Not only had Gregory changed in appearance, but his demeanor was now cold and uncaring. For many nights at a time Gregory would disappear and return days later as if nothing had happened. She continued to play her role as the loving and faithful wife catering to him and making love to him when he wanted it. And through it all, Dorothy hoped that things would get better and the love that they had once shared would return, but she had no such luck.

Gregory had been home six months, when Dorothy found out she was pregnant again. Gregory acted unconcerned about his second child, and even more indifferent when he found out that Dorothy was having another girl. He didn't do anything for his wife during her pregnancy. He refused to bring her food when she complained of being hungry in the middle of the night, calling her lazy and ungrateful. He was so emotionally detached that he would allow one of his workers to accompany Dorothy on her doctor's visits.

He pushed her out of his business dealings completely, feeling slightly jealous of the credibility she attained during his prison term. While Dorothy struggled with work, Monica, and being pregnant, Big G was running the streets with various women and had even started smoking his own product. He had only been out for two years when he was arrested again, this time for trying to pick up an undercover cop posing as a prostitute and for possession of cocaine. During his short stint in prison, his dependence grew and as a result his handle on business was starting to slip.

Once again Dorothy was left to have a baby alone and pick up the slack of Gregory's illegal endeavors. In 1981, Erica Renee Payne was born and Dorothy wondered how she would handle everything with a newborn baby added on to her responsibilities. Luckily she still had her sister to lean on.

As the girls grew older, Dorothy noticed extreme differences between their personalities. Monica was always the more reserved of the two. Although not shy and introverted, Monica didn't come close to Erica's daring and outgoing personality. And as much as their childhoods were alike, their lives could not have been more dissimilar. Monica was very focused in school and always talked about going to college to become a lawyer or a famous doctor. She spent little time socializing and more time with her head in the books. Meanwhile, Erica lacked in the education department, not because she wasn't smart enough, but because of her behavior. Erica loved to learn and was a very bright girl, but she hated being cooped up in a classroom all day and usually caused disturbances in class or didn't go altogether. Things were even worse when her father was around.

When Gregory returned home from prison, Dorothy was determined to make her marriage work. For years she had tried to be a better wife, cooking and cleaning, caring for their children and working to support her family, and all the while Gregory made things worse by spending the family's money on his drug habit and having his other women calling and harassing Dorothy at home. If that wasn't bad enough, he had also started becoming verbally abusive. He would degrade her in front of the children, yelling and screaming in tirades of curses and anger. His late nights would usually end with him coming home in the morning drunk and high, screaming obscenities and picking fights with Dorothy. Monica tried to be supportive of her mother, hugging and consoling her when she cried after their father's outbursts, but Erica stayed away, building anger and hatred for her father who only brought pain and strife to the one person who tried so hard to make everyone happy.

As Monica tried to appease her father and be the good daughter, Erica lashed out which often resulted in physical altercations with Gregory. Dorothy would try to intervene, telling her husband that their daughter was just a child and didn't deserve his lashes of anger and instead of continuing to lash out on Erica, he would take his anger out on Dorothy, leaving her body emotionally and sometimes physically scarred. But all of this only made Erica stronger, and she vowed that one day she would get the evil bastard back.

Erica's life continued to be conflicted. While other kids in the neighborhood were going to the local public school, Erica was being driven to elite private schools where she didn't fit in with her rich white classmates, so she usually stayed to herself.

Holidays were usually glum. Christmas' were spent quietly in the Payne home when Gregory was there. Erica and Monica weren't allowed to make any noise or any kind of mess while opening presents. A lot of the time Dorothy would have to sneak the girls extra gifts because Gregory thought showering them with toys was going to spoil them rotten. Dorothy usually made plans for them to go somewhere fun like Miami Beach or skiing in Utah to help make the holidays memorable.

Dorothy believed that sending her daughters away for school would make up for the stress that G caused when they came home. It didn't make sense to him and this was an ongoing issue, but nevertheless Dorothy felt it was her best effort at protecting her girls from sharing her disappointing life.

Compared to other children in the projects, the Payne sisters' were considered royalty. They attended the best schools, had nice clothes and always had food on the table. Despite all the niceties that separated Erica and her family from other families in Fort Greene, her father refused to move them to an upscale residence. He was so fixated on being this hood celebrity that he didn't see how foolish it was to continue staying in the projects when they could afford to move somewhere better.

"The grass is always greener," seemed to be the motto that Erica lived by. People looking in thought she had it pretty good. Big G looked as though he was taking care of home and carried on a good front in the streets. Yes he lived at home, and yes he paid the bills, but not much else came with that but abuse, anger and pain. Erica witnessed more than her fair share of life's so-called ups and downs. With all the perks and benefits of being her father's child, also came the distractions and pitfalls. Erica's major fault with her father was his treatment of her mother. In today's society, what might be called bipolar disorder was then known as being "just a little off". She would see her father treat her mother like his queen one minute and then treat her like a worthless bitch, the next. She often wondered how one person could take so much abuse from another. She knew that her mother had to have a breaking point, but so far she hadn't come to it. Erica saw her mother's devotion to her father as a weakness and knew that wasn't a trait she possessed.

Although being what was considered the more subservient of the two genders, she vowed to dominate all the men in her life; all but one… her father.

Chapter 2

As soon as Erica made it to the top step of the subway stairs, the warm summer breeze slapped her in the face. She ran her fingers through her long hair trying to keep it from becoming a bird's nest on top of her head, New York summer wrecked havoc on the tresses. She always had to look her best and she had a ways to go before reaching her parents' apartment. The all white Reebok Classics made her light on her feet, as she moved silently through the noisy streets of Brooklyn. Erica traveled along in an easy but swift gait, passing over broken concrete, glass bottles and crack vials that lined the streets of Myrtle Avenue. Covering the final two blocks of her destination, she stopped for a quick moment to catch her breath. She was so deep in thought that she hadn't even realized how fast she was walking. She stared into a calm puddle of water that was left from an early morning sun shower and wondered what her life would be like if her father wasn't around. In her heart she built tower of anger and resentment towards the man she knew as her father.

She quickly snapped out of her thoughts and began admiring her reflection in the puddle. She noted, to her dismay for probably the hundredth time that her size was diminutive compared with other girls her age. At seventeen, Erica barely stood four-feet-ten inches and weighed a mere 105 pounds. Her petite frame was willowy and lean.

Her dark colored hair was finely textured and long, usually pulled back in a tight ponytail, which accented her almond-shaped brown eyes, set in a smooth milk-chocolate face. For her frame, Erica had full breasts and an "apple bottom" that usually caught the attention of the opposite sex.

The light buzz of a dimly lit street light overhead brought Erica's attention back to the present surroundings. Normally, Erica would not be in the streets alone. The Fort Greene Projects of Brooklyn was usually too dangerous for solo treks, even for someone brought up in the streets like her. Continuing on her way, Erica noticed the soft blue glow of her entrance way. The hue was a mixture of the iridescent light and shitty industrial paint that adorned the project doors.

Erica was always nervous when she came to this point of her journey, which consisted of tunnels, back allies, and passages that she used to get there. She turned down the volume on her headphones, slowed her pace, and looked around to make sure it was safe before entering. There have been many occasions when local hustlers and gamblers were known to have shoot outs in or around the building and unfortunately there was only one way to get in or out and that was the front entrance. Erica knew that she had to come to this place—the place that she feared to spend a minute more than she had to; a place that brought her nothing but pain and misery … The place that she unfortunately called home.

Since her husband refused to move, Dorothy Payne decided that she would "trick" out her apartment like the rich and famous, making her meager project residence into Fort Greene's rendition of the Taj Mahal. The entire right wall of the apartment was designed with elaborate imported mirrors, and the other side was a sophisticated accent wall with a mural of the ocean. The furniture in the living room was comprised of a blue subtle suede sectional and an Italian glass coffee table. The kitchen was canary yellow with fully loaded matching LG appliances. Dorothy Payne's apartment was the definition of ghetto fabulous in vision and in persona of those who lived with all of the drama and ass "whippings" that went on.

Erica had made it through the building unscathed and rushed through the door of the Payne home. She carefully closed the door behind her, trying not to make a sound. The apartment was quiet, which was a rare occurrence. Silence in the Payne house was a small prelude to the arguments between her mother and father that constantly filled the air. Silence, Erica learned early on, was something to be treasured, but not for long.

Taking a deep breath, Erica closed her eyes and stretched out her senses. She could feel uneasiness in her spirit as she moved from room to room. As she walked through the house to her bedroom, she could feel it... his presence was all around her. Her drunken bull-headed father was home. The sound of his heavy intoxicated breathing was clue enough, but it was his smell that told her for sure that he was there. It was a mixed smell of musk from fading cologne and Hennessy, and a distant sound that came from the muffled sobs of Dorothy crying in another room. He was waiting for Erica and she knew it, but she thought that if she could make it to her safe-haven she would be alright and escape yet another altercation with this monster.

Erica rushed into her bedroom and closed the door behind her. Staring at her empty bed, she thought back to the times that she would find Monica curled up under the covers trying to escape the screaming, arguing, slaps and punches of their parents' bickering. But now Erica was alone... to deal with the drama on her own. Monica had made her escape to Howard University earlier the year before and came home as little as possible. She had even decided to stay for the summer sessions just to avoid coming home to the ongoing drama.

Hoping to make it through the night without dealing with her father's bullshit, Erica threw down her Louis Vuitton backpack and MP3 player on the bed and walked towards her closet to get undressed for the evening. She had some last minute homework assignments to do and then she was going to call it a night. She had already picked up something to eat on the way home to limit the amount of face time that she had to spend with her parents. As she began to undress, she went to open her closet door and was awe struck. All of her clothing was gone. Erica's clothes were her mark on the outside world. They were her most prized possessions and now her closet lay empty. All of her cashmere sweaters, Bebe dresses, Fendi handbags, vintage leather coats, dozens of Jimmy Choo strappy stilettos, Cole Haan loafers, Hermes and D&G belts, Puma, Nike and Adidas, kicks, her impressive jeans collection which consisted of Rock and Republic, Seven, Antik, and True Religon , everything was gone.

What the fuck is this? She thought to herself as the anger and fury filled her. For a second she thought that maybe someone had been playing a cruel joke and that her clothes would be hidden somewhere like under the bed. Unlikely however, because no one in the house had a sense of humor, and emptying her closet wasn't her idea of a joke. She raced towards her twin-sized bed, dropped to her knees and searched vigorously for the clothes that she knew weren't there.

"Shit!" She screamed out not knowing what to do. Erica walked back to her closet making sure that her eyes weren't playing tricks on her… they weren't. All of her things were missing

"Mom!" Erica's voice echoed through the house. She had to get to the bottom of this. Erica paced the floor as she waited for her mother, only her mother didn't come. Instead it was him, her father, standing in the doorway with a twisted smile on his face.

"What's the problem Erica? Are we missing something?" He snickered.

"Where are my clothes? I know you took them? Why the fuck would you take my clothes?"

"Bitch, who the fuck do you think you're talking to? I run this house, I pay the bills. When you start paying for shit around this house, then maybe you might have some kind of say, but until then shut the fuck up. You ain't need all that shit anyway. What the fuck does someone your age know about Jimmy Choo or whatever the fuck that shit is? You are walking around here like you some kind of Princess Diana or some shit. This will teach you to stay in your lane and act your fucking age. I know that little nigga's been buying you all that shit. Tell that youngin' he best keep it moving 'cause you're my responsibility and I takes care of this."

Erica was so upset she couldn't even speak. All she wanted to do was knock the shit out of Gregory and then find out where all her clothes were. She forced herself to speak through her tears of anger and rage. "I'm going to ask you one more time. Where is my shit?"

"I gave that shit to the Salvation Army. I'm sure there are more fucking deserving people that would appreciate that shit," he said, slurring his words and showering Erica's doorway with saliva.

Erica had enough. Without thinking, she grabbed her cheerleading trophy off of her dresser and heaved it in Gregory's direction with all her might. Whether it was intentional or not, a corner of the trophy connected with the right side of her father's head as he attempted to duck, leaving a jagged gash above his eye.

Before Erica could take advantage of the opening, Gregory recovered and was on her like white on rice. His large frame towered over her body as he unleashed his drunken rage blow after blow. Despite the fact that this was his own flesh and blood, it was beyond a father's attempt of discipline. He was going to beat her like a complete stranger.

Although Erica was quick and nimble, her dad being the far more experience fighter easily cornered her against her closet door. She continued swinging as hard as she could with but rarely connected while trying to block his relentless attack. While she managed to cover her head and face, he began to systematically break her down by pummeling her arms and legs until she was barely able to protect herself at all. She had clearly started something that she could not finish. It was becoming more than obvious to Erica, it was a no-win situation.

"That's enough!" screamed a voice from the hallway. Dorothy rushed in and jumped on Gregory's back, trying to get him away from their youngest child. Though Erica had been disrespectful, she didn't deserve this. He was going too far. Struggling to remove Dorothy from his back, Gregory was so distracted he failed to see Erica rise to her feet. However, the throbbing agony from a well placed kick that all but crushed his testicles got his complete attention. Overcome with pain, Gregory finally gave up, lowering Dorothy to the floor; he hobbled out of the room. Erica dropped to the floor crying, trying to figure out what she was going to do. Sooner or later, her father's pain would subside and there was likely to be a rematch. As much as she wanted to stick around for her mother's sake, she couldn't continue to live like this.

Dorothy stood over Erica, looking behind her to make sure that Gregory hadn't decided to come back and finish off the job. Once she was sure that he wasn't coming back, she turned her attention to her daughter. The fire and fury in Erica's eyes scared even Dorothy, but she was just relieved that her daughter was OK outside of a swollen lip and a few scratches and bruises on her face and arms. She wasn't hurt as bad as she had been in the past.

"It's all right, baby. It's all right," Dorothy cooed. But Erica knew that it wasn't alright and she wasn't sure if it ever would be.

Chapter 3

Erica woke up the next morning with a pounding headache and soreness all over her body. She grimaced in pain as she slowly rose from her bed. She reached into her drawer happy to find that at least the bastard had left her some underwear and a few sundresses that couldn't fit in her closet. After getting her things together for a shower, Erica opened her door slowly and looked from left to right making sure the coast was clear. When she was sure that things were quiet, she moved as fast as she could towards the bathroom for a hot shower and some aspirin.

After her shower, Erica walked into the kitchen. Sunlight poured through the room as Dorothy finished the last of breakfast on the stove and served it to Erica. Erica was usually excited to eat her mother's cooking, but one problem she noticed was that her mom fucked up everything when she and Gregory had serious issues. There was too much salt in the eggs, the pancake batter was rubbery, the grits were lumpy, and the biscuits crumbled. Aside from that, she just wasn't in the mood to eat anything after last night.

The two women were alone in the house, safe from Gregory who was out in the streets, probably drinking and getting high. Dorothy fully expected this moment with Erica. Gregory and Erica's fights were common sights in her home; a fact that only saddened her more. Gregory had swept Dorothy off her feet when they met, but it was clear by now that the Payne's lives were far from perfect. They damn sure were no Cliff and Claire Huxtable. Dorothy thought back to when Gregory promised that he would take care of her. She cringed at the thought of her life. Between Gregory's time in jail, drinking and getting high, and spending time in the arms of other women, he had yet to fulfill his promise. Dorothy had been hurt and humiliated so many times, she was beginning to wonder if she would ever recover.

"Listen, your father was just trying to teach you some humility," Dorothy tried to explain. "I'll talk to him later about trying to get some of your clothes back." Erica looked at her mother in disbelief.

"Do you really believe that crap that he tells you? Wake up Mommy; he was just doing it out of spite. He doesn't give a damn about my stuff. And what's the point of even bringing it up, all he gonna do is beat on you again?" Erica grumbled back.

"You have got to work with me Erica," Dorothy pressed, desperate for her daughter to calm down.

"But, I don't want him to keep hurting you," Erica replied. Her tone carried the weight of her emotions. Dorothy sighed, taking a seat next to her daughter.

"Listen, it is going to be alright. He is a difficult man, but all he's trying to be is a good father." Erica could not believe what she was hearing. Her mother was her world but she couldn't help but feel like the bitch had lost her mind.

Rising from the table, Erica walked back to her room. She grabbed her keys and book-bag and headed for the door. Before her mother could ask where she was going she shouted angrily, "I'm going to Aunt Kat's", slamming the door behind her. Dorothy, realizing her error, stared at the untouched plate still on the table.

Erica was tired of fighting at home and in the streets. The fight with her father was her second altercation of the day. After school she had a fight with a girl named Chante over her boyfriend Victor. It was already known that Chante had been trying to get with Victor, but on top of that she had been throwing dirt on Erica's name and even had the nerve to step to Victor in front of everybody, knowing that it would get back to Erica. To Erica, that was blatant disrespect and the bitch had the ass whooping coming to her. To have to deal with the nightmare of the events with her father and mother left her stressed.

Erica walked through the streets of Brooklyn, with all types of things going through her mind, but the most pertinent thought was of how she was going to get her father back. Erica shook away the feelings of tears and focused on getting to her destination. Although she was just seventeen, she had seen her fair share of the world but at times she felt that she knew nothing. Feeling confused and alone, Erica knew that there was only one person she could talk to... Victor.

Erica had known Victor Davis most of her life. They had attended middle school together, along with Antwan Robinson also known as Twan, and her best friend Tracy Fields. Twan and Victor were just two little boys who loved music. Even from back in the day Victor and Twan would sit at the lunchroom table pounding their little fists on the table making beats. Victor's dream was always to own his own record label.

Although Erica and Victor had known each other, they didn't get together until later on. They were just really cool and she cared deeply for him, as she did for all of her friends. She was just happy to be out and about and away from all the drama at home. Whenever Gregory would go away to prison, Erica's life was better and it showed in everything that she did. Her attitude was better and her friends were actually allowed to hang out at her house. As junior high school came to an end, Victor and Erica were almost inseparable. Victor was the only man that Erica trusted and every time she would get into a fight with her father, Victor promised that one day he would take her away from it all.

When junior high ended, Dorothy sent Erica to Bishop Loughlin, which was a private high school in downtown Brooklyn. Her friend Tracy also attended that school and that's where they both met Kim Johnson and Crystal Pierce. The girls became fast friends and did everything together. They became known as the "Diva Squad" because they never let anyone else into their crew and they had a way about them that screamed diva. The girls shared great passion for coveting designer clothing they saw in fashion magazines. Even though Twan and Victor didn't attend the same school, they all stayed in touch. Victor had started dabbling in the street life and took his boy, Twan along for the ride. By the twelfth grade, Victor had made a name for himself and used the money that he was making in the drug business to start a small record label, signing all the acts from around the way that he thought he could make famous. All in all for a boy Victor's age, he was doing big things. He dropped out of school citing he was already making money and school was taking up to much of his town. He already had a brand new car and a two family house in Clinton Hill section of Brooklyn.

By Erica's sixteenth birthday she and Victor was a real item, and everyone knew it. Victor couldn't stand what Erica had been going through at home and threatened to take Gregory out on several occasions. But for whatever reason Erica never allowed him to act on his anger. Instead she took whatever it was that Gregory had to offer, in hopes that one day things would get better.

The phone rang twice before Katrina, also known as Kat, answered.

"Hello?"

"Hey Kat, it's me," Dorothy's voice uneasily came through the phone.

"Hey sis, how are you doing?"

"Fine… I mean, I don't know."

"It's him again isn't it?" Kat already knew the answer before she even finished. There was silence on the other end, as Kat waited for Dorothy to finish. Dorothy sighed, as she started to regret having to call her sister. She was feeling bad enough without having to hear Kat go through her usual lecture about Gregory and their children.

"Yes, it's him. Erica and Gregory got into it last night again."

"Really who won?" Kat asked amused.

"Neither, I broke it up. But listen, Erica is on her way to your house right now. Could you please talk to her? Watch her for me," Dorothy said as she began to cry. No longer amused, the pleading tone in Dorothy's voice was enough to break Kat's heart.

"Sure love, anything else?" Kat loved her sister so much and there was nothing that she wouldn't do for Erica and Monica, but she couldn't understand her sister's devotion to her slime of a husband. She could only hope that he wouldn't harm her sister or nieces worse than he had already done and she prayed that they wouldn't make the same mistakes as their mother had.

"No that's it. Thanks Kat. I love you."

"I know… I love you too. I will call and check on you later."

"Yeah, bye."

"Bye." Kat hung up the phone and went into the kitchen to prepare for Erica. Kat had been a mentor and a friend to Erica for many years. Dorothy's younger sister was wild and took things to the extreme. In all honesty, Kat was just like Erica, and these characteristics made Erica love her even more.

Kat had just finished making breakfast, when she heard the key wrestling in the lock. The door opened and Erica walked in.

"Hey Aunt Kat," she said. The smile on her face represented the happiness of seeing her favorite relative. Kat embraced her niece with a warm hug, which was promptly returned. Erica was so wrapped up with greeting her aunt that she almost paid no attention to the freshly prepared food in the kitchen. Her favorite breakfast of homemade apple cinnamon pancakes that Kat had been making for her since she was three, sat on the table. For her to have some of her famous pancakes already prepared, meant something was up. Moving into the kitchen Erica shrugged and sat down. Kat finished cooking the last of the stack before adding a dab of butter on top, then glossed it over with maple syrup. A small satisfied smile appeared on her lips as she saw Erica's reaction to the scent of the meal before her. The pancakes were all made from scratch and took some special preparation; Erica had a real weakness for the dish. The willful girl gave her a small nod, which told Kat that the price for information had been met.

"Hungry?" asked Kat.

"A little," replied Erica, remembering her mother's food at home, but her stomach felt otherwise. Kat served the pancakes and sat attentively as Erica told her story. When it was all said and done Kat let out a breath of relief as she reflected on all that her niece had told her. The situation was not too bad, but definitely not good either. All and all Erica was safe as long as she stayed with Kat. Erica finished her meal scraping her plate clean. Kat gave her niece an astonished look, taking into consideration that her niece only had the food in front of her for less than five minutes.

Satisfied, Erica rose from the table. “Aunty, can I use your phone?” Kat nodded her approval. Erica hurried into the living room, as Kat looked at the empty plate. Damn that girl can eat, she thought.

* * *

“Dorothy, where the hell is that daughter of mine!” Gregory yelled as he returned from his “errands”, once again being loud and demanding. Dorothy had hoped that it would be different this time when he came home, but it only seemed to get worse, and she wondered why she even put up with him.

“Dee, are you listening?” Gregory growled. Dorothy met his stare with a smile.

“Yes dear,” her tone dripping with sarcasm. But Gregory hardly noticed and continued with his ranting.

“Dee, you know this shit is all your fault! You are always letting her do anything she wants.” Gregory stopped for a moment to consider his next words. “But that shit is going to stop right here and right now, the minute she gets home.” Gregory sat in his favorite chair with confidence, waiting for round two with Erica if and when she finally decided to come home.

Erica walked out of the front door of her aunt’s four-story brownstone on Bedford Avenue and was grinning from ear to ear. Victor was the only person that made her feel complete and seeing him sitting in front of her aunt’s apartment building made her forget her problems if only for that split second. The smile that lit up his face when he saw her told her that he felt the same way.

"What's up, Ma?" he said, jumping out of his truck walking towards her. Victor was fine. He had light-brown eyes and a dark-brown complexion that washed over his chiseled body. He had a smile that lit up Erica's world and a short fade that he always kept fresh. He stood at about six-foot-two and had the look of an NFL quarterback. "Your mother told me you were over here, what's going on?"

"I need to talk to you." Victor knew Erica very well— well enough to know that there was something bothering her and suddenly a concerned look covered his face.

"Hey Ma, let's go sit in the truck so we can talk." As soon as they got inside the truck, Erica began to explain all of the shit that happened the day before. Right in the middle of her tangent she paused suddenly, "Hold up. Where the hell were you at all day?" Victor gave Erica a look like "where the fuck did this come from". He answered, slightly irritated at the sudden shift in conversation.

"At the studio, why?" he responded.

"Oh, I guess you haven't heard what happened up at Wingate yesterday?"

"No why? What's with all the questions?"

"Oh, your bitch ain't call you!"

"Ma, what's really good! I ain't got time for this bullshit."

"Well, I went up to Chante's school yesterday and kicked that bitch's ass."

"For what? You know I don't fuck with her."

"Well, she always in your face putting the pussy on parade, I hear. Plus she told me to keep you out of her face and was talking shit about me. What's up with that?"

"Girls are gonna talk. I don't have time for that shit, Erica." Victor was getting upset and just wanted Erica to finish telling him about what happened with her pops. He loved her with all his might, but her jealous streak was starting to put a damper on things.

"Yeah, well she'll be calling."

"What is that supposed to mean?"

"Anyway, like I was saying, I had just come home from school and was about to get comfortable so that I could do my homework. I went straight in my room and opened my closet to hang up my uniform and my shit was empty. All my shit was gone. Victor all I had was the clothes in my drawers and a pair of shoes. So of course I went off. I yelled for my mother and my father showed up, talking all this shit about he gave my stuff away to people who deserved it more. He just had this look on his face and I couldn't take it. I threw my trophy at him and shit just popped off.

"Then after my mother broke it up, she had the nerve to try and take up for him again. Sometimes I just don't know what's wrong with her. She knows that shit ain't right, but she still tries to convince everyone that he's not wrong and justify what he does. Monica's so lucky that she got out. I'm just waiting for it to be my turn," Erica said, sighing as she looked out the window.

"I couldn't take the shit no more, so I grabbed my shit and bounced to my aunt Kat's house to get everything off my chest. That's when I called you, but you didn't answer. I needed you V. Why you didn't call back?"

"I did, that's how I knew you were over here."

"Oh!" she said looking out the window. "I just can't take it anymore," she said in a whisper to no one in particular. Victor knew that she was upset about the fight, but most of her anger was about her clothes. Victor let out an exasperated sigh.

"Every week it's some shit with this nigga. I'm tired of you going back and forth with this shit. What are you going to do? Nah matter of fact, I'm going to tell you what you going to do. Either pack the rest of your shit like I told you before and move in with me, or don't complain to me about this shit."

"Victor, it's just my mother you know? I worry about her."

"Baby I understand all that, but your mother is grown. She chose her path. If she decides to stay there and take all that shit your dad dishes out, then there's nothing you can do whether you stay there or not. You know I love your moms, but she has to fight her own battles. Things aren't going to get any better with all of you fighting all the damn time. Now you know I love you E, and if that nigga keep putting his hands on you, I'm a have to touch him. The only reason I ain't touch his ass yet is 'cause you asked me not to, but I can't keep standing by watching you go through this shit. So you gotta make a decision. I know you want to help your moms, but you got to do what's best for you. Now I gotta go handle some business, but by the time I pick you up from school on Monday, you need to have this mess figured out, okay."

"Victor, why are you being so mean?"

"I'm not! Erica I love you and you and I both know that the shit at your house ain't working and we need to stop faking with our relationship and take it to the next level. I been told you, I need my woman at home with me. So like I said, think about it and let me know when I can come get you on Monday OK?" Oh, so you gonna be home now? Erica thought to herself. "You are staying here at your aunt's place for the rest of the weekend?"

"Yea, most likely," she said as she looked into his eyes. She knew he was serious about her moving in with him.

"So you have a whole day to make up your mind baby, but you know where you need to be."

"Yea V… OK. And don't be late picking me up; you know how I hate to wait."

"I'll be there."

"So are you gonna tell me where you was really at?"

"In the studio, I told you!"

"Yeah, uh-huh." Erica loved to see Victor mad. She liked to push his buttons. His anger was so sexy to her and as she saw the emotion and irritation on his face, it made her pussy wet. She reached over to bite his bottom lip, looking at it as if it was the sweetest chocolate she had ever seen. They shared a long passionate kiss that almost made her get naked right there in his truck in front of her aunt's apartment building.

"Are you ready?" he asked her with a serious look on his face.

"Ready for what?"

"This… every night?"

"No, the question is are you ready for me?" She stared into his eyes and knew his answer before he even opened his mouth. She got lost in his eyes, day dreaming about what it would be like to live in peace with the man she loved the most; waking up to him every day, marrying him and having his babies.

Erica kissed him again, sucking on his bottom lip before releasing him from her grip. She looked back at him as she got out of the truck.

Victor winked, rolled up the window and pulled off. Erica went back into her aunt's apartment to lie down, calling it a night. She was emotionally and physically exhausted. That night she dreamed of what tomorrow would bring and hoped that she would make the right decision.

Monday came before Erica knew it. She had never been happier to wear a uniform in her life, since she didn't have very many clothes left. Victor had stopped by the day before and brought her a few things, but it didn't compare to collection she lost. As Erica walked through the halls towards her locker, she heard someone calling her name.

"Yo, Erica!" She turned around and saw Tracy jogging down the hallway.

"What's up Tracy," Erica replied.

"Why you walking so fast?"

"Girl, 'cause it's Monday and I'm trying to get the hell outta here."

"So what's up with the weekend Erica? Are we doing Justin's or what? 'Cause you know Kim and Crystal gonna wanna know what's up so they can get their appearances together."

"Naw… maybe. I gotta take care of something with Victor first, but you know I stay ready for Justin's. Victor just brought me some new clothes so I can be ready to hit Manhattan in a moment's notice

"I know that's right," Tracy said as she gave Erica a high-five.

"Speaking of Victor, his ass should be waiting outside on me now."

"Alright Erica, just hit me later and let me know the deal."

* * *

As Victor drove down DeKalb Avenue, all Erica could do was stare out of the window. She was so confused. She really wanted to be with Victor, but was she ready to live with him? She only had one more month before graduation and she promised her mother, whom she loved dearly, that she would stay home until then. But she just couldn't live another day in that house with her father. Erica was caught between a rock and a hard place. She wanted to be there for her mother, but after thinking about what Victor said, she was starting to think that she should move on and start her life with him. Anything had to be better than what she was going through at home.

"What's up E? Why you so quiet? Something wrong?"

"Naw, everything's fine, Boo. Just thinking that's all."

"Thinking about what?" Victor asked, worried about her.

"Us, school… my mom."

"Look E you ain't having second thoughts are you? 'Cause my time is valuable and I ain't got time to be bullshitting. I know you got a lot to think about, but what you really need to be thinking about is if this is what you want. I ain't gonna have you running back and forth home to your mother and shit. I want to take care of you. You know I always take care of mine. You are mine, right?"

"Yes baby, you know I'm yours," Erica said, staring at him softly. "It's not that I'm having second thoughts, it's just that in a matter of two days my life has been flipped. This shit is crazy yo. I don't need pressure right now. You know that I love you and that I am yours, it's just not that easy for me. But fuck it, I'm ready. I want to be with you… always," Erica said, hoping that she was making the right decision. Something in her gut was telling her to rethink this just a little bit more, but she was tired of the bullshit and she wanted to spend her days with Victor, the one person who made her happy.

Her mother would just have to handle her father on her own. She just hoped she was strong enough to do so. Shit she lasted this long… I gotta grow up sometime, Erica thought to herself as they pulled up to Victor's house.

"Aight just checking," he said with a confident smile. His smile always made her feel better and she couldn't help but smile back as she reached over to kiss his lips.

"Well I need to go to my mom's house to get the little bit of stuff that bastard left me and say goodbye to my mother, and then I'll be ready to make my move." Just as Erica finished her sentence, Victor's cell phone rang. He picked up but didn't say much to the person on the other end, but she could tell by his tone that he was getting ready to leave her. That was the only downside to this whole set up. Victor was always on the move and she wasn't sure if she could deal with it. Erica was the jealous type and she didn't trust too many people and she knew that this might one day cause some static, but right now she didn't have the energy to argue. Plus she had some homework that she had to do when she got in the house.

"Baby I gotta make a run I will be right back!" Victor said, dropping Erica off at his house.

"Well then drop me at my mom's house and pick me up on your way home."

"Sorry E, I don't have time to go all the way over to the Fort. Just wait here, I'll take you as soon as I get back. You got your key right?"

"Yea," Erica said exasperated, stepping out of the truck. She could barely get the door closed before Victor pulled off. She walked inside with all kinds of thoughts flowing through her mind. How was she going to tell her mother that she was moving in with Victor? She didn't want to let Dorothy down, but she knew that she couldn't deal with being there anymore. Erica stepped into Victor's modest three-bedroom home and dropped her book-bag onto the floor. She plopped down on the butter-soft leather couch and grabbed the cordless phone off the table beside her. She needed some help and a call to her girls was sure to do the trick.

* * *

"911, what's the emergency?" came the voice on the other end of the phone.

"I need help! Please! Something is wrong with my mother," Monica yelled out in a panic.

"Look calm down dear, where is your mother now?" the attendant replied in a professional tone.

"330 Hudson Walk. Apartment 1C in the Fort Greene projects!" Monica replied

"Help is on the way. Now tell me, what happened to your mother?"

"I think my father beat her again, I think she's dying please help me! Please!"

"Ma'am, where are you?"

"I'm on my way home from school. I'm on the Greyhound bus."

"There's an ambulance on the way to your mother, would you like an escort Ma'am?"

"Yes, please. I should be pulling into The Port Authority in about 10 minutes!"

"First what is your name, ma'am?"

"Monica Payne."

"I'll send an officer out to you. Can you tell me what you have on, so that we can alert the officers?" Monica gave her all the information she needed and hung up the phone, wishing the bus would hurry up. She nervously dialed her aunt Kat. Kat answered on the second ring.

"Yes Monica. What's wrong are you crying?"

"It's ma! Something's wrong with ma. I called to check on her and let her know that I was close to the station and she could barely talk. She sounded bad Aunty. I think he beat her again. The police are on their way!" Monica said, as she scrambled through the aisle and off the bus. She grabbed her carry-on and rushed towards the escalators, leading to the street level.

"Oh God no! I'm on my way? Have you talked to Erica?"

"Last time I spoke with her she was at Victor's. I am going to call her now!"

"OK sweetie. Bye."

Monica dialed Victor's number and got the answering machine. "Shit the damn answering machine came on!" She left a panicked message for Erica and hung up. She was frantically trying to remember the car number of the patrol car sent to pick her up. Looking up and down Eighth Avenue, Monica spotted the squad car with its lights flashing. She rushed towards the car.

"Hello, I'm Monica Payne, are you my escorts?"

"Yes ma'am," the officer answered. He took her luggage and placed it in the trunk before helping her into the car. With sirens on, they raced through the west side, heading for the Brooklyn Bridge and to the rescue of her beloved mother.

* * *

Erica got out of the shower and went to check the caller ID to see who had called. She was feeling quite relaxed and refreshed and planned to go and see her mother as soon as Victor came back from running his daily errands. Before picking up the phone she noticed that she had a message. It was from Monica. After listening, she got a little worried, but figured it was probably nothing because Monica had always been the dramatic type. She picked up the phone to call her sister back, but her call went straight to voice mail. Damn, what does my sister want with me, let me try her again, she thought to herself. She was a little irritated that Monica didn't just state the issue on the answering machine, but that was one thing they did have in common. They were both very private people.

"Hello. Hey Monica you called me? What's up Sis?"

"Erica, something is wrong with Ma."

"What do you mean?" Erica asked as her heart dropped to her knees.

"I called there and Ma didn't sound too good. I think dad beat her again! I called the police to go over there because, as we were talking, the damn phone went dead. I'm on my way with a police escort and Aunty is taking a cab to meet me."

"What! I just spoke to Ma last night and everything was fine. Shit! That no-good motherfucker! If he put his hands on her I swear... Alright I'll be there." A furious Erica slipped on a Juicy Couture sweat suit and some new white Air Force Ones and slammed the door behind her. She ran up the block to the corner of Lafayette Avenue and Clinton and flagged down a cab.

"Myrtle and Prince please."

"Five dollars," the cab driver snapped back in a grumpy tone. Erica gave the man a ten and sat back praying her mother was okay.

Suddenly Erica felt guilty. She knew deep down that something was wrong the night before and she should have gone with her gut and went back to her mother's house. Maybe if she had been there she could have protected her mother from that monster. Maybe if she would have had the guts to tell Victor that she needed to go home to her mother and stayed with her for just a little while longer, everything would have been OK. As the cab crossed Ashland place, she told him to pull up in the middle of the block.

"Keep the change," she shouted as she ran through the projects to her building. All she saw was what seemed like a million flashing lights everywhere. As she turned the corner she saw the EMS workers carrying her mother out of the building on a stretcher.

"Ma! Ma, what happened?" Erica yelled.

The EMS worker turned and said, "Ma'am do you know this woman?"

"Yes that's my mother!" Erica screamed with tear-filled eyes. All Erica could do was feel guilty because she wasn't there and she knew her mother had most likely been defending her.

"What is her name?" the EMS attendant questioned Erica.

"Dorothy Payne."

"What is your name?" the worker asked.

"Erica Payne," she answered in a trembling voice. She needed Victor at that very moment, but she knew that he probably hadn't gotten home yet.

"Do you know what happened?" Erica was getting impatient and the technician was asking her too many damn questions. Her only concern at this point was making sure her mother was OK. Ignoring the EMS attendant, Erica ran over to her mother.

"Ma, answer me!"

"Ms. Payne your mother is unconscious. Although she may be able to hear you, she can't answer you back."

"Is she going to be okay?" Erica couldn't help but let the tears flow down her face. She couldn't stand to think that anything like this could be happening to her mother. Her mother was her world. Things were bad but Gregory had never put her mother in the hospital before. Speaking of which, she wondered where that bastard was. She knew he couldn't have been in the house because he definitely would have gotten arrested.

"Well as of right now, she is on a respirator just for her breathing," said the EMS attendant, trying to sound reassuring. "Her vital signs are stable. I'm not going to lie to you Ms. Payne she has been beaten pretty badly. We are going to take her in for some tests and X-rays and monitor her." As the man finished talking, Erica saw Monica running towards her from a squad car.

"Erica what's happening?" Monica yelled as she approached the scene.

"He beat her up. The fucking bastard beat her." Erica could not contain her anguish. Monica just stood there shaking her head and crying. Erica had the look of a killer, standing there with her hands balled up in tiny fists as the tears continued down her cheeks. The EMS worker rushed over to the two women.

"Ms. Payne," he said looking at Erica, "are you coming?"

"Monica you go, I'll stay and wait for Kat." Erica could not bear the thought of seeing her mother connected to all those machines being poked and prodded at her. Besides Erica now had a mission to find her father and kill him.

"Okay," Monica responded, but she had a worried expression on her face. "Erica be careful and please don't do anything stupid." Erica ignored her sister and asked the attendant what hospital her mother was being taken to. He told her Brooklyn Hospital. Erica embraced her sister and whispered to her in a hoarse-cracking voice, "I'll meet you there, Monica. Don't worry about me I'll be fine. Just be strong for Ma." Monica kissed her sister. She knew Erica was going to look for Gregory and she feared that she would never see any of her family again. She feared that one or both of them would end up dead or in jail. Monica walked towards the ambulance but turned towards her sister with a great look of fear and concern one last time before stepping into the van.

"I'll be fine," Erica told her, as if reading Monica's thoughts. She knew Monica was worried and afraid. Erica watched as the ambulance and police cars pulled out of the parking lot with her battered mother and worried sister. The squad car that Monica had been riding in had dropped off Monica's bags and followed suit with the rest of the entourage. Erica walked over to the bench and sat down to immerse herself in guilt and anger. Man how could I let this happen? She thought I want to kill him! Her inner monologue could only entertain the plot of murder. There was no mercy for what Gregory had done. Father or not….he had to go!

The courtyard was full of local dudes posted up on the gate watching all of the commotion. As soon as the paramedics pulled off with Erica's mother and sister, Juju, a guy Erica knew from the projects, walked up.

"What's up E? What happened to Moms? I saw your pops pull off just before 5-0 came."

"So why the fuck ya'll ain't do nothing?" Erica exploded. "His bitch ass beat her."

"Man, E I ain't fucking wit Big G, that's a crazy motherfucker yo!" Juju responded. He didn't sound afraid, but acted as if stopping G would have violated some type of street code. Erica's father was notorious in the projects and throughout Fort Greene. He was fucked up and totally absorbed with his own agenda, doing whatever it took to serve his own purpose by any and every means necessary." Monica and Erica bared the stigma of being "Big G's Girls". Erica knew that there was legitimacy in Juju's response, but she didn't give a fuck. That was her mother in the ambulance laying there half dead, and she felt like somebody should have done something. They could have stalled the nigga until the cops came, bucked some shots at him, something. She continued to lash out.

"Man, ya'll know my mother don't deserve that shit. Ya'll let that old bitch ass nigga do that shit and ya'll was sitting right out here? I can't believe this shit! Man, fuck all ya'll! That's why I don't fuck with none of ya'll niggas anyway. That's why I fuck with them Bed-Stuy niggas, if ya'll really want to know. That's exactly why I never gave ya'll coward asses no play. Bitch ass niggas," Erica vented.

"Fuck you Erica, and all those Bed-Stuy niggas," Juju snapped back, "Them do or die niggas know better than to step up in the Fort!" Erica dismissed Juju with a final response.

"Yo all that talking… do that shit while walking that way. Go the fuck on. We're done here." Erica dismissed Juju with the fling of her hand, and stared aimlessly into the parking lot at all the activity going on in front of the building. Ju knew better than to push it any further. After all, Erica was Big G's daughter and she had her own reputation for being extreme. No one in their right mind wanted to be on the receiving end of her wrath. People in the projects thought that Erica was crazy, men and women alike.

Erica walked away mad as hell not wanting to hear shit from anyone except where she could find Big G. She went into the house to get her mind right. She sat in her mother's room deep in thought. About five minutes later the door slammed!

"Erica, Monica?" It was Aunt Kat. Erica called out, "I'm in Ma's room Kat!"

"What happened? Where's your mother?" Kat surveyed the apartment already filling in the blanks from the looks of disarray.

"They took Ma to Brooklyn Hospital."

"Is she alright?" Kat questioned, with panic in her voice. She had no idea that things were this severe.

"Nah Aunty, she's messed up pretty bad. I almost didn't recognize her. Her eyes were swollen shut, her lips were all busted and she had knots all over her face. I'm guessing after it all happened, she panicked and had an asthma attack. That's probably why she could barely talk on the phone, but thank God Monica called when she did! They found her unconscious. My mother was in here fighting for her life, Aunty. All because she was trying to protect me and for what? I wasn't even here to help. Instead I was over at Victor's house trying to figure out a way to tell Mommy I was moving in with him. I feel so selfish Kat," Erica said as she began to cry again. The sight of her Aunt evoked another moment for Erica to shed her emotions. Envisioning her mother so badly beaten up Erica's anger quickly resurfaced and replaced her sadness.

"That nigga has been locked up all my damn life. I mean outta the seventeen years I've been living, what? He's been in our lives maybe six of that. And he thinks he's such a big man and he can come in here trying to run shit! When he's not around, I run this! I take care of Mom. I do the shit that he wasn't man enough to do. I was Mommy's backbone. That nigga ain't shit! My mother means the world to me and if she doesn't make it, I swear anyone who gets between me and that nigga is going to feel my pain!"

"Erica, don't talk like that. Your mother is a strong woman, she'll make it." Kat knew that Erica was serious and she was afraid because she also knew what her niece was capable of. Kat attempted to comfort Erica but to no avail. "Right now we got to be strong for her sake. We'll take care of him later." It was not going to work because Erica was too far gone in her own vengeful thoughts.

"Naw I got him!" Erica's voice was cold and steady, almost calm.

"Go fix yourself up, so we can go to the hospital," Kat said trying to change the subject. That was not going to work either. Erica responded in a firm voice. "No you go Aunty; I'll stay here and clean up the mess. I can't see my mother like that again, I just can't!"

Kat let it go. "Okay, baby I understand, I'll call and check on you when I get there."

"Okay, please tell her I'm sorry and I love her."

"I'm sure she knows that baby," Kat said as she embraced Erica with a reassuring hug and headed out the door. After Kat left, Erica went into her mother's room to clean up the mess that was made as her mother was fighting for her life. When Erica finished cleaning up she went into her room, grabbed her pillow and curled up on her bed and cried.

"My father ain't shit! She should've known that shit a long time ago!" Erica sobbed aloud, clinching her pillow as she began her conversation with God, venting her frustration. She hoped He would hear her anguish. "She doesn't deserve this. She took care of me and my sister all these years damn-near by herself. It's bad enough she had to raise Monica and me, but then she had to work so hard just short of selling her ass to keep us in private school after my father left and this is the thanks she gets. This nigga better pray 5-0 catches his ass before I do." Convinced that God was not listening, Erica fell silent. She jumped at the sound of the ringing phone and picked it up immediately.

"Hello? It's Aunt Kat, Erica pack up something for your mother."

"How is she?"

"She's—" Erica held her breath awaiting her aunt's response, "stable but the doctor said she'll be here for at least a week. But when she's released she won't be coming back there. So just get her some things and bring them to my house." Erica dared to breathe as she responded, "Okay."

"How are you doing, you holding up okay?"

"Yeah I'm trying, I'm trying. I'm just going to pack the rest of my stuff too. Then I'm a go back to Victor's. How is Monica?"

"She is still a little shaken up but she's coming along. She went to the cafeteria to get some coffee." Erica hurried her aunt off the phone. "Aright let me finish packing so I can get outta here?"

"Okay bye Baby."

"Bye." Erica finished packing and threw her Gucci back pack over her left shoulder, her mother's Tumi suit case in her left hand, and Monica's carry-on in her right. She opened the front door and turned around to take one last look. From that point on Erica knew there was no turning back. She knew that she would have to make sure that she found a hustle to support herself, even if it was just a simple 9-5. She wasn't going to have to depend on her man like her mother did. Although Erica didn't want to go to college, she did want to find a good job making good money. That would be the first thing she would do after graduation.

Erica struggled down the steps and out the building and hailed a cab to her aunt's house. Sad and broken hearted she knew that this day would forever change her. It was the re-birth of Erica Payne.

Chapter 4

"Wake up, birthday girl," Victor whispered, softly into Erica's ear.

"I'm tired, leave me alone," Erica mumbled, not wanting to move. They had a long night and she felt that she still needed a few hours to re-cooperate.

Erica had been living with Victor for almost six years now and things were as good as they could be. Victor's hustle was going strong and his record label had made great strides in the industry. When she graduated from high school, she got a job in a small public relations firm. She wasn't sure if that was what she wanted to do long-term, but for now she was meeting people and putting some extra money in her pockets.

All in all, Erica liked her life with Victor but they had been through some rough times. Yet, no matter what they went through, it was nothing compared to her life in the projects with her father.

"Wake your ass up," he said louder with a hint of pleading. Erica felt the weight of his hard body as he leaned over to kiss her. His breathing quickened as he made an effort to be tender. Besides that he wasn't sure if his vibe of love was felt yet. Erica could be an evil bitch when she wanted to be. Yes she was petite, but shit, she hit like a prized fighter. Now 23, Erica had only grown a few inches in the past years.

She now stood at an even five feet, but she was still as beautiful as when they had first gotten together, if not better, now that she was stress-free.

Erica shifted uneasily in her bed. She knew she was about to give up her last minutes of sleep. Victor was not adhering to the "leave me alone" plea. As Victor opened the drapes the sun came beaming through the windows, Her plans to sleep in were now a thing of the past.

"What! I'm up", Erica said in a groggy voice, pretending to be pissed off. Victor anxiously lifted the silver tray from the night stand and placed it on Erica's lap as she squirmed to sit up in their California king-sized bed.

"I made breakfast for my birthday girl."

"Thanks baby. What do you have here?" Opening the lid of the covered dish, the aroma of stacked pancakes topped with whipped cream, cinnamon and brown sugar hit her nose. On the side stood a single red rose in a crystal vase. "Wow this looks great baby."

"Soooo…" Victor teased, waiting for something else. A mischievous grin was on his face as he eased behind her and began tickling her. Erica exploded in a fit of laughter.

"Stop, stop. You know I'm ticklish!" Victor continued to tickle and tease her.

"You better not knock over that tray after I slaved in the kitchen first thing this morning for your fine ass. Shut up and kiss me, Baby Girl," Victor said in a fake Jamaican accent. Erica leaned in and Victor gave her a kiss filled with the love and passion that only a man can have for the woman he loves.

Breaking the embrace, Erica started in on the food that Victor prepared for her. He slid down towards the end of the bed reaching for her feet and started to gently suck on her toes. The intent behind his actions strengthened as his massage took on a rhythm— a rhythm that spoke of possibilities.

"So how does it feel to be twenty-three?"

"I don't know yet, why don't you show me?" Erica replied in a coy little girl's voice.

"In due time," Victor said as he stiffened and pulled away. Although she and Victor were only months apart, he liked to act like he was a lot older. He stood up and walked towards his closet.

"You are going out?" Erica asked sarcastically, taking notice that Victor was fully-clothed. Him pulling away gave no indication that he was about to disrobe and come back to bed.

"Yeah, I got a few moves to make before your big night," he said glancing at his watch, Erica noticed, for the second time. Somehow, whatever his reasons for leaving did not seem to matter at this moment. He was fucking up her birthday dick. Erica had plans for the whip cream that topped her pancakes. Victor knew that Erica was pissed because he had his own ideas about the whip cream as well. However, his thoughts were that she would have to get over it because he had a lot of shit to do if he was going to pull off Erica's birthday bash in grand style. Victor was reminded of Al Pacino in Scarface. He thought of the scene when his wife was pissed that he was about to leave and he said she'll take some Quaaludes and love him in the morning. Instead of drugs, Erica's addiction was shopping. Victor knew sending her shopping all day would be a good way to get her out his hair and off his ass. That seemed to be his antidote for everything, but Erica was tired of shopping.

Victor placed his hand on the wall triggering the biometric sensor, which opened the safe. He was such a technology whore. He reached inside and pulled out five large stacks of bills. He dropped three stacks on the bed beside Erica and put the rest in his satchel. Erica was sitting up in bed giving Victor the "I don't believe this motherfucker" stare. Victor caught the look, but chose to ignore its meaning.

"Go, get yourself something nice. I'm taking you out later to celebrate your birthday." The idea that Victor always provided for Erica used to be appealing, but for some reason she felt a little cheated. Though she was happy with Victor, in a lot of ways it reminded her of another relationship. One that nearly destroyed a beautiful woman and her two children. She loved him with all of her heart, but she had seen how bad things could get. She loved him so much she would try to overcome her past.

Since this was her day she felt that by all rights, everything should go according to her desires. Sleep late, wake up to some good loving, eat, bathe and then go shopping. After all, this was her princess party.

"Fine, I'll go shopping, but where did you say that you were going again?"

"I said that I have shit to do. What part of 'it's a surprise' don't you get?" Victor replied. "Just be ready by nine-thirty." Victor gave Erica a kiss on the forehead and headed for the door.

Erica brushed him off and finished her meal. After placing the dishes in the kitchen, she was up and running before she knew it. She hopped in the shower and was dressed in 20 minutes. Heading into the kitchen, Erica fixed herself a mimosa. She decided to call Tracy, her best friend and partner in crime, to go and terrorize the stores with her. Tracy's phone rang twice before she answered.

"What's up girl? Happy Birthday! You're up awfully early on a Saturday morning."

"Whatever. I have a pocket full of money and I am ready to do some damage. So get your ass over here."

"Nah you come and get me. You know it takes me a minute. I should be ready by the time you get here." Tracy was one of the few people that Erica could count on.

Tracy hopped out of bed immediately. She knew that a day with Erica promised to bring excitement. She grabbed her silk head wrap, and rushed to the bathroom to take a shower. Tracy was almost ready when Erica pulled up in her black SL500. Victor had just had it detailed; making sure that it was in show room condition for her tour around town that day. Tracy's phone rang a second later.

"Tracy you ready?"

"In a minute, bitch did you teleport here?"

"Hurry up!"

Tracy finished primping, putting the final touches on her Mac sponsored face. Finally she came out grinning wearing a short denim Levi mini, with some suede Bruni Magli wedges and a printed deep-cut V-neck blouse from Barney's that left way for her Bvlgari four caret diamond monogrammed necklace to take the spotlight.

"I can't help it that I am a little slow. Perfection takes time", Tracy remarked as she put her Gucci clutch on her lap and closed the car door."

"Whatever bitch," Erica retorted as she peeled out of the driveway. Tracy pulled down the mirror over the visor to add on a little more Prrr lip gloss. “Please don’t get any make-up in the car. Victor just had it detailed.”

“Happy birthday girl!” Tracy said again. Without acknowledgment of the birthday greeting, Erica immediately started to interrogate Tracy.

“Where is Victor taking me tonight? And bitch, don’t act like you don’t know. I know you all are planning some shit.”

“What are you talking about? I am not in on shit. I don’t know what you are talking about.”

“You know, because if Victor didn’t tell you, Twan did.”

“Twan? What are you talking about?”

“Bitch, do not play games. One of you knows! Twan is Victor’s man and you are fucking him, and you are my best friend so one of you knows something. But I will go along with the shit.” Erica adjusted her mirrors as she got on the Brooklyn Bridge crossing over into Manhattan. Not long after crossing the bridge, they arrived at Sak’s Fifth Avenue.

Entering the store, Erica and Tracy strolled in like Paris Hilton and Nicole Richie on Rodeo Drive. Heads turned, as they moved through the aisles systematically scanning the racks and making mental notes about items of interest. Erica made a detour straight to the shoe department. Tracy took this as an opportunity to start looking for something to wear to Erica’s surprise party, which was taking place that evening at Jay-Z’s 40/40 club. She spotted the perfect dress, and stuck her size in the back of the stack of dresses to retrieve later. She then walked over to where Erica was in the shoe department.

“Damn Erica those shoes are the shit.”

“You like them?” Erica replied.

"Yeah, but let's go upstairs so that you can get something to wear first."

"Aight, let's go then."

"Go ahead I am right behind you"

Approaching the couture section, Erica recognized her favorite sales person. A white girl named Jennifer greeted her with a warm hug.

"Hello Ms. Payne, I have not seen you in a while." Erica corrected her. "It's Mrs. Fletcher these days." Jennifer apologized and offered her immediate congratulations. "Thank you. Jen you don't have to apologize, you had no way of knowing. We have not told anyone, yet. We wanted to try the situation out before we brought others on board. I have a feeling that tonight is the night we will be coming out and letting everyone know. I wanted you to be one of first to be informed." Jennifer was a girl from Long Island. She knew her shit when it came to fashion and most importantly, she knew what Erica liked and how to style her.

"I got a few pieces I would like for you to check out," Jennifer said pointing to the Vera Wang section.

"Okay, but I'm looking for something sexy… I mean spectacular. It is my birthday and I am going out tonight."

"Where to might I ask?"

"I don't know it is supposed to be a surprise. However, we would not want to ruin the surprise by me not being on point."

"Oh no never that," Jennifer remarked. She loved styling Erica because she had excellent taste and was not afraid to take a risk with her look.

Jennifer went to the back to pull a few things in Erica's size. She found the perfect little number to compliment Erica's petite frame and killer legs. It was a short, black hand-beaded number, with a plunging V-neck and low back.

"Try this on Mrs. Fletcher," Jennifer said, holding the dress. "This is you." Erica took one look at the dress and knew this was it.

"Tracy what do you think about this?"

"Girl that is definitely the dress. Try it on." Erica went into the dressing room and slipped the dress on. She stood there for a moment admiring herself in the mirror. She started reminiscing about the day her father got rid of all of her clothes. That situation was one of the worst that she had been through, but she had got through it and couldn't imagine anything being worse except if she had dresses like this in her closet. Erica stepped out of the dressing room in runway fashion.

"So ladies what do you think?" she asked confidently, already knowing that she looked fabulous.

"Girl where ever Victor takes you tonight, you are certainly going to stop traffic," Tracy remarked.

"Mrs. Fletcher I knew this would be it. You look stunning!"

"OK girl go get changed, I got this. Happy birthday," Tracy said following Jennifer to the register. Erica looked stunned, but didn't bother to ask any questions. Instead, she quickly put her clothes back on and met the two women out front.

"Will you need this to be gift wrapped?"

"No, that won't be necessary."

"Tracy, are you sure girl, Victor gave me money?" This is a seven thousand dollar dress and that bitch does not even pay her damn phone bill, Erica thought.

"Naw, I'm serious I got this. You know you are my girl."

"How will you be handling this today"?

"Charge." Tracy pulled out a Discover card and handed it to Jennifer, who immediately swiped the card and waited for it to go through. Erica stood there thinking if this shit does not go through, she was going to kill this bitch. Just then the card was approved.

"Sign here Mrs. Penn." Jennifer returned the card and placed the slip and pen on the counter for Tracy to sign. Jennifer handed Erica the bag with the dress. "I saw a pair of Jimmy Choo shoes downstairs that will go perfect with this dress," she said handing the receipt back to Jennifer and placing her copy into her purse.

"Thanks Jennifer I will see you soon," Erica said as they walked towards the escalator. When they got off, instead of heading to the shoe section, Erica headed towards the door.

"Where are you going Erica, I thought you wanted to look at the shoes?"

"Yeah bitch I do, but right now I have something else on my mind." They left the store, heading back towards the parking lot.

"Bitch, who the fuck is Mrs. Penn?" Erica questioned Tracy.

"That's my thing, when the fuck did you start using 'Mrs. Fletcher'," Tracy responded in a sarcastic tone. "Just giving the bitch a storyline. She's my best friend." Erica Responded

They both busted out laughing.

"Well I gotta know more about what you got goin on," Erica insisted, not wanting to dismiss the subject.

"Well, while you were home playing wifey, I was out makin moves. I got my own little side hustle set-up, that don't rely on my man's money. What the fuck you care anyway, you still have a purse full of money and a seven thousand dollar dress to wear."

"Let's get something to eat. We need to have a board meeting."

They walked into Ruth Chris on Broadway and asked for a table for two. The hostess grabbed the menus and told them to follow her. A very thin woman in her late twenties sat two glasses of water down on the table.

"What can I get you to drink?"

"I'll have a chocolate martini with a shot of Belvedere," replied Erica.

"And you ma'am?" she asked, looking at Tracy.

"I'll have a blue martini with a shot of Grey Goose." Once the waitress was out of ear shot, Erica started in on her questioning.

"Yo, Tracy what the fuck was that stunt back at Saks? I know you ain't gonna keep me guessing."

"Nah, it ain't like that E. It's this dude I met up with in Queens that put me down with this plastic game."

"Damn shit sweet like that?" Erica asked in an amused voice.

"Yeah, everybody's down with this shit. I'm telling you E, shit is sweet." Just then, the waitress walked over with their drinks. After she left, Tracy continued. "See I buy the credit cards from him and he already has them hooked up with real account numbers and shit. All I have to do is memorize the name on the card and make my purchases. It's sweet situation. See if your ass would hang out with a bitch more often, you could have been hipped to the game. But you're too busy playing house Mrs. Davis."

"Whatever, how can I get down?"

"You fo'real?"

"Yeah bitch I'm for real!"

"Well all you have to do is give me fifteen thousand and I'll get you some plates with an ID number." Damn, this dude is making fifteen off just my head? This bastard is getting paid! Erica thought to herself.

"Damn where is the waitress? I need another drink," Tracy said. Tracy's phone rang and interrupted their conversation. "Girl, hold up, this is Twan. Hello."

"What's up boo, where you at?" Twan asked through the phone.

"I'm having a drink with Erica at Ruth's on Broadway, where you at?"

"I'm about five minutes away from there. I'm in Soho getting my pants tailored for tonight."

"Hold on Twan", Tracy paused to question Erica, "What are you getting ready to do when you leave here Erica?"

"Get my hair done why?"

"Because I am going to tell Twan to meet me," she said putting her drink down as she invited Twan to come get her. "Come up to Ruth Chris."

"I'm on my way," he said hanging up.

"Well since I don't have to take you home, I can go pick up some shoes and go to the salon from here," Erica said reaching in her purse. "Here's some money for the drinks, I'll see you tonight."

"You know how I do," Tracy said pushing Erica's money away and pulling out her platinum card. "Charge it to the game!"

"Girl you silly. I will see you tonight and thanks for the dress."

"It's all good, see you later birthday girl," Tracy responded, pleased at impressing Erica with her own brand of hustle. "Wait, Erica do you want me to get you some plates from my guy?"

"I'll see you later Mrs. Penn. We will talk. I'll have to move on that later."

"Later? Mmhmmm I know that you are up to something."

"You just don't know," Erica replied with a mischievous smile.

Chapter 5

Erica left her meeting with Tracy, not believing what had just happened. This was the opportunity that she had been waiting for. Although her job helped her with a few things here and there, it was nowhere as big as what this game might lead to. And if what Tracy said was true, it seemed less risky than the drug game that Victor was a part of. All she had to do was learn, and that dude Tracy was talking about was going to be her key to financial freedom and success.

Erica knew that this had to be easy if Tracy was doing it. She had no prior hustling skills, so for her to be involved in something like this, said a lot. Yeah she knew people with illegal hustles but, she was never down. Erica wondered how many other Tracy's there were running around town with these fake credit cards, charging up shit from meals to heels... If Tracy was being fueled by some nigga that posed as the King of Plastic, then Erica definitely needed to meet him. This kind of power in the wrong hands could be lethal.

Erica took a look at her Cartier watch and noticed the time. Victor told her to be ready by 9:30pm and from the looks of things this was not going to happen. Erica headed back downtown to The Village to pick up some shoes on 8th Street and make her hair appointment with her stylist Vonda. If she did not get caught in traffic, she just might pull all of this off.

* * *

"Hey Victor, what up? Long time no see," Crystal said giving Victor a big hug. She hadn't seen Erica or Victor in a long time, and was so excited to be back in the city.

"So how was your flight?" Victor asked.

"Shit I guess it was OK, I'm here aren't I?" They both laughed lightly.

"Damn, you still crazy girl," Victor said. Crystal smiled.

"You know Victor, I really can't wait for the party tonight," she said as they walked out the gate towards the parking lot of JFK airport. "It's been so long since I last saw you and Erica, plus I needed a serious break from this school shit. Damn, I almost didn't recognize you," Crystal said smiling.

"Shit you ain't change too much," Victor said giving her the once-over, taking in her light-skinned shapely body that was topped off with a pretty face. Although Crystal was thick, she was proportioned nicely. She kind of reminded Victor of Tocarra, from America's Next Top Model.

"I have changed. Maybe not physically, but I am not the silly young girl from back in the day."

"I don't know about all that," Victor remarked jokingly. Crystal nudged him playfully.

"Looks like you put on a few pounds in the mid-section," she joked as she poked at his abdomen.

"Nah that's just good living, Shorty. You know my baby takes care of a nigga," Victor said rubbing his stomach as they approached his truck. He threw her luggage in the back, and then walked over to let Crystal in the passenger side. Once she was safely inside the truck,

Victor walked to his side, jumped in, and started the engine.

"Victor your truck is nice," she said admiring the smooth leather interior with his first initial V in the headrests, and the twenty's it was riding on weren't bad on the eye either.

"Yeah it's just a little something, something. One of the fleet," he said smiling, truly proud of his accomplishments. They were all strapped in and headed out the parking lot towards the Belt Parkway entrance.

"OK, what's the game plan for tonight? What do you want me to do?" Crystal asked, ready to get everything started.

"First I need you to take Erica's gift to Maxwell's Bakery on Atlantic Avenue and give it to Jill. She is waiting for it."

"Alright where is it?" Crystal asked, looking excited.

"Reach behind me in the back of my seat," Victor replied, changing the radio station. Crystal followed his instructions and found a small jewelry box. Opening it, she found a four-carat diamond solitaire with diamonds around the band. She sat there staring at the ring for several minutes, unable to say a word.

"Damn Victor. You're really serious aren't you? I mean damn this ring is...it's, it's, it's—" Victor gave her the "I know" type of look.

"I mean I know ya'll been together since junior high school, but this really puts things in perspective," she said giving Victor one last look before closing the box and placing it safely in her purse.

"Look I'm gonna jump on the North Conduit and go to the garage on Atlantic Avenue and get my car. I'm going to give you the truck so that you can go and pick up Kat and Monica from Kat's house at about 8:00pm. Bring them to the club with you. We should reach there about

10:30," Victor said. He looked over at Crystal. "You got me Crystal, right?" She nodded. The rest of the ride, the two of them caught up on each other's lives, as Crystal thought about how lucky her girl was to have found true love in Victor.

* * *

Crystal walked into the club, laying Erica's gift on the table.

"What did you get her Tracy?" she asked, as Tracy was putting the finishing touches on the decorations.

"Oh I got her a pair of Christian Laboutin boots all those Hollywood bitches have them."

"And I brought her this Cavalli jacket," Kim said sipping on some cognac. "It's fire girl!"

"Oh aight. Well I bought her this vintage Chanel bag," Crystal said. "I hope she likes it," she added under her breath. She knew how picky Erica could be, and hoped she would be pleased with her present. "They should be here any minute." They all rushed to put the last minute touches on all the decorations and make sure things were perfect for their girl's arrival.

Erica arrived back at home around 8:15, which was barely enough time for her to take a bubble bath, get dressed, and put on her make-up. She stood in the mirror admiring her brand new dress, wondering what surprise Victor had in store for her birthday. She watched him from the mirror running around the room like a mad man trying to get his self together as well. He had just arrived fifteen minutes prior and was headed for the shower.

"Do you like what I'm wearing?" Erica asked.

"Yea Erica. You look beautiful. But baby I'm about to jump in the shower and get my clothes ready. We have to hurry up."

"Ready for what? Hurry up for what V?" Erica asked hoping that Victor would give her a hint. "Where are we going? Am I over dressed? Should I wear these shoes? Come on V I need to know something so I know how to dress."

"Erica you are fine," Victor said scooping her up in his arms and giving her a peck on the lips. "You look beautiful as always. Now can you help me get ready?"

"What are you wearing?" Erica asked in a frustrated tone. She was mad that he was really keeping her surprise under wraps. Usually she was able to break him by now, but Victor was holding out for real.

"It's hanging on the door. Just get my jewelry out the safe and put it on the dresser," he yelled heading for the bathroom. Ain't this a bitch! I bust my ass getting home and now I have to help him get ready, Erica thought.

Once they were dressed and ready, they both headed out to Victor's shiny clean car. The two of them looked like a superstar couple headed to the GRAMMYS. They jumped in the car and headed towards the club. Erica sat in her seat quiet, still trying to figure out where Victor was taking her. She was excited and tried not to make a fuss anymore about where they were headed.

"Yo Erica, I have to make a quick stop," Victor said, hoping that his plan would work.

"What! A quick stop where Victor? I mean damn it's my birthday Boo," Erica said pouting and getting more upset as the night went on.

"I know E, but it will only take a second. I just have to drop something off to Twan. He's at the 40/40 Club, which is right by the spot that I want to take you," he said smiling, hoping that the small hint to her birthday surprise would get her off his back long enough to make it into the club. Great! Take a second? He'll probably take about twenty minutes. He always does his damn business on my time. It could never just be me and him. It's always me, him and everybody else. I'm so tired of this shit. I have to share you on my birthday too? On my day! Erica thought as she rolled her eyes and sat quietly. The rest of the drive was taken in silence as the radio blared. The car came to a stop outside of Jay-Z's 40/40 Club, a known hot spot for celebrities and other important figures. It was always packed with hustlers, record label types, Wall Street dudes and chicks trying to bag themselves professional athlete. Victor got out of the car and ran to hold the door for Erica. The pavement was slippery and she was trying to make sure that she didn't slip getting out of the car.

"Could we please hurry this up?" Erica asked, growing more impatient. The front of the club was filled with double-parked cars and people standing around waiting to get in. Cars lined the streets for at least a mile down towards 6th Avenue. Victor walked right up to the bouncer and flashed him a smile. The bouncer smiled back and moved the ropes, allowing Victor and Erica to enter. Erica was so engulfed in her thoughts, she didn't even catch the smirk that the bouncer gave her, which definitely would have tipped her off that something was going on other than what Victor told her.

"Don't worry, we will be having a good time before you know it," Victor said softly, inches from her ear trying to use a soft whisper to calm her down. "Trust me you are going to have so much fun tonight baby," he said placing a kiss next to her ear. "It will be a night that you will never forget." Erica wanted to be angry, but Victor always knew how to get to her. For a moment she started thinking that they might have to make a stop in the ladies' room before heading to their destination, because Victor had her feeling hot. When he put on that raspy phone-sex voice, along with his soft sensual kisses, it always sent her up the wall.

Before she knew it, Victor was opening a set of double doors and the crowd yelled, "Surprise! Happy birthday!"

Erica jumped back, startled and surprised. Victor gave her a kiss as the crowd went wild. She didn't know what to do. All she could hear was people requesting the champagne and Hennessey at the bar, and Beyoncé's song "Crazy in Love", playing in the background. Erica was speechless. Victor had definitely outdone himself.

"Did you think we forgot?" Crystal asked, walking up to Erica giving her a hug.

"Crystal! Oh my God girl what are you doing here?" she screamed grabbing her girlfriend and giving her a big hug. "I mean damn I hoped ya'll bitches didn't forget, but I didn't expect all this," Erica said, glancing Victor's way as he winked his eye at her. She was so happy she couldn't even begin to handle the emotions that were rolling over her. Tears were streaming down her eyes before she knew it.

"Oh, so you only got love for this hoe!" Kim said, pushing her way through the crowd.

"Ahhhhhhhh," Erica screamed as she broke away from Crystal, and headed for Kim. Tracy came through the crowd as well, and the four girls embraced in a four-way huddle happy to be together again after being apart for so long.

"Well, since we're here. Let's do the damn thing!" yelled Victor gently leading Erica forward. She had many guests to see. As Erica made her rounds through the party greeting her guests, a very attractive gentleman approached Tracy from behind.

"What's up, Tracy," he said, trying to speak over the loud music. As soon as Tracy heard her name, she turned around.

"Hey Ty," Tracy said giving him a hug. The smell of Cool Water cologne and Irish Spring soap filled her nostrils and she had to take a deep breath in order to compose herself. "I wanted to introduce you to my home girl Erica, the birthday girl, but as you can see she's a little tied up at the moment. I'll make the introductions as soon as she's done greeting her peoples. So what's up with you?" she said trying to spark conversation while they waited for Erica.

Erica was done greeting her party guests and was standing around chatting with one of her co-workers when she caught a glimpse of Tracy talking with a man she had never seen. Erica put two and two together and figured that he must be the guy that Tracy wanted to introduce her to. She politely ended her conversation and walked over to Tracy and the gentleman.

"Hey Tracy what's up?"

"Oh, hey E. We were just talking about you. Ty this is Erica, and Erica this is Ty, the guy from Queens that I was telling you about." Tracy looked at Erica with a "you know" expression on her face, and she understood immediately.

"Oh how are you?" she said catching on fast. She had to admit Ty was sexy as hell and her birthday shot was already making her body and hormones hot. Ty was tall like an NBA basketball player. He was dressed like a GQ model in all black and accessorized his outfit with a modest chain, two diamond studs in his ears and a simple Rolex watch, with some Gucci shades. He wasn't flashy, but definitely dressed with style and his curly hair complimented his pecan brown skin tone. Erica wasn't quite sure how she felt at the moment because she was never one to mix business with pleasure, but this man had it going on. She couldn't help but be surprised at her attraction to Ty since this had only been their first meeting. This made him that much more intriguing to her and she wanted to know more about him. The two of them just stood there in an unexpected silence staring at each other.

Tracy broke their silence. "So Ty, when are my prices going to drop? You promised me that they would." Erica looked at him curiously.

"Oh, so are you telling me that he isn't a man of his word? Hmm," Erica said, flirting with Ty and pretending to be questioning his credibility. Ty gave Tracy a look that could kill.

"Now Tracy, why would you say something like that? You got me looking bad in front of your girl. If I said I would cut your price, then you know that's what I'm going to do." Tracy took a step back. She realized that the timing for her little clever remark was all wrong. She didn't mean to make Ty upset. She was only trying to be as sarcastic and cunning as Erica, but it wasn't working to her advantage like she had hoped.

"Hey you know me, I call it how I see it," she replied, attempting to make a quick come back. Instead she further annoyed Ty, and he completely ignored her.

"So what can I do to help you Ms. Erica?" he asked facing Erica, completely tuning Tracy out. She knew she had fucked up royally and decided to keep her mouth shut. She didn't want to mess things up with Ty.

"Well I think you already know what I want from you," Erica flirtatiously responded back.

"No I don't Miss Birthday Girl, so tell me what a brotha can do for you on your special day".

"My girl Tracey told me about your product and I was thinking I start out with twenty cards or better and I need you to drop fifty bills off each one. You know what? On second thought you just keep the price as it is. Just bring me twenty-four plates I can do this."

Ty thought for a minute. "Listen, since Tracy already told me about you, I'm going to jump out there on the strength of her and give you the plates without doing a thorough background check."

"Oh, so you only fucking with me on the strength of Tracy? Money talks, bullshit walks. I'm about business. You should be able to tell from my demeanor that I'm straight up. If anything, you should be fucking with me on the strength of that." Ty fought to keep a snicker to himself. He liked Erica's style.

"Maybe we can—" the sound of Tracy clearing her throat stopped him in mid-sentence.

"I don't mean to interrupt but there goes your man at the bar E." All three of them glanced over and Erica knew it was time to wrap things up. She didn't want Victor to know anything, until she got her shit together. Ty lifted up his shades to get a closer look at the dude buying drinks at the bar.

"Oh, you're Victor's girl?"

"Yeah, why?" Erica asked boldly.

"Nice to know that's all," he said in a cool manner, as he nodded his head. He took in a deep breath and polished off the last of his drink and then very incognito he backed away and said, "Look I'll check you later Shorty." Ty turned and disappeared into the crowd. Erica stood there unsure of how to respond to what had just happened. The whole day had presented an interesting turn of events.

"Damn girl what's up? Why were you grilling him like that? I told you he was cool." Tracy asked Erica once Ty was out of sight.

"Tracy I love you girl, but you are clueless to how niggas get down in the streets. I grew up in this hustling shit. I don't know him, so I have to take every precaution no matter what you say. I got to get a feel for him before I can really trust him, but I do know one thing. He is going to work with us and bring those prices down. That's the main thing we need to be worrying about right now." Tracy's ego was a little bruised, but she knew how Erica was and she loved her for it.

"You sure you're serious about this?" Tracy asked.

"I'm telling you if it's as sweet as you led me to believe back in the mall then, I truly want to begin make some power moves. Are we in this together?" Tracy nodded her head in agreement.

"Yeah, well let me handle this nigga because I see straight through him. His ego is going to get him caught up and then I'll make my move." Erica stated cunningly.

"Alright Erica... Do you girl," Tracy said. She was excited to have her girl join her in this new hustle. Erica's mother approached the two girls looking tired.

"Erica, when are you going to cut the cake? I'm ready to go home. I'm tired."

"OK, Ma, I'm going to get Victor. Just have a seat and chill out for a minute." Erica looked around and noticed Victor chilling with his boys at a table close to the bar. She came up from behind him and wrapped her arms around his neck. "Hey Babe. Ma is ready to leave, so make the announcement for us to cut the cake."

"I don't want any cake," Victor said, obviously drunk.

"OK Victor, just make the announcement baby. If you can't do it, we can ask Twan to do it." Victor nodded and Twan made the announcement.

All gathered around and sang the Stevie Wonder version of the Happy Birthday song to Erica. Raising their glasses they all cheered and she cut into her three-layer strawberry and pineapple sheet cake that Victor had designed in purple and pink with a 4" inch high diamond like version of the letter "E" sitting dead center with smaller renditions of diamond jewelry including a tiara, drop earrings and several necklaces with pendants sprinkled across the top. Strawberries the size of large eggs, were grouped together in 3's in all four corners. The cake read "HAPPY BIRTHDAY E". It was a work of art, almost too pretty to eat.

Erica got a piece of cake and tried to share it with Victor.

"E, I told you I don't want any cake, Baby. I can't mix that sugary shit with all this liquor, You trying to have a nigga sick as a dog tonight?" Erica thought about Victor's statement and realized that he was right. She decided not to eat any cake either, but she did eat the strawberries off the top. As she cut through the cake, she bumped into something hard.

"What's this? Victor what's this baby?" she said half-smiling and half-confused. "Give me a napkin." Victor handed her the napkin and just watched her and smiled. She worked anxiously through the cake cutting bigger and bigger slices and found what she was looking for. She screamed and a few people turned their heads to look in the couple's direction. She wiped the ring off and placed the four carat rock on her finger, staring at it admiringly. She jumped into Victor's lap and started showering his face with kisses.

"Damn that shit is blinding me over here," Tracy said.

"That's all you boo. I love you," Victor said to Erica, killing the last bit of Cristal in his champagne flute.

"Erica I don't think I want Victor taking me home like that," Erica's mother said, interrupting their intimate moment.

"Don't worry Mrs. Payne, I'll take you home," Crystal said.

"How did you get here," Erica asked Crystal, knowing that she didn't drive from Atlanta.

"I got Victor's truck. Let's put all these gifts and stuff in the truck so that we can get out of here. Your moms look a little tired." Twan got up and started helping the girls to the truck with all of Erica's presents.

"Where are you staying, Crystal?" Erica asked when Crystal returned.

"I'm going to my mother's unless I get that two-way from Dezo. I might be at the W hotel tonight in Times Square."

"Well … come to my house in the morning to drop the truck off."

"OK."

"You and Victor get home safe," Erica's mother interjected with a worried look.

"We will Ma, I'll talk to you in the morning," she said kissing her mother on the cheek. They proceeded to leave while everybody else kept partying. Erica walked over to the bar to chat with Tracy. Twan sat next to Victor.

"Yo V, you see that nigga over there? The dude in the black? Doesn't that look like that nigga Ty?"

"Yeah that's that bitch ass nigga! What the fuck is he doing up in here?"

"I don't know, but I think I saw him talking to Tracy and Erica earlier, but I wasn't sure until now. What the fuck is up with that shit?"

"That nigga was talking to my girl? Yo Twan you strapped?"

"I stay that way," Twan answered with a smile, tapping the 9mm he had on his hip.

"I'm about to lay his ass down for disrespecting me!"

"Nah Victor hold up, nigga."

"What the fuck you mean? Hold up!" Victor barked with slurred speech.

"This nigga took my loot and now I see him talking to my girl, fuck that! It's a private party anyway how he get up in here?"

"Look, man it's a time and a place for everything. This may be the time, but it damn sure ain't the place. We'll catch that nigga slipping again."

Erica returned to where the men were sitting.

"Yo, Erica, what the fuck you doing talking to that Queens snake?"

"What?" she asked unsure of what she had just walked into. Twan pointed in Ty's direction. "Oh him? That's Ty," she responded wondering why he was so upset.

"I know who the fuck it is! I asked what the fuck you doing talking to him?"

"He's Tracy guest, she introduced me to him, all I said was hi, and that's all."

"Where Tracy know him from?" Victor asked steaming.

"I don't know, Boo. Why what's up with you, why you acting all detective like?"

"Just don't let me see none of ya'll talking to him again. That nigga is a snake and I don't trust him," Victor said never taking his eyes off of Ty.

"OK Boo calm down," Erica said putting her arm around his neck and kissing him. They kissed and embraced for a while and slowly Victor was calmed down and almost forgot what he was beefing about.

"Alright, Ma. See what your lips do to me? You better stop before I have your ass bent over up in the club rest room."

"Ohh baby you better stop. You know how I do," she replied with a mischievous grin on her face.

"I see you liked your gift baby."

"If you take me home, I'll show you how much."

"You ain't gotta tell me twice, let's bounce," he said palming her ass.

"Stop, Victor," she said giggling.

"Be quiet, this is mine. Give me a minute, let me holla at Twan alright."

"Boo, hurry up, I'm ready to go."

"Twan, what's up, you straight?" Victor asked

"Yeah, I'm aight, why?"

"Me and E 'bout to bounce, what you gonna do?"

"I'm going to stay for a minute, and then I'm gone. Keep your eyes open nigga and be safe."

"No doubt," Victor said, giving Twan dap. The couple said their goodbyes to everyone and made their exit out of the club.

Chapter 6

Victor and Erica had finally arrived home. They were quickly undressing so that they could jump into bed and end the party with a bang.

"Baby I really had a good time. I don't know how you pulled all of this off, and I love my gift. I'm sorry for acting all crazy earlier, but you know how I am about surprises. I still can't believe you flew my girls in!" Erica spoke to Victor with her slurred, intoxicated "I love you" tone.

"Baby you know I'd do anything for you. We've been down far too long not to take the next step. E, you know how much I love you right?"

"Yeah Victor. And I love you too. I love you so much," Erica said feeling overwhelmed by her emotions from the day's events. Victor walked over to her and kissed her gently on the lips. He helped her ease out of her Black dress and stared at her beautiful body glistening in the moonlight. Erica grabbed his shirt and practically ripped it open. The liquor had their hormones raging like drunken college students at a fraternity party.

Erica pushed Victor back onto the bed and started to slow-grind on his dick as it sprang to attention through his slacks. Victor took a handful of her breasts and reached up to place them into his mouth, ravishing them like a starved babe. Their breathing increased and moments later they were both butt-naked making their headboard sing. He kissed her lips and made his way down her body placing soft sensual kisses down her breasts, to her stomach and stopped right above her belly button. Victor lifted Erica's left leg over his shoulder and placed his middle finger slowly into her love. She was dripping wet. He reached up and placed his wet finger into her mouth so she could taste herself. Erica sucked all her juices off his fingers and sat up to return the favor. She couldn't wait to have him in her mouth. She devoured his fat dick and worked the magic of her tongue, almost putting Superhead to shame. Victor didn't want to come yet so he pulled out. Erica rolled him on to his back and prepared to mount him. He looked up at her to see if she was ready for what he was about to give.

"Damn ride that dick baby. Damn," Victor called out. "Mmm you like that dick? Huh E, you like that dick?"

"Yea baby. I love it. Oh shit," Erica said as she began to climax. Sensing she was about to explode, Victor increased his pace to meet her stroke for stroke which drove Erica wild.

"Oh my God," Erica said as she exploded and engulfed Victor's dick in her juices. Victor continued to thrust into Erica, until he too was on the verge of climax.

"Oh shit E, I'm about to let it go."

"Yeah baby. Let it go. I want it all." Erica tightened her pussy walls around his swollen dick and started riding Victor as if her life depended on it.

"Oh shit Erica! Shit!" Victor couldn't take it anymore, and erupted inside of Erica. She collapsed on his chest as he was trying to catch his breath.

"I love you boo," Erica whispered into his ear before kissing his lips.

"I love you too baby. I love you too," he said still breathing heavily. He placed his hands on her ass and massaged both cheeks before wrapping his arms around her.

They started kissing again and moments later, Erica felt his dick getting hard again.

"Damn you didn't get enough huh?" Erica asked laughing. Victor jumped up and pushed Erica up and turned her around to get it doggy style.

He slid his dick deep inside her wet pussy walls for the second time and pumped until they climaxed. They cuddled in the spoon position and fell asleep.

Erica woke up at about 11:00am and fixed some turkey sausage, cheese eggs, home-fries, toast and coffee. She knew she was going to have to be serious about her wifely duties, not only because of Victor's proposal but also to pump Victor for more info about Ty. She and Ty had some pending business and she needed to know what the issues were between the two. Unfortunately, she already knew she was not going to be able to accommodate Victor by staying away from Ty like he demanded. Ty was giving Erica the opportunity of a lifetime and she couldn't imagine giving that up. Although she loved Victor with all her heart, she didn't want to have to depend on him for everything. Yes she had a regular 9 to 5 but with her spending habits, she'd go through her small paycheck in less than a week. She needed more, and Ty was the key to her financial independence.

Victor started tossing and turning as he smelled the delicious aroma from the food Erica was cooking. After a night of partying, drinking and fucking, Victor was more than ready to get his eat on. Erica fixed a tray of food and took it up to him.

"Wake up V. I made you something to eat."

"OK baby, two more minutes."

"Now V! Come on I fixed breakfast the least you can do is get up and eat it. I got shit to do. I want to go hang out with the girls before they leave town and I want to spend some time with you before they get here."

"Aight E, I'm getting up now. Damn! You drain a brother, and then you don't let him get his proper rest."

"Whatever, just get up," Erica responded with a sarcasm. Victor got up to go to the bathroom and relieve himself. He put some water on his face and washed his hands.

"It smells good baby, what did you fix?" Erica recited the menu. "I tink I luv she," Victor responded jokingly in his rendition of a Jamaican dialect. He finally positioned himself to eat, and removed the cover from the plate. "Are you going to join me?"

"Nah I'm not hungry. I'll probably get something to eat with the girls."

"So who are you diva bitches going to terrorize today?" Victor commented, knowing first-hand that Erica and her girls were dangerous when they got together.

"Nothing we'll probably just get something to eat and talk—"

"And shop," Victor said, finishing her sentence.

"You think you know it all don't you? I just might be going to meet my boyfriend." Erica responded baiting him into the question about Ty.

"Oh really? Tell that nigga, I said what up."

"Oh, so now you are going to act like you're not jealous?"

"Jealous? E you know that ain't my style."

"Oh, really? I can't tell the way you were tripping last night about that guy Tracy introduced me to."

"E, that wasn't jealousy. That was my love and concern for you. That motherfucker is grimy."

"Victor what is your issue with him? We both know grimy motherfuckers and you know that I can handle myself."

"Erica, I know where you are going with this and I'm not falling for it. I am telling you to stay away from that nigga. I mean it. Don't test me on this one, trust me." Victor's whole demeanor changed and it was clear that he really hated Ty.

"OK baby if you say so. But what's up."

"What's up is what I told you. STAY-THE-FUCK-AWAY-FROM-THAT–NIGGA!" Erica blew out a deep breath. This conversation was going nowhere and she was tired as hell of all Victor's secrecy. She had already heard around town that the two had been bickering over some turf war shit about which crew had what corners. What the hell is so secret about that? Why can't the nigga just tell me what I want to know so I can be on my way? Erica just stood by her dresser watching Victor eat. The more she thought about things, the angrier she got. Victor had become more secretive and demanding in the past year and she was getting really sick of him and all his bullshit.

Erica snapped out of her train of thought and started rummaging through her drawers for a pair of panties and a bra. She took her things and went into the bathroom for a quick shower. She was ready to go in 30 minutes flat. She grabbed her car keys and LV purse from the dresser, and headed for the bedroom door.

"I'm out," she said walking past Victor.

"I thought that you were going to spend some time with me and they were going to meet you here?"

"Nah I am going to go catch up with them. You pissed me off with this shit. I don't understand why you can't just tell me what the big deal is and why you beefing with some motherfucker from Queens."

"Yeah and I don't know why you can't just take some things for face value."

"Whatever," Erica said and walked out, slamming the door behind her. She hopped in her car and drove off.

* * *

Erica had driven for what felt like hours, but it was only a few miles. She was furious that Victor would dare belittle her to her face, implying that she could not take care of herself and he could control her by telling her whom she could and could not speak to. Caught up in her anger, she barely noticed that her gas tank was nearing empty. Sighting a gas station up ahead, she quickly pulled in to refill.

Dropping twenty-five to the cashier, Erica began to pump her gas when a voice came from across the way.

"Hey, what's up?" She looked over her shoulder and saw that it was Ty. He was standing across the way in all his fineness, pumping gas into a silver Lexus GS300. Ty looked at Erica with keen interest. Seeing him now in the light, Erica took notice of his hazel eyes, which she couldn't see during their first meeting. She was happy to see him because she had been thinking about him ever since Tracy introduced them. Not necessarily in a romantic way, but she wanted to get to business as soon as possible.

"Hey what's up, you pumping gas too? What brings you to this side of town?" Erica responded, looking him up and down.

"Baby I'm like crack, you can find me everywhere."

"Yeah? Flies are everywhere too, what's your point?"

"Oh you got jokes. You fine as hell and funny too." Ty looked at Erica as if he would consume her at any minute. He took notice of every curve of her petite body, especially how her fitted skirt hugged her curvaceous hips and thighs.

"Uh excuse me, my mouth is up here," she said, making a gesture with her hands to direct his gaze to her face. Ty was distracted from his moment of lust and continued the conversation.

"So, you ready to be a member of my team and handle a little business?" Erica let out a slight chuckle. Thinking about how right she was about him having a big ego.

"Didn't you get the news baby, I am your MVP. I am like the queen of England. I stay down for my crown."

"Really? Then that's what's up. Can I interest you in a cup of cappuccino? There's a Starbucks near here."

"That sounds delightful, but I have a previous engagement." Erica responded with cynicism in her voice. She shook the pump and placed it back into its cradle. She closed her gas cap and clicked the lock.

"Well let's get together later, give me your cell phone number." Ty was already plotting on how he was going to get at Victor through Erica, but Erica was already ten steps ahead, as she always was.

"Nah baby, you will get a number one day, but not this one."

"Well then plug my number in your cell, 917 872-" Erica interrupted him before he could finish.

"Sweetie just like my G-spot, I know how to get at you. I'll be in touch." Ty smiled that sexy smile, and walked away mildly defeated. Erica stood there smiling, watching him retreat, but they both knew that this was only the beginning. She jumped into her car and sped out of the gas station before he could, making sure that he was still watching her every move.

"This is going to be more fun than I thought," Erica said to herself and laughed as she noticed Victor's name on her caller ID.

Chapter 7

Erica sped through the streets of Brooklyn with thoughts of both Victor and Ty on her mind. On the one hand she was about to marry the man who had stood by her and taken care of her for all of her young adult life, yet on the other hand there was another man whom her fiancé hated, that would help her get ahead and make money. Erica had so many decisions to make that she was bombarded with feelings of confusion and emotion. She thought that at any second her head would explode—the beginning of a hunger headache no doubt. As she drove along she felt her stomach growling and remembered that she hadn't eaten any breakfast. Her little chance meeting with Ty had thrown her off completely. She decided to call her girls to see if she could catch them before they left Junior's. She dialed Tracy's cell phone.

"Y'all bitches are crazy—" Tracy said, as she answered her phone in mid–sentence, "Hello?"

"It's me Erica. Are ya'll still at Junior's?"

"Yeah why what's up? I thought we were meeting you at your crib?"

"Naa, I'm on my way there and I'm hungry. Can you order me the fried shrimp platter and a chocolate martini? I'm on my way. I'm headed down Atlantic Avenue now."

"How long is it going to take you? Are you in traffic?" Tracy asked, looking at Kim and Crystal.

"Nah, I'll be there in 10 minutes. Just make sure my food is on the table when I get there."

"Aight E, anything else?" she asked sarcastically.

"Nah, friend, I will see you in a minute. I just hope that I can get a parking space." Fifteen minutes later, Erica pulled up on Flatbush Avenue and found a parking space right on the corner of Junior's restaurant. She was relieved, because with the way she was feeling, she really didn't feel like having to look around for a parking space. Downtown Brooklyn was notorious for ridiculous parking meters and ticketing traffic officers, so drivers had to be very cautious with where they parked their cars. She also didn't feel like going out too far being as though she was wearing a very high pair or Manolo Blahnik boots that were made for sitting, not walking.

Erica walked into the restaurant to find "The Meeting of the Diva's" already underway. Apparently, Erica had missed a real funny joke because Tracy and Crystal were laughing hysterically and Kim was damn-near about to choke on her food.

"What the hell is so funny?" Erica asked as she sat down. Kim decided to do the honors and fill her in.

"Erica our waiter is a trip. You have got to see this guy. I think he is Russian or something and he keeps flirting with us with these corny ass lines, but that is not the half. Girl you have got to see him. He has on these tight ass pants, I mean booty chokers. His toupee is propped on his head flopping around like it's fanning his scalp. Now I know what it means to peel someone's cap back. And wait… he has this big bulge in his pants, but we think it's a sock," she said still laughing hysterically.

"No, I think it is a pair of socks," Crystal interrupted. Erica scooted over closer to Kim, observing the spectacle of her girlfriend's amusement.

"Umm before you finish bitch, where is my drink and my food?" Erica questioned, as if she was having a mini-tantrum, while giving her girls the look as if a pimp slap would soon follow.

"Erica he just went back to get it," Tracy responded calmly. She knew how Erica acted when she was hungry, so she paid her no mind.

"OK, what about my drink? Damn, Tracy I am not trying to be a bitch, but I am hungry as hell. I thought that you had me." There was a brief silence as a waitress placed a drink on the table.

"Your waiter will be out with your food in a minute," she said before walking away.

"As you were saying," Tracy snapped sarcastically. Erica realized that she was being a little over the top, but they knew she didn't mean anything by it. She figured they'd be a little edgy too if they were as famished as she was, besides they grew up together and regardless of how old they got some things would not change.

"Thank you girl. After the morning I had, a girl needs her nourishments." This was Erica's way of bringing it down to a dull roar, as she took a sip of her chocolate martini. "Mmm just what the doctor ordered. Thanks Tracy." Erica now turned her attention back on Kim. "Now, what the fuck were you talking about?"

"You'll see in a minute." Just as she finished her sentence, the waiter approached the table with a piping-hot plate.

"Here you are ladies. Be careful, it is hot like me." He could barely speak English and here he was trying to be clever with words.

With a deep accent the waiter initiated Erica with one of his lines. "Ah I see we have another beautiful woman with nice rack." His eyes went straight for Erica's chest. Erica's eyes were fixed on the plate of shrimp, but she looked up for a moment to witness this buffoon. When she established eye contact with the waiter, he immediately became nervous. His playful mood had changed. In fact, his whole demeanor changed. Before he could speak, Erica dropped her napkin. The waiter bent down to pick it up, never taking his eyes of her. It was as if he was mesmerized.

Erica's actions were just the opposite. She refused to continue to engage him with conversation, much less eye contact. To Erica he was below her and for that she would not acknowledge him. She waited impatiently as he bent down to retrieve her napkin for her, and quickly offered them a fresh batch of napkins from the pocket on the front of his apron.

"Uh, I hope everything good," he said nervously as he looked around the table awaiting their responses.

Erica paid him no mind as she gulped down her fried shrimp and martini. The girls simply shrugged off her behavior as being typical Erica—stuck up. Once she deemed someone a nuisance, she would refuse anything connected to them. Kim, not quite as in tuned with anything that was going on, hadn't even realized that Erica had dropped her napkin in the first place. She was still humored by the waiter's whole costume and cartoon antics. Being the clown that she was, she purposely spilled her drink on his pants. The waiter, stunned by the cold drink, backed away from the table. Kim, continuing with her prank, grabbed her napkin and began to wipe his pants.

"Oh I am so sorry. I don't want to wake the anaconda," she

humorously commented, taking a cheap shot at the infamous bulge. Her efforts were focused on his crotch. She was determined to prove that the bulge was some type of falsity. The sock in his pants was now at the bottom of his right pants' leg. After witnessing the vanishing "anaconda," the girls were once again hysterical in laughter. The waiter rapidly retreated to the kitchen in embarrassment.

Now everyone in the restaurant was staring at them wondering what had caused the commotion, Erica grew weary. She hated to bring too much attention to herself.

"I thought that we were here to catch up on some things and take care of business, not be concerned about this sock-dick motherfucker," she snapped with the look of annoyance in her eyes. Her statement only incited more laughter from the crew. Erica was not amused and only wanted the attention from the restaurant patrons to cease. This day is turning out to be too full of foolishness! She thought to herself.

Tracy noticed that Erica appeared a little offset and not at all joining in on the fun, so she moved in to change the mood and conversation.

"So E, what's up with you and Victor?"

"What do you mean what's up with us?" Erica responded a little on the defensive side.

"Ya'll getting married or what? Bitch, you know what I mean. Last night you got that big ass rock, so what's up?"

"How do you know that we're not already married?"

"Well, shit you right, I don't know, as much as you are under that nigga," Tracy said before sticking out her tongue at Erica.

"Whatever, I know you ain't talking Tracy, not the way Twan got your ass on lock down."

"OK, OK. But you're right. We don't know the deal, so why

don't you enlighten us? We're listening," Tracy said with a big smile on her face. Erica looked around and noticed everyone staring at her.

"Shit, they might as well be married the way she be playing house and shit," Kim said laughing and breaking the silence.

"And besides bitch, you can't talk about me. I still got my friends, you cut everybody off for Victor," replied Tracy defending her relationship with Twan.

"What are you saying? I'm with you bitches now." They all started laughing. Crystal chimed in.

"Kim you just mad 'cause you don't have a man hooker."

"I might not have a man, but I got plenty of sponsors that keep a bitch fly!" Kim retorted.

"I know that's right," Tracy said as she gave Kim a high-five.

"See that's your problem. You bitches are looking for a social security plan in these niggas. You better start thinking about getting your own dollar and a dream," Erica responded, directing the conversation to business.

"Erica, please. Like Victor is not a part of your retirement plan," Tracy retorted attempting to put Erica in her place, but Erica was not interested in getting into a bullshit tit-for-tat with Tracy. She knew that she was a little envious of her and Victor, but she had to respond if she was going to complete her mission for the day.

"Listen Victor is a part of my retirement plan, but not financially. He is what he is to me because of what we are to one another. Please don't get it twisted," she said in a serious tone. "That shit is not a fairy tale all the time, but it is worth it. I love Victor but trust, I am worth more than he can provide and so are you… all of you. That is what I want to talk to you about. Now are you all ready to get down to business?"

"OK, E what's up?" Tracy asked, curious to see what Erica was going to say.

"Listen up ladies. Tracy introduced me to this guy named Ty who is supposed to be a major player in the credit card game. I am not quite sure how deep his game runs, but I am sure as hell going to find out."

"But Erica, what about that shit between Ty and Victor? What's up with that? You know Twan don't tell me shit about his business," Tracy asked with concern in her voice.

"Tracy, don't worry about that. I have the tea for that fever."

"You always do E," Crystal chimed in. Although they were best friends, Crystal had always been a fan of her girl Erica. Crystal was two years older, she admired Erica because she seemed to be fearless, and in Crystal's eyes, living life with the absence of fear was one of life's most incredible feats.

"Would you bitches let me finish?" Erica was exasperated and anxious to finish laying out her game plan. She continued. "The bottom line is that everyone wants to be able to acquire a few needs and desires, and credit is a commodity that everybody wants, but few people have, at least to the extent that we will be able to provide for them," she said pausing for effect. "For a small fee of course," she added with a smile.

"OK, OK," Kim yelled out. "You got my attention. What do you have in mind?"

"Well, the way I see it is if Ty is currently charging five hundred dollars for the works of the card and matching ID, we should be able to get him to cut that price in half by ordering in bulk. I know that it sounds like a lot right now but if you think about it, it's all worth it. Say you buy a card for five hundred; you could get yourself a cash advance to get your money back and then spend on another mark's credit. Feel me? Plus, with the volume of clientele that we can produce in all the locations we know people, he'll have no choice but to cut our price. The numbers are official so technically these cards aren't fake. We are just taking that information and creating new cards with pre-existing accounts from god knows who.

"Listen ladies once we get in, this will be a piece of cake. We stand to make a small fortune if we play this smart. This ain't like the drug game where you on street corners constantly putting your ass and the asses of your team members on the line. By using credit cards we won't need to supply ID. How many times have you gone into a store and used a credit card without having to show ID?"

"Shit, all the time," Crystal said with a chuckle.

"Exactly my point. However, you have to remember that you're supposed to be someone else so you can't slip up and write your own damn name on receipts. It's imperative to get that point across to anyone that you sell the plates to. Ain't that right Ms. Penn?" Erica said looking over at Tracy with a smile.

"Right, Mrs. Fletcher." The other two girls looked at them like they were crazy.

"What the fuck? Never mind," Crystal said as she started to ask what the hell they were talking about.

"Why don't we need ID?" Kim asked.

"I will get to that later. I have a plan," Erica responded.

"Crystal, I know you can get Atlanta on lock between those bitches at the colleges, the mall Diva's and the queens."

"Please, that is a gold mine right there and that is just the obvious market," Crystal said with a laugh. "Whatever E. You know that I'm with it."

"Kim, I want you to take Maryland to North Carolina. I want you to target the doctors, lawyers and CEO's and don't forget the bankers in North Carolina." Although Kim seemed silly, she definitely had a way with the suit and tie set. Kim was like the pretty dumb blonde who was really a genius underneath it all.

"That's what's up," replied Kim.

"Tracy, I want you to handle New York, New Jersey, Philadelphia and Connecticut. I know that Victor and Twan are making some moves with some major players in the recording industry. I want you to tap that market." A waitress came over to the booth and the women fell silent.

"Ladies can I get you anything else?" Everyone, at the table looked at each other in agreement.

"No, thank you we're done," Erica said. "Could you just get us the check please?"

"What happened to our waiter? We thought he was cute," Kim asked.

"Oh I'm sorry, he had to leave. He had an emergency. I am going to close you out if that is oK?"

"See what you did Kim, you done ran the motherfucker off. Is that what you do to all of your men?" Crystal taunted Kim.

"Fuck you Crystal, I did not run him off. It must have been one of you bitches."

"Whatever," Tracy snapped back. "I got the check."

"By the way Tracy, let me get that card when you're done. I need to do some research. And while you're at it I want you to call that nigga Ty tomorrow and set something up. I will call you later with the details," Erica said.

"How did you know that I was going to charge it?"

"Why would you do anything else?" she responded, with a sly look on her face. Tracy smiled.

"Yeah, you know how we do… just charge it to the game."

"Exactly!" Erica retorted. The waitress returned to the table with the bill and Tracy handed her a Discover card. The waitress took the card, which she enclosed in the leather bound encasement. Erica's attention was now on Crystal.

"Crystal, bring Victor's truck by the house later."

"No problem E." Erica slid out of the booth.

"Crystal, Kim how long are you two going to be in town?"

"I'm leaving tomorrow night," said Crystal.

"Me too," added Kim.

"Aight, I will definitely touch bases with you before you leave. Start making a mental note of a client list. I want to have some product in your hands by the end of next week. You ladies be safe, and thank you for a wonderful birthday surprise and the beautiful gifts." The waitress returned with the case and pen enclosed to sign the credit card slip. Tracy signed the slip and handed the card to Erica. Erica leaned over and gave them all a hug and a kiss before making her signature departure with her runway swagger; one hand extended in the air and her pointer finger up. "I'm out!

Chapter 8

Erica's brain was working over time. It was a wonder that there wasn't smoke coming from her ears. While on her way home, she wondered if Victor would be there. More importantly she hoped he was over their little spat about Ty. Erica realized Victor and Ty's beef wasn't all that important. At this point she had accepted nothing. She was definitely going to get at Ty at least on a business level and Victor didn't have to know everything that she did.

Erica thought about how far she and Victor had come together. Victor and Erica had been through so much in their relationship. After Erica left home, she found it a little hard to get over leaving her mother to deal with the monster she called a father. Erica had waited patiently for Gregory to return home after her mother's hospital stay, but he never showed up. A month later he was found at a local crack house, high and laid up with some crack whore that he probably picked up in the streets. He was arrested and sent back to prison, which was nothing new to Erica and her family. Erica didn't know what upset her more; the fact that he could care less about what he had done to her mother, or the fact that the police found him before she did. Either way she was pissed that she couldn't get at him like she had planned. How could a man go from being the ruler of the streets and a loving husband, to some abusive psycho who lays up with crackheads? All respect for her father was completely demolished as far as Erica was concerned.

Dorothy returned home shortly after Gregory was convicted and once Monica was through with college, she too decided to return home to the Fort to watch over their mother. Erica, however, remained with Victor. She enjoyed being able to go to sleep and wake up by his side every day. She had also learned so much from him. He showed her so many things on the business side, both with his record label and his drug dealings. He made sure that if anything were to happen to him, she would be set financially. She knew where all of his stash houses were, as well as the locations to all his safes and important people to contact should anything go wrong. Despite their constant bickering the two shared a tight bond and Victor knew that he could trust Erica with his most prized possessions. Briefly this made her feel a little guilty about not letting him in on her new dealings with Ty, but she quickly brushed those thoughts off. She would just take things one day at a time. While her new venture was not to Victor's liking, she knew all too well that it was not in her best interest to be so dependent. If necessary, she had to be prepared. At this point things could go either way and she may not be dealing with Ty at all if he wasn't willing to agree to her terms.

Erica took a deep breath and focused on the drive. She decided to give some consideration to her upcoming wedding. It was already March and she needed to start making the arrangements for an end of summer ceremony. She was thinking maybe late August or September. She had a lot of planning to do and had no idea what church she wanted to wed in, much less where to have the wedding party, get her dress, the reception hall… she had a lot to think about and this shit with

Victor and Ty wasn't helping any. She started to think that if she could square away her business dealings with Ty in the next month or two, and have the girls set-up with their supplies and clientele she would be completely free once the wedding came around to be able to enjoy the ceremony and honeymoon.

She smiled at the thought of her and Victor visiting someplace they had never been to, like Greece or Italy and making love on the beaches as man and wife. She even thought about the day she would give birth to their first child and whether or not they would have a little boy or girl.

With everything going on, she decided that it would be best to hire a wedding planner. She had taken a few days off from work to continue celebrating her birthday so she had some time to research wedding planners, look into the credit card she had gotten from Tracy, and meet with Ty to settle their business. All Erica needed was to sit down and map everything out. She always worked well with a game plan. She spent the rest of her ride home mapping it all out in her head.

* * *

Ty sat at home chilling with one of his side hoes, Tiffany. She was in the kitchen trying to live out her fantasy of being a permanent fixture in his home and in his life. But that wasn't going to happen. He was not the settling-down type. He had too much larceny in his heart and quite frankly, he didn't trust women. For him, women had been a diversion for brief amusement and an occasional sexual release.

In an effort to play psychologist, Ty's friends always blamed his treatment of women on his mother. He was born and raised in the streets of Queens, bouncing from place to place. He lived in Far

Rockaway, Cambria, Laurelton, Jamaica, St. Albans, and finally as an adult he had moved to Jamaica Estates. He wasn't the product of your typical urban street story. His mother wasn't a crack head or a prostitute, she was just selfish. At 15, she had gotten pregnant, after hooking up with an older boy in her neighborhood who had promised her everything under the sun until he found out. Immediately after, he kicked her to the curb and left months later to attend college out of state. By the time his mother realized that his father would have nothing to do with them, it was too late. She was too far along in her pregnancy to get an abortion and even if she wanted one she couldn't afford it.

Being blessed with a small frame, she was able to hide her belly until her eight month when she suddenly blew up like a balloon. Her parents, being heavily into the church, pointed the finger at her and told her that she would have to leave once the baby was born. After having Ty, her parents gave her a few dollars and sent her on her way. She went from place to place until she found a room nearby to rent and was happy to know that an old woman who roomed next door to her, didn't mind watching her crying baby. His mother worked and worked to support herself and her baby, but she couldn't help but feel like Ty was to blame for all her misfortune and never missed an opportunity to tell him so, although he was just a toddler. She would just rant about her misfortune and gave cold love to Ty. At the age of 30 she committed suicide. By then Ty was old enough to take care of himself and had found his way in the street life, doing stick-ups and selling drugs for local dealers. .

Nothing made Ty's dick harder than the thought of digits in his bank account and he did any and everything to get it. He wasn't like your average guy who played mind games with women to get some ass. He wanted more and for some reason women flocked to him. They all wanted to believe that they had that special something to gain Ty's trust and love, but that was never the case.

Ty sat at his desk staring at the computer, trying to analyze some data codes for a new batch of cards, but his mind kept drifting. He was thinking about her. He was also thinking about how he was going to get back at Victor, using Erica as the piece de résistance to make his revenge even sweeter. His mind wandered with all the possibilities as to how he could make money off of Erica and then do whatever he wished to her to get revenge back on Victor. Kidnapping, murder, whatever his heart desired. But right now he had to hold off on harming her because her business seemed too vital. He could tell just by their first meeting that she was about getting her money.

But as much as he thought about ways of using her as a tool, he started to wonder about her. What type of person she was. What her favorite perfume might be. Her smile when she was happy. What kind of flowers she liked. His imagination started running wild with the possibilities of ways to get her to let her guard down, until he heard his door bell ring. It was his two boys, Troy and Phil. They had stopped by to give Ty an update on how things were progressing with his empire. Ty couldn't even focus on what they were saying. He was more upset that his thoughts of Erica had been interrupted. What the fuck is wrong with me? He asked himself. You know we don't waste time thinking about no bitches.

After the update, Troy and Phil sat down to watch TV. Ty tried to refocus his thoughts to the computer screen, but Tiffany came out of the kitchen.

"Hey baby, dinner will be ready in a minute. Is Troy and Phil staying for dinner?" Now Ty was really annoyed. Her whole happy homemaker routine pissed him off.

"Thanks, Tiff I really appreciate you coming over and fixing dinner, but Troy and Phil are not staying," he said blowing her off. And neither are you, he thought. "But I do need to talk business with Phil and Troy. Do you mind if we resume another time? I'll call you tomorrow," he said and focused his attention back to the computer screen. Tiffany could only stand there with hurt and disappointment in her eyes. She had just spent all that time making her famous broiled salmon cured in whiskey, Black beans, yellow rice, leaks and zucchini, with the hopes of being his dessert. But those fantasies had been shattered. She had just been dismissed.

Ty didn't even bother to see if she was still standing there or not. He didn't care. At this point he didn't even like her anymore, so he probably wouldn't eat her food. He was funny like that; once he was done with something he was completely through. Tiffany knew better than to express any disappointment regarding her plans. Instead she took it like a trooper.

"Good evening gentlemen," she said as she grabbed her bag and coat and left immediately.

"Damn Ty, you are deep," Troy said. Ty didn't respond to Tiffany's departure or Troy's comment. Instead he interjected with a question.

"So what do you know about that Erica chick?"

"Who, the shorty from the party the other night? Victor's girl?" Phil said, already making a B-line to the kitchen.

"Yeah the one with that fine heart-shaped ass," Troy said smirking, but Ty was not amused. His expression never changed and he did not blink from his eye contact with Troy.

"Man I don't know what's up with her, I mean she is known as Victor's wifey, but there is no real story behind her. I mean, what are you trying to know?" Troy asked noticing Ty's irritated expression.

"In other words, you don't know shit right?" Ty asked.

"Nah man, I mean just surface shit. I know this; she ain't nothing to fuck with!" Ty was pissed. He was satisfied with Troy not knowing, but all his adlibs were getting on his damn nerves.

"Troy, do me a favor man. If you don't know specifics, shut the fuck up and go and find out. Don't repeat that weak ass shit. 'Not something to fuck with'? Nigga how you know that if you don't know shit about the broad? I fucks with anything I wanna fuck with, you feel me?"

"Damn Ty oK… what's up with you nigga?" Troy said staring at Ty like he was a mad man.

"Hey Ty man whatever you want to know I'll find out about the bitch. It's whatever you want to do. You want to kill her or kidnap her? Either way it leads a path straight to that nigga Victor and you know we got to get him by any means necessary," Phil screamed out from the kitchen. Parts of Ty mirrored his sentiment, but he was having second thoughts about Erica. He had not yet defined his feelings, but the puzzling factor was that he was even thinking twice about this woman. This was an entity within itself. Maybe it was just her "I don't give a fuck" attitude, or the fact that she wasn't a dick rider like most of the women that he met. She actually seemed to be about business and business only.

Ty gave some thought to what Phil had suggested, which had already crossed his mind that way. What should be done about Erica?

No matter what, unfortunately she had to get hers whether it be physical or mental. Either way Erica was a direct path to get to Victor. Ty looked at Troy and Phil moving around in the kitchen and thought about the people that he surrounded himself with. At least in the inner-circle of men there was always one or two in a bunch that was either down for anything or always trying to see a way out. Troy and Phil were always down for anything. Ty decided to let the Erica topic go. He wanted to explore whatever this new thing was without influence.

Erica finally arrived home and Victor wasn't there. As usual duty called and he had to leave. Erica was happy for a moment of solace. Not yet finished with her evaluation of the day's events, she sat down on the couch and put her feet up. She noticed a piece of her expensive birthday dress by the coffee table. She had a brief vision of how good the sex had been the previous night. Just before she could indulge herself in a re-creation of the events, she remembered that she had work to do before Victor got home. In a spry manner, she got up from the couch and went down to the basement, eager to complete her list of tasks for the girls' new business venture.

The house had a finished basement where there was an office complete with a library of software, movies, and books on various subjects, including law and financial management. Notwithstanding manuals on importing and exporting, fine wines, rare coins, graphics, cases of ink cartridges, reports on numerology and complex mathematical concepts. She also had a copy of The Art of War by Sun Tzu, and a chess game already in progress, in which she battled herself.

Instead of shopping away all of her free time, she decided that she would utilize her days learning. Going back to college somehow seemed too restrictive. Sitting in a classroom all day so that a high-paid professor could half-ass teach subjects that weren't even important to her field of study and then to pay for it all, didn't seem appealing to her. There was something sacred about her self-teachings that allowed her to escape… escape from all of the pain that she had experienced and witnessed in her lifetime. She faced the daunting elements of her insecurities with her plans to conquer the world.

Erica's mother was similar to her in her younger days before she met Gregory. She too was young and curious about life. She was bright and loved to learn, always creating things to stimulate and increase her intellectual capacity. Erica vowed that she would never become so complacent with the chimera of security of what a man could bring and would accomplish financial security for herself. Victor was not at all like her father, but she was not sure how he would react to her unquenchable thirst to have a hustle all her own.

Erica knew Victor well and knew that he loved being the breadwinner of the household and feeling needed. She didn't mind letting him feel that way, but deep down she wanted more. She loved Victor with all her heart but in her lifetime she saw that love sometimes didn't last forever, nor was it everything. Erica also knew that with the power of knowledge she could always free herself, just in case in the future Victor became like her father. She sat down at her desk and examined her fortress of solitude, finding everything she could want in life in this one place. She pressed the button on her MAC G4 and waited for it to boot up. While waiting she began to craft her plan.

While the world looked for weapons of mass destruction, Erica would build her own.

Chapter 9

Ding dong. Ding dong.

"Who is it?" Erica asked over the intercom.

"E it's me, Crystal."

"Aight, I'll be right there." Erica made a quick move on the chess board and rushed upstairs to answer the door.

"Hey girl, I had Dezo follow me over here to drop off Victor's truck."

"OK, good so I don't have to drop you off," Erica responded, glad that she didn't have to go back out. Besides, she was just in the middle of something that she wanted to finish before Victor got home.

"So I see you didn't have a hard time finding your local piece of ass for the night?" Erica taunted Crystal with a smile.

"I ain't fucking with Dezo, I just asked him to follow me over here," Crystal snapped, with a smirk on her face.

"Yeah bitch but where you staying tonight?"

"I'll be in my room at the Marriott."

"Great!" Erica was determined to try to get Crystal to confess to being with Dezo. "I'll be over there later to hang out with you before you leave. Uh what time should I come through?" Erica laughed.

"Look, I know you love me, but I also know that you are not trying to see my ass tonight," Crystal responded.

"Well if you know so much, then why won't you just cut the

bullshit and tell me what's good?"

"Mmm hmm, whatever." Crystal handed Erica the keys to the truck and headed for the door. As she was leaving she looked back at Erica and laughed. "Cock blocker!"

"Bye girl you are too crazy! Don't hurt 'em now," Erica yelled as she closed the door and went back to the basement to work. She was almost done and was very pleased at the things she found out.

With the credit card, she was able to play around on the Discover website. She found that the card itself was a fake, but the account number was valid, which was a plus so far for Ty. She called Tracy soon after and asked her to make arrangements for her to meet with him as soon as possible. She then called around a few of the wedding planners she had searched online and made appointments to meet with them before returning to work that Wednesday. There were only two on the list that were closed on Sundays, so she would have to make the calls first thing the next morning. As Erica finished jotting down notes in her notepad, she heard the door slamming shut. Victor was home.

"Hey baby," he called out to Erica. She hadn't moved from her position in the basement.

"What's up boo, I'll be right there," she yelled back to him through the intercom. She shoved her notebook in her desk drawer, locked it and placed the key under her favorite book on the book shelf. Then she quickly shut down her computer and scurried up the stairs to meet Victor as he was on his way down to get her. Erica, moving too fast, fell right into his embrace and planted a big wet kiss on his luscious lips.

"Seems like you missed me?" Victor said, holding her in his arms.

"I sure did," she said smiling. Erica noticed a woman's perfume on Victor's coat, but decided to disregard it. She wanted to make sure it was what it was before she started to make a fuss. She knew how Victor was about her jealousy and didn't want to start another heated argument for the day. Besides, she was aware that there was always some bitch in Victor's face. So, she decided to conduct a little test of her own. It was one thing to have a woman's scent on the outside of your coat, which could be caused by brushing against someone or giving a hug, but it was another thing to have it on the inside of your coat, especially in the frigid, New York weather.

Erica stood on her tippy-toes as she reached up and under Victor's jacket holding him close. Low and behold, the scent was all on his shirt and neck. Erica felt the anger building up in the pit of her stomach and couldn't help but question him.

"So, where have you been?"

"I was just out taking care of some things." Here we go again with this damn mystery shit! Erica thought, getting frustrated. Whatever!

"You hungry?" she asked trying to change the subject.

"Nah, I grabbed something while I was out, but I will go and get you something if you want?"

"No that's all right." Erica accepted Victor's answer, but she knew her man, and knew damn well that something was up.

Victor knew Erica as well and was still leery because of the way things had ended that morning concerning Ty. He knew he had to see what Ty was up to and went on a little fact-finding mission of his own. But strangely enough nothing had turned up. It appeared that his quarry was keeping a low profile, but Victor knew how niggas were … eventually they had to show their asses and he would be in the background waiting patiently.

Ty was almost ready. His money was flowing, his product was in place, and the promise of bigger and better things weren't far beyond the horizon. All that was left was to organize the troops.

Stepping into the next room, Ty acknowledged his entire crew. Everyone was waiting to hear what his master plan was. Ty walked to the center of the room and paused in order to make eye contact with everyone. He then began his speech.

"Who are we? The days of the drug wars are passé. There is a new product that is coveted and more powerful than anything that we have undertaken before. The beauty of it is that it is not just limited to a destructive addiction. Everyone wants it and everyone needs it. Parents, doctors, lawyers, the music industry, the good Christians and their pastors, even politicians; no one is exempt. In fact, it is what drives our society. Can anyone tell me what that is?" No one answered.

"Money," Ty said as he shifted uneasily in front of his crew. To Ty, this was a day to remember; the beginning of the end for Victor. While it had only been two years, it felt like twenty since Victor murdered his brother.

Chapter 10

Although Erica was mad as hell about the perfume smell on Victor's clothing, she decided to play her position and keep quiet. As her mother used to say, "what's done in the dark, will come to light" and she knew that it would be a matter of time before Victor's sneaky ways would catch up with him.

"Erica, are you coming to bed?" Victor called out.

"Yeah I'll be there in a minute." Erica was downstairs catching the last part of her favorite movie Heat. No matter how many times she had seen the movie, it still fascinated her. It was as if she was enjoying it for the first time.

"What are you doing?" Victor asked growing a little impatient. He wasn't sure if Erica was paying him back for not stating where he had been earlier, but he noticed that she was acting a little strange. Erica had been known to wild out, so when she acted so calmly about him not revealing where he'd been, he was a little shocked. He also couldn't shake the feeling that their conversation about Ty earlier wouldn't be the last.

He knew how headstrong Erica was, and his worst fear was that she would continue pursuing any contact with Ty or find out what had happened two years prior. Yes he had told Erica about his money and drugs, but never once would he tell her that he had killed the man's brother.

Erica worried enough about him being in the streets, without having to think about gun fights and killings. Besides the less people who knew, the less likely he would get locked up. He also found it a little unsettling that Ty had so easily gotten into Erica's birthday party and had snuck under the radar. What if he decided to retaliate then? Would Erica have been killed? Victor pushed his thoughts aside for a moment. I'll get that nigga when the time is right.

He glanced at the clock and noticed that it had been ten minutes since he called Erica to bed. What the fuck is going on? He asked himself. OK if she's mad, she won't do shit for me, but if she's not, she will.

"Hey baby when you come upstairs, can you bring me something to drink?"

"Sure boo," Erica responded, just like the dutiful wife. "I'm on my way up, what can I get for you?"

"Uh, could you bring me a beer?"

"Do you want it in a frosted glass or just the bottle? Whatever is not too much trouble?" Erica looked up at the ceiling and smiled. Men were so stupid sometimes. She knew what he was up to and his little test wouldn't work. She was ten steps ahead of him. She turned everything off downstairs, except for the hall light and went to the kitchen. She picked up two Coronas and placed lime wedges in each bottle, then headed upstairs.

"Here you are," she said in a soft sultry voice, handing him the beer. "Baby, don't forget to use a coaster. I'm going to get in the shower."

"Why don't you just run us a bubble bath?" Victor asked, looking for an opportunity to seduce her. Erica thought he was really pushing it, but she decided to play along.

"No problem," she responded. Erica ran the hot bath with some bath salts and lavender oils. Victor sipped on his beer as he eyed Erica's silhouette leaning over the tub, testing the water making sure that it was just right. Erica decided to give Victor a little show since she could feel his eyes on her. She crossed her arms and lifted her shirt over her head slowly to show off her tight abdominal, slender waist and curvaceous hips. She undid her belt and slowly zipped down her jeans, sliding them off as if she were shedding a second skin. She stood there in a laced thong and matching push-up bra.

As she loosened her bra, she threw her hair back and looked over her shoulder towards the bedroom.

"Victor the water is ready, are you coming?" Victor was mesmerized. At this point he didn't care that he had lost this round. Erica would have her way with him.

Victor joined her in the bath tub, sliding down behind her. "Baby you know how much I love you, right?" Victor asked, rubbing Erica's shoulders, massaging the oils into her moistened skin.

"Yes baby, I know. I love you too." She extended her hand from the bath water, showing off the diamond ring that he had given her on her birthday. Victor smirked.

"Oh is that why you love me?" Erica laughed.

"Come on now, you know better." She turned around to lay on Victor's chest. He massaged her ass rubbing the oils and bubbles in. Erica kissed Victor so passionately; it felt as if her mouth were on fire. She could feel him rising beneath her.

Victor continued to massage Erica's ass, letting his finger slide down between the crevices, massaging the forbidden hole. Erica squirmed a little avoiding the tickle of the water and bubbles. She slowly eased up, arching her back. As she slid up and down letting the movement of the water swish between them, Victor clutched her breasts with his hands and massaged their fullness. Her nipples glistened as drops of water christened them. As her breasts became firm with pleasure, Victor took them into his mouth one by one, tasting the bitter-sweetness of the lavender. Erica arched her spine forming a half circle as she leaned her head back wanting to experience every aspect of being transformed into a morsel. As she closed her eyes, she allowed herself to drift into ecstasy releasing everything that had happened that day.

Victor's manhood was as hard as a metal rod and Erica could not wait to mount him. As she straddled him, Victor rose up making sure that she took all of him in. Erica contemplated letting him in from behind, but decided to see how well things progressed.

"Sssssss," she hissed, "mmmmmm, oh baby," she whispered. He was feeling so right, so good. He was hitting all of her spots. "Oh shit, Victor, give it to me harder! Show me how much you want this pussy." Victor responded by clamping his hands on her waist and holding her firm and still while he plunged her with quick shots of raw hard dick. Erica wanted to move in order to meet his strokes, but Victor kept her pinned. He wanted to make sure she felt every blow. Erica took it like a champ.

"More, more, more," she chanted and he gave it to her until they finally climaxed together. With Erica screaming and Victor moaning, they held on to each other as he exploded inside of her.

Later while lying in bed cuddled with Victor, Erica could not stop thinking of Ty. She found herself more than preoccupied about their possible business dealings. Erica was curious about all of her new associate's undertakings. She wondered where he was and what he was doing. She found herself anxious about their next meeting. Tracy had called and told her that Ty would reach out to her the next day. She had put together a tight plan, one that he couldn't refuse. She had also secured her team and was ready for anything. All Ty had to do was give her the plates and the green light and the rest was history.

"What are you thinking about, baby," Victor asked, interrupting her thoughts.

"I was thinking about why you're being so secretive these days. There was a time when I didn't have to ask you questions about anything, you would just share your day, your thoughts… everything."

"Erica, I still share everything with you; everything that's important."

"Victor I'm not going to even go there with you, you know what I mean. If you keep this shit up, I'm going to start wondering."

"Baby there is nothing up, I am just trying to make some moves."

"Make some moves or make a move?" Erica asked, twisting Victor's words.

"Why would you even say some shit like that Erica?"

"Because lately you've been the fucking man of mystery!" Erica retorted. "Coming home smelling like another bitch!"

"Erica you're reaching, Ma. You know I don't even get down like that. Another bitch taking your place is something that you would never have to question."

"Victor, trust I am not worried about a bitch, although you did have the hint of perfume on you earlier and all of a sudden you have become a man of few words, at least when it comes to your whereabouts."

Exasperated, Victor blurted out, "The only other bitch I was with today was Crystal, your girl and you know she is like a sister to me." Erica didn't expect to hear this shit. She was only trying to pick a fight with Victor, so he would leave her alone to ponder her thoughts.

"What the hell were you doing with Crystal?"

"I wasn't with her, I just ran into her and that dude she used to mess around with from back in the day, and I gave her a hug."

"Yeah and?"

"And, I told her just like I told you and that damn Tracy, to stay the fuck away from Ty." Erica didn't respond. His statement spoke volumes. Ty really had Victor on fire. She was already determined to get to the bottom of it all; she just wasn't sure how deep it would take her. Her silence made him wonder. He knew that Erica didn't normally retreat from an argument so quickly.

"Oh so now you have anything to say?"

"Victor I'm tired and I told you that I am not going to argue with you, especially about a motherfucker that I don't even know."

"Fuck it," he said frustrated, not imagining how a simple question could lead to such an argument. Victor got up and left the room. Erica rolled over and went to sleep.

Chapter 11

The next day Erica could not wait to call Tracy, so that she could make arrangements to meet Ty. As soon as Victor left out that morning she called her. Tracy picked up on the third ring.

"Hey E, I knew this was you."

"Of course you did, you see my number."

"Yeah, smart ass hold on; I have someone who wants to speak to you."

"Hey you," a voice said from the other end of the phone.

"Uh, hey yourself. Who is this?"

"This is Ty." Erica placed her hand over the phone and started gagging. She didn't know the nigga was gonna be on the phone. She hadn't mentally prepared herself but she quickly got it together.

"What's up? So you working out your prices with Tracy?" she asked in a calm voice, although she was freaking out on her end of the phone.

"No, I thought you and I already worked that out."

"Did we?" Erica responded in a coquettish manner.

"Yeah we did. Or did you forget?" His confidence caught her off-guard.

"OK Sweetie, well I guess there's only one thing left to do."

"Yea, you're right. That's why I came over here early to catch up with you so that we can discuss some things and get everything set up. What is your day like?"

"I'll be available after 2:00, where do you want me to meet you guys?"

"Actually, it will be just you and I," Ty said matter-of-factly.

"Really?"

"Yes, I came all the way over hear hoping to catch your call."

"OK, so where do want to meet?"

"Do you know where—" Erica listened intently.

"Yes, I know it. I'll meet you there at 2:30."

"OK, I'll see you then."

"Alright, tell Tracy I'll call her later," Ty didn't respond, he just hung up. Erica looked at her phone and smiled. She jumped up and got dressed. She had her wedding planners to see out in Long Island and then she had to hurry back to the city to meet up with Ty. While starring in the mirror she reflected back on her life. Aside from her abusive father, things weren't as bad as they could have been. She always had food to eat, a roof over her head, and until her father's act of "humility", clothes on her back. Yet, Victor had still been her knight in shining armor and pretty soon they would be married.

She knew that nothing was perfect but once she got her shit together with Ty, she would be set. She wouldn't even have to work her little bullshit job anymore. Shit maybe she could start her own PR firm or even go into being some kind of an agent. She already had some connections in the industry and with all her free time, she would be able to find a mentor in the business to learn the day to day and then start her own. She smiled at the thought.

Erica put the last touches on her make-up and completed her outfit with her expensive Michael Kors boots that gave her at least four inches, and threw on her Chanel shades. She gave herself one last look in the mirror. She was looking sharp as always, hair done, lips glossed, and dress to the nines

"Let the games begin," she said as she traveled down the stairs and out the door to start her day.

She was lucky to have found the perfect wedding planner at her first go see. Rochelle had a fabulous portfolio. He had coordinated many weddings for A-list celebrities like, Catherine Zeta Jones and Michael Douglas, Russell and Kimora, Carmen Elecktra and her rocker boyfriend. He was a chocolate complexioned, metro-sexual man dressed very GQ with a hint of Glamour magazine. He reminded Erica of a toned-down version of Jay Alexander from America's Next Top Model. His posh agency was located out in Oyster Bay, Long Island. They spent the morning going through several wedding books in order to pick out the essential things for the wedding including themes, colors schemes, dresses and most importantly a date. Finer details in the planning process would come later. Erica set the date for Saturday, September 18, the very end of summer, where the weather wouldn't be muggy hot nor would it be cold yet. After picking out invitations and writing down a task list of important information that she had to supply him with, Erica left for her meeting with Ty, promising to Rochelle call him tomorrow with all of her info.

She arrived at the meeting spot at about 2:15pm and began looking for parking. Of course there was none on the upper west side of Manhattan, so she opted to find a parking garage. Luckily there was one nearby and Erica handed her keys to the attendant and sashayed around the corner to the Bar and Grill. Upon entering, she spotted Ty seated at the bar.

"Hey you," she said, approaching him from behind. Ty turned around immediately.

"Oh hey girl. I already reserved a table for us. Let's go have a seat." After they took their seats at a secluded booth in the corner, they both ordered drinks and food, and then began to chat.

"OK, so is there anything you want to know before we get this thing going?" he asked, looking at Erica with a raised brow.

"Umm I don't think so. As far as I know, we're pretty much up to speed. I need about 50 plates to distribute and I promise you won't regret putting me onto your team," Erica said confidently.

"Well alright," Ty said picking up his drink. "A toast… to good business, and even better partners." Erica raised her glass to his, but couldn't help the underlying message behind his words. Was he really trying to get at her on a personal level? She knew that he was aware of her connection to Victor and it didn't take a dummy to know that he was probably willing to use her to get to him. She pushed those thoughts to the back of her mind. As of right now that was irrelevant. All she wanted to do was secure their transaction so that she and the girls could get started. They had already made their lists of prospects and it was just a matter of time before business would take off. Erica could feel the excitement racing through her bones.

"If everything goes as it should these next couple of months, I would like to invite you on a little business trip. It's an annual thing me and my colleagues do around July. Kind of like a conference to catch up and meet and greet everyone in our organization. The location is confidential of course and if things go well, and I think they will, I'll be sure to see you and your girls in attendance, am I right?" he said looking at her intensely with his eyes.

"Oh I will be there. Make no mistake about that," Erica said, taking another sip of her drink. Their food arrived shortly after and the two spent the rest of their lunch chit-chatting and planning the start of their take over.

* * *

"Boo wake up! Somebody's at the door," Erica yelled to Victor.

"Well get it, I'm tired shit!"

"Well I'm tired too. Shit!" Erica said as she got up to open the door.

"Who is it?" she screamed out groggily.

"It's me bitch open the door."

"Damn Crystal, what the fuck are you doing here so early?" Erica asked irritated as she opened the door to let her in.

"Early? Girl it's a quarter to one ya'll need to get up. Nobody told ya'll to be fucking all night," she said with a smile, as she pushed her way in.

"Shut up and you are too loud Victor is still asleep."

"Come on E get dressed, I want to spend some time with my girls before I leave. I at least want to hang out."

"Did you call everybody? Where's everybody at?" Erica asked trying to wake herself up.

"I haven't talked to Kim, but Tracy is ready for whatever. We tried to call you but you ain't answer. So I came over."

"OK, well I wanted to talk to ya'll anyways."

"About what E?" Crystal asked as she went into the kitchen.

"Nothing big. I just got some things finalized and I wanted to go over them with you and Kim face-to-face before you left."

"Damn you don't have any bottled water?" Crystal asked with her head stuck in the fridge.

"No bitch this ain't the grocery store, close my refrigerator."

"Aight, how long is it gonna take you to get dressed?"

"Bitch just wait, I ain't gonna be long," Erica responded, taking the stairs two at a time.

"Whatever!" Crystal said as she sat on the couch and turned on the TV to wait for Erica to get ready.

"Boo, that's Crystal. She came to get me so we can do the girl thing before everyone leaves."

"Aight baby, could you get me a Tylenol before you leave I got a fucking hangover."

"Aw, poor baby. Next time you go out you should only get soda, since you can't stomp with the big dogs," Erica said laughing as she retrieved the Tylenol from their medicine cabinet.

"Oh you got jokes huh? That's how you gonna treat your man?" he asked, pretending to pout.

"I'm sorry baby gimme a kiss." She pecked his lips and went into the bathroom for a quick shower. When she came out fully dressed, Victor had fallen asleep. She managed to sneak passed him with some skin-tight jeans on and a shirt that showed way too much cleavage. She felt like being sexy and she didn't want to hear his mouth.

"So Crystal how you liking ATL?"

"It's cool. Pouring with ballers, but you know I like to get my own shit. The one thing I can say is that it's hot as hell down there."

"How is school?" Erica asked as they drove.

"Same old shit, I'm still busting my ass. I'm gonna transfer from Clark next semester. Not too sure where but I got to get out of there. Speaking of college, you decided where you going yet?"

"Girl, I wanted to come down to Atlanta with you but I can't convince Victor to go down south. You know that's my baby, I can't leave him, and he can't leave his damn music."

"That's ya boo."

"Yeah, I love him, but sometimes I wish he would just forget about the music shit."

"Well E, you know that ain't happening. That boy has been loving music since 6th grade. I remember all those damn stories that you and Tracy used to tell us about them beating on the lunch tables and shit back in the day. I can't even picture serious ass Twan beating on a desk, with his short ass. He lucky he so damn cute, otherwise Ms. Tracy wouldn't have gave him the time of day," Crystal said laughing.

"Cute? Please, that nigga's slanging that dick that's what got her there," Erica said joining in the laughter. "Yo, hit Tracy on her chirp and ask her where she at? Tell her I'll be at Sugar Canes in about 10 minutes." Crystal reached into Erica's purse to get her Nextel and began to chirp Tracy just as they pulled into the Exxon station. "Let me get some gas, you want anything?"

"No, I'm straight." Erica got out of the car to pay the cashier and get a pack of gum. As soon as she got back in the car, her Nextel began to vibrate.

"That's probably Tracy," she said. Crystal opened up the phone and saw that it was a text message. It said, "We're on our second drink where you at?"

"Oh shit, she there already? Aight tell her we are on the way and to order me some baked clams 'cause I'm hungry as shit, and I don't feel like waiting." Erica pulled up on Flatbush Avenue and found a parking space, down the block from the lounge. "Come on Crystal and grab my purse for me please."

As they walked in the door of the restaurant they saw Tracy and Kim sitting at a booth in the back. "What's up ya'll?" Crystal asked, as she approached the entourage. "Ain't shit, what's up with your talkative ass?"

"Fuck you Tracy. Move over, I'm starving."

"Me too," said Erica. "Did you order my clams?"

"Yeah, it should be coming out shortly. So E, what's up with you and Victor?"

"What do you mean, what's up with us?"

"I mean you're making moves without him. So I thought I would ask. I know you," Kim said looking at Erica sideways.

"Nothing is going on. There are just things I need to do to move forward in life. I can't take the way I'm living. I mean I'm not broke or anything like that, but I feel like I can do so much more with just myself alone. You guys know how I feel about having my own."

"Well Erica we understand all of that, but you cut everyone off though. We're your girls and we don't know shit that's going on with you," Crystal said looking worried and everyone shook their heads in agreement.

"That's what you think. Just because I play the role of wifey doesn't mean I'm totally out of the loop. Everything I had is still in position. I'm sorry if I've been distant lately, but I'm just trying to get some things together. Once I get everything situated I promise I will stay in touch more and even come out to see you bitches," she said looking her girls in the eyes. "You just mad 'cause you don't have a man Crystal," she said trying to lighten the mood. Everyone started laughing.

"Like I said before, I may not have a man, but I got more sponsors than the Super Bowl," she said matter-of-factly.

"I know that's right," Tracy said.

"Oh, that's what I wanted to holla at ya'll about," Erica said, suddenly remembering what she wanted to say. "OK first thing... from now on we gonna call Ty, T-Boogie in public. You know there's ears everywhere and I don't need anything getting out," the girls nodded their heads in approval. "OK great. I met up with T-Boogie and everything is in place. I should have the goods by the end of this week. I ordered 50, so each of us will get 12 plates. There will be two left over that I will keep in my drawer in the basement. Those two will be left for whoever sells the plates the fastest. That person will be able to make two extra sales." There was a brief silence as the waitress placed their food on the table.

"Would there be anything else, ladies?"

"Yes, I'll take a chocolate martini," said Erica, and Crystal asked for a strawberry daiquiri.

"Coming right up," the waitress said politely, while walking off.

"Since we all have a list to work off of, it should be easy to get the plates out there. We should be making some real paper in a few months. Like I was telling Tracy earlier, this nigga is the key. I think that he be making them shits on his own and selling them to people. Imagine where we could be if we knew how to do that shit for ourselves. We wouldn't even need him anymore and we'd be able to pocket most of the money, except for supplies and what not.

And then maybe we could even branch out and start finding our own distributors. This thing is so much bigger than just getting a few plates here and there. This could be a lucrative business, ladies." Erica had everyone's undivided attention and she could see each of their minds ticking, so she kept going.

"Crystal, with extra cash you'll be able to go to any school you want and won't have to worry about paying no damn loans. You could just pay that shit off one time and be done with it. Tracy, you won't have to beg that nigga Twan for shit no more unless you just feel like it. You could take the time off from work to finish at Baruch and then get the job that you really want. Kim, fuck that nigga Charles out in Maryland. You know he don't treat you right anyway. You could use this money for a new start. Get yourself a little spot, a nice car and just start over like you want to. As for me, I think I'm going to just stack my ends and start a business. I think I want to stay in publicity. I kind of like knowing the "who's who" of the industry and being in the middle of shit. Ya'll know how I do," she laughed as everyone laughed with her.

"So ya'll down right? 'Cause once we get in this shit, we in," she gave everyone a serious look. They all held hands around the table and looked at each other.

"We in E," they said in unison as big Kool-Aid smiles popped up on everybody's faces.

"OK. Well now that that's settled, on to bigger and better news. I finally started planning the wedding." Kim started clapping with excitement. "We're still in the first stages but you know how I am. Now before you guys leave tonight I need you to help me with a list of guests, food ideas, church and reception hall ideas, dresses… pretty much every damn thing. I have to call Rochelle tomorrow and get shit straightened out before I go back to work on Wednesday."

"Wow E, oK that sounds good," said Crystal. "But uh, what's the date?"

"Oh shit," Erica laughed, "that's a good point. September 18, so ya'll bitches got time to stack that paper, lose weight or whatever else you want to do before the time rolls around." All the girls started chit-chatting about the wedding for a while, until Kim had something to say.

"E, no offense, but how the fuck you gonna do business with this nigga and Victor told you not to fuck with him," Kim asked, trying to sort everything out in her head.

"Kim let me worry about that."

"I'm saying though Erica. It's not like you're talking about this being a one-shot thing. You're trying to make this our hustle. Wouldn't it be a whole lot easier if you didn't have Victor against this?" asked Kim.

"Look, where there is a will, there is a way."

"See, bitch there you go. Just don't call me, when Victor put his whole foot in ya ass!" she said laughing. Tracy and Crystal started laughing as well.

"Shut up, I got this one. I hope to only deal with this nigga for a short minute. As for right now he's just the middle man. He's going to take us where we need to go and then he could drop dead for all I care. I'm not fucking him, although he is fine as hell," she laughed, "but we need him for the time being to get this shit straight. Like I said, he might be able to show us how to do this shit ourselves."

"OK I was just checking because we all know how you are E,

and I think that sometimes you temporarily lose your mind when it comes to something you want and I just don't want there to be any unnecessary problems, you know what I mean?"

"Yeah I feel you Kim. But hey, if we don't say shit, how would anyone find out? Besides if we sell this shit quickly and I get in good with Ty, we may not even need him in a few months."

"You really think he's gonna put you on where you won't need him anymore? I've known Ty for a little while now, and he doesn't seem like the type that would just set you up and then let you go making money without him," Tracy said.

"That's a good point. Well we'll cross that bridge when we get to it. By the way Tracy, you never did tell me how you met that nigga."

"I was out with one of my friends from work, you know that girl Neeka? Well anyways one of her peoples was messing with him and we bumped into him at the club. He caught my eye with his fine self, and was ordering drinks at the bar for everyone. So you know me, I'm all in the mix 'cause I'm like damn this nigga got bread where did he come from? So at the end of the night when he pulled out his card to pay, I noticed that the name we were given wasn't the name that appeared on the card. So now we leaving out the spot and I whisper to him how much I wish I could spend like that. He says, 'maybe you can', and smiles. So I'm like hey I'm listening. So he tells me how he knows this guy who could get me a card if I was willing to spend the cash for it. We exchanged numbers and a week later I had my own card. It wasn't until about a month after that that I found out it was him who was supplying the cards."

"Oh oK. He was probably trying to feel you out and see if he could trust you enough to reveal that information. Smart man," Erica commented. The girls finished off their meals and continued to chat. Erica told Tracy to hit up Ty so that they could set up a meeting place to get the cards. Crystal wanted to set something up before she left to go back to Atlanta. She knew these queens that lived uptown that would love an opportunity like this. They would love and opt to do some 5th avenue shopping on someone else's dime. As Crystal made her call, Tracy dialed Ty. He didn't answer, so she left a message.

"They're in," Crystal said with a smile, hanging up her phone. My uptown crew is in, they each want a plate. Just in case you can't meet with Ty before I have to leave, here is their information. Their names are Ronny and Joe. You can call either one and they'll meet you anywhere. Ronny and his thirsty self said he has the money right now.

"See, that's what I'm talking about," Erica responded with a smile on her face. Shit this might be easier than I thought, she thought to herself. "Let's do the damn thing. Tracy call Ty again and see what his schedule is like for today. I can't afford to miss out on this money these chicks with dicks got for me!"

"Bitch you are sick," everybody said laughing.

"Ya'll bitches can say what ya'll want, but them queens are gonna be our #1 clientele. Watch what I say. They can shop unlike any woman I know. "

"Shit I agree with you. You know how them queens from uptown be dressing their asses off, Fendi this Dior that, they be having stuff I ain't seen before." Crystal added.

"Hold up ya'll be quiet," Tracy said, while waiting for Ty to answer his phone.

"Yo who dis?" he said in that sexy voice of his.

"Yo Ty what's up? It's Tracy."

"Tracy, what's good wit' you?"

"Ain't shit, my girl Erica wanna holla at you."

"Yeah, aight," he responded nonchalantly, but deep down he was happy to talk to Erica anytime. If for nothing else he knew Erica meant business, so if she was calling that meant something was up her sleeve. He heard Tracy calling Erica to the phone, then her voice came through and Ty couldn't help but wonder what she was wearing as she spoke to him on the phone.

"What's up Ty?"

"How you doing Shorty?"

"I'm doing fine, but I'll be doing better if I was on your team."

"Oh! Is that right?" he asked as he stroked his goatee. "What position you want to play?"

"What position you got?"

"All positions for you boo."

"Well, I wanna be the star player if that's okay with you."

"Your wish is my command Shorty, but let me ask you a question. Do you think you can handle that?"

Erica smiled. "I can handle whatever. Look we're at Sugar Cane's right now. My friends came from out of town for my birthday, so I'm hanging out with them before they leave. If you want, we can go out tonight around 11 and do a mini-birthday recap. Plus you have something that I want and I was hoping that you could give it to me today, or at least half."

"Oh oK. I got you. That sounds like a plan. I'll take ya'll out tonight and we can talk then," he said with a smile on his face. He couldn't wait.

"Aight. I'll call you back around 9:30pm, oK?"

"Aight, Shorty do that."

"Bet. I'll be waiting," she said as she closed the phone, glancing over at Kim.

"You sure this is just about business? 'Cause your ass looked a little too happy while you was making those plans," Kim said looking at Erica quizzically.

"Yes heifer, not everyone is a little hooch like you. Besides I have Victor, what could that dude offer me that my man can't aside from some new dick and a new headache?"

"Well if he hustling like I think he is, then I'm sure he could offer just as much as Victor minus the years ya'll have been together," Tracy said. Erica gave it some thought. Who could be better than Victor? For so many years he had been her everything. She had never given anyone else a half of a thought…until now.

"So where ya'll trying to go tonight?" Tracy said, breaking into her thought process.

"It's whatever, I told him I'd call and let him know. But hold up, what time are ya'll going home?" Erica said.

"Oh we both got a flight at the crack of dawn in the morning. As long as I'm back before class starts, I'm good. Check please," Crystal said with her hand in the air.

"Thanks for lunch, Crystal," everyone said.

"Where you headed now, Kim?" Erica asked getting her things together, ready to make her exit.

"To the city. Where ya'll going?"

"I got to call Victor. He asked me if I wanted to go see that Levert concert, so I want to see what he wants to do. Plus since we're already on this side of town, I'm a ride over to Ma's real quick."

"Yeah, alright we'll touch bases around 8:00pm."

"Look at this fool," Crystal said, as she watched Dezo drive up and down the block looking for the small lounge. "I should hit his ass." She turned her attention back to Erica, "So when you coming down to Atlanta?"

"I want you to work up some orders for me first and in the meantime I'll work on Victor. I was thinking possibly like June or July."

"Cool. Erica I have one question. Why are you chasing money like this? You and Victor are set. With his music and side hustle, I know you guys got dough. What's up?" Crystal said concern.

"I never want to be caught without, you know? I mean Victor gives me whatever I want but I have to ask for it. It's never been 'this is yours Erica'. Everything I get I have to ask for. It's like it's all accounted for. I want to have my own. I want to be able to do as I please without feeling like I'm being watched or that I owe him anything. I mean I have my job but it's nothing compared to this. I just want my own security you feel me? Plus he thinks I don't know what's going on with him. Coming in at all hours of the damn night? He even had the nerve to come in smelling like some other bitch last night!"

"Damn are you serious? I swear niggas ain't shit."

"Plus my game is much better and safer. You don't shine forever in that drug shit."

"Well, you know whatever you want to do I'm with you," they all gave each other a hug. Crystal finally got up with Dezo and told him she would link up with him later. She decided to take the ride with Erica to see Dorothy. She could always see Dezo.

On the ride to her mother's, Erica tried to think of a way to get Victor to accept her hustle. She also had thoughts of what the night would bring at their meeting with Ty. As Erica parked her car, they got out and walked towards the building.

"Hold that door!" Erica screamed out to the man entering the apartment building. "Thank you. My mother takes forever to answer the door," Erica said to Crystal standing in the hallway. They made it to Dorothy's apartment and Erica started banging on the door.

"Who is it?"

"It's me Ma." As Dorothy opened the door, a sweet aroma wafted into the girls' noses. "Dang Ma, what are you cooking? It smells great."

"Hey baby," she said giving her daughter a hug and kiss. "And hello to you too Crystal. It was such a great surprise to see you at the party," she said also giving Crystal a hug and kiss.

"Same here Mrs. Payne."

"You girls make yourself comfortable. I was making some chicken and baked macaroni. So Crystal how's school and life in Atlanta?"

"It's fine Mrs. Payne. I'm trying to debate whether I want to come back home and go to a local college or transfer to Spellman because I'm changing my major."

"Well just remember no breaks. It's best to get it over with now. Don't wait. The longer you wait, the longer it will take you to finish if you ever do finish. The mind is a terrible thing to waste," Dorothy said, thinking back to how she had wasted her education so many years back.

"Where is Monica?" Erica asked.

"Oh, she went to the mall."

"Dang I can never catch her to spend some time together," Erica said slightly disappointed.

"OK well let me call her. She might be on her way home now. She went quite a while ago. Do ya'll want to eat?"

"Oh no Ma, we just came from Sugar Cane, we're not hungry."

"So where's Victor, Erica."

"He's home. I left him asleep. He was tired from too much partying and hanging out," Erica said thinking.

"Were you surprised?" her mother smiled, happy that her daughter was finally at peace.

"Yes, Ma I was. Thanks for helping him. He told me you helped with the guest list. And I also want to thank you for your present. See I'm wearing the bracelet you brought me."

"You are so welcome baby. So what are ya'll doing for the day?"

"Well I thought I might catch up with Monica and take her with us to Manhattan to do some shopping and just hang out, but she's not here."

"OK, well, if ya'll are not too busy, come back and see me before you leave," just as Mrs. Payne finished her last statement the phone rang. Erica looked at the caller ID and rushed to answer the phone.

"Hey Monica I'm at Ma's, where you at?" But before Monica could respond, the other line beeped. "Hold on a sec Monica, someone's on the other line. Hello?"

"I have a collect call from 'Gregory'," Erica frowned as she listened to the options on the automated telephone prompt. She quickly pressed the number 5 on the keypad to block inmate calls. How dare he call here? She thought, and clicked back over to finish her conversation with her sister.

"What's up Monica, it's Erica. Where did you say that you were at?"

"Oh I was taking back some shoes that I brought at Sunrise."

"Oh damn. Well I guess I should have called before I came, to let you know I was trying to go to the city to do some shopping and I wanted you to come," Erica said with disappointment on her face.

"It's okay. We can go next weekend because I get paid then."

"Oh aight cool. I'll pick you up Friday night, and we can stay at my house. We'll leave in the morning and spend the day together okay?"

"Sounds good. Love you."

"I love you too," Erica said before disconnecting the call. "Okay Ma we're getting ready to leave. I'll get at Monica next weekend," she said as they got up to get their things together.

"OK, baby, drive safe."

They gave Mrs. Payne a hug and walked out of the apartment and back downstairs to the parking lot. The girls were chatting about the day they had ahead of them, when they heard a voice calling out to Erica.

"Yo Erica, why you always dissing me?" Crystal and Erica stopped to turn around and see who had called out to them. It was Juju.

"Hey look, I just call it how I see it. Don't take it personally, Juju," she said as she got into her car and prepared to back out of the parking lot.

"Come on E; don't do your boy like that. We used to be tight at one time. What's up?"

Erica stopped her car and looked Juju in the eyes. "Aight then. You want to be down? I need you to do something for me. Come here." Juju got closer to Erica's car, as she rolled her window all the way down. "Find out who needs that plastic, you feel me?" Juju nodded his head. "Then holla at me."

"But how do I get in touch with you E?" Juju asked.

"Yo here's my number," Erica handed Juju a folded piece of paper with her number on it. "Also, give me your number, so that I know it's you." Juju gave Erica his number as well.

"Aight so what you working with?" asked Juju excited to have gotten some play from Erica.

"We got that America Express, Discover, Visa and MasterCard. You name it, we got it. They go for $500 each, in cash you feel me?" Juju stood there listening with an impressed look on his face.

"What's in it for me?"

"Every twenty cards, I'll give you four," Erica said. Juju nodded his head.

"Sounds good. I got you!"

"Aight my dude, just hit me when you got something," Erica said, as she pulled out of the parking lot of the Fort Greene Housing Projects.

"Damn Erica, you're serious about this money, huh?" Crystal asked, smiling.

"Girl I told you. I'm not playing. This is an opportunity of a lifetime, and I'm about to make the best of it."

"So where are we going now?"

"I gotta ride through Sumner Projects to see if Victor is out there, so I can get some money," she said pulling up to a red light. I'm so tired of asking him for money every time I need it. I can't wait 'til I get my own shit popping majorly, Erica thought.

Victor pulled up in front of the projects and rolled down the window.

"Yo V!" Twan yelled. "Where the fuck you been at, man? I been hittin' you all day."

"My bad dog, I been at the crib sleep. I had the worst fucking hangover."

"Man that bitch Toya be buggin' son. That bitch wouldn't even let me in to cook up my shit, and Black was trying to get 64. You need to check that bitch, 'cause she fucking with our paper."

"What the fuck you mean," Victor snapped back. "She ain't let you in?"

"Nah she ain't let my ass in. I told her stupid ass that you was outta town. She talking about fuck that she know Erica had a party and you was with her. And ain't nobody getting shit 'til you come," Twan yelled angrily.

"What the fuck is wrong with her ass? It ain't like she don't know you. Damn. Let me go holla at this bitch," Victor said getting out of his truck. It's always some shit, Victor thought to himself as he walked in the building and pressed the button for the elevator to go up. When the door opened, the strong aroma of piss and shit hit him right in the face. Victor tried to hold his breath in the elevator, which was only big enough to hold about four people comfortably. He looked around as the doors closed, trying not to touch anything. Damn, niggas is nasty in the hood.

The closet-sized elevator was covered with graffiti and all sorts of trash from kids eating junk food all day. He looked up and waited impatiently to reach the fourteenth floor, because the elevator wouldn't stop at eleven, twelve or thirteen. As soon as the doors opened, Victor took flight to the staircase and practically jumped down the three flights of stairs. Fuck this; I need a bitch on the first floor. I can't keep doing this shit, he thought.

When he finally reached Toya's apartment, he started banging on the door.

"Who is it?"

"It's me Toya, open the door!"

"Who the fuck is me?"

"You know who the fuck it is. Open this motherfucking door," Victor yelled, getting more and more irritated by the minute. Toya opened the door and started in on Victor before he could enter the apartment.

"Oh so Erica tired of ya ass? Why the fuck are you here Victor? I'm tired of being your leftovers!" she shouted, as the tears welled up in her eyes.

"Man shut the fuck up. I ain't trying to hear that shit, and leave my girl out of this," he said, with his hand wrapped around her neck as he pushed her away from him. As soon as he let her go, she started up again.

"Well, if it's like that, you can get your shit and get the fuck out! If you ain't wanna be with me, you could have just told me."

"Bitch I was never with you. You knew I had a girl, so why the fuck are you tripping? You know what? You ain't gotta say no more. I will get my shit and leave! I don't have to put up with this dumb ass shit. I don't need you. On top of that, you fucking with my business. You lucky I don't beat ya stupid ass!" he yelled as he walked down the hallway of her two-bedroom apartment to her bedroom. Victor opened up his safe to get his shit. As he sat on the edge of the bed, Toya walked up behind him.

"Toya, I'm tired of your little stunts and shit," he said, while packing up a bag with his stuff. Toya threw her hands up helplessly.

"What did I do Victor? Why can't you understand that I want to be with you? I love you."

"Don't play stupid. Why the fuck you ain't let Twan in? I told you before don't play with my money." Toya took her hand off of his shoulder and walked around in front of him while he was counting his money.

"So are you going to let me make it up to you," she asked seductively, trying everything that she could think of to get Victor's attention. She started rubbing his leg, and kneeled down in front of him. She knew Victor had always been a sucker for some good head, and she definitely gave some good head. She had a technique about her where she sucked on his dick like a suction cup and he loved it. It was the only reason he put up with her shit in the first place. He knew exactly what she was trying to do.

"Handle ya business," he said, dropping his pants to his ankles. With no hesitation she picked up his flaccid penis and started sucking on his dick as if her life depended on it. Victor got rock hard in a matter of seconds, which only excited her more. He couldn't even concentrate on what he was doing. He sat his money down on her bed, and grabbed her head as he began fucking her mouth. She couldn't wait to taste his cum and knew that when his knees began to buckle, he was about to explode. Moments later, she could feel him releasing in the back of her throat. Victor held her head to make sure that she got every bit of it and she loved it. Sure that she had him right where she wanted him, she began to undress.

"I gotta go," he said, rising and pulling his pants up, while stuffing the rest of his shit in the bag.

"You gotta go? What the fuck you mean you gotta go? Where you going?"

"Didn't you tell me to get my shit and get out?" Victor asked.

"But… but—"

"Ain't no fucking buts. I told you before Toya, you ain't my fucking girl, so you either gonna accept that shit or you not. But you ain't gonna keep interfering with my paper Shorty. It's not fucking happening. I told you before don't fuck around with my money, but your dumb ass ain't wanna listen. Now look what happened."

"I said I was sorry Victor," Toya said as the tears streamed down her face.

"Sorry ain't gonna bring back the money I missed, is it? Oh. Now you ain't got anything to say huh? Yeah that's what the fuck I thought. Shorty you need to get your mind right and figure out what you gonna do, 'cause trust me when I tell you what you won't do, the next bitch will," he said smiling as he walked back down the hallway with Toya crying and pleading behind him.

* * *

"I hope his ass is out here," Erica said, as she looked around.

"Yo E, ain't that his truck right there?" Crystal asked as Erica pulled up in front of the projects.

"Yeah that's it," she said when she suddenly saw Twan. "Yo Twan where's Victor?"

Twan saw Erica approaching and began to panic. He knew that Victor was upstairs with Toya and had to think of something fast to get her out of there just in case Toya decided to come outside and show her ass. Twan told Black to run upstairs and tell Victor not to come down, while he got rid of Erica.

"Hey Ms. Erica. What's up?"

"Nothin' up. Where my boo at?"

"Oh, he left wit' that nigga Tony like 10 minutes ago, you just missed him."

"Damn. Aight well let me call him." Damn, I hope this nigga don't come out this building man, Twan thought. "Hello, Boo where you at?"

"I'm around the way, what's up?"

"Who you with?"

"I'm with Twan, why you ask me that?" Victor said, wondering why she was calling him to question his whereabouts.

"'Cause Twan is standing right here. So what? We lying to each other now?" Erica was pissed off and hurt that Victor would lie. She knew for sure that he must have been with another bitch.

"What the fuck is this? What's with all the questions?"

"Where the fuck are you, Victor?" Erica yelled. Twan knew his boy was done for, as he shook his head and walked away from Erica's car. That was Victor's shit to deal with. He was out of it.

"Don't be calling, questioning me. You know where the fuck I'm at," he said trying to think of something to tell Erica. Just then there was a knock at Toya's door. Toya went to answer it, while Victor continued on the phone. It was Black. He walked in and pointed to the window. Victor looked outside and saw that Erica sitting out in front of the building. Black mouthed the lie that Twan had told her and Victor nodded, letting him know that he understood.

"No I didn't know where you were at. But I know where you gonna be, if you don't quit fucking lying!" Erica screamed into the phone piece.

"Go ahead Erica and stop trippin'. I was just with Twan. I had to ride across the bridge with Tony to take care of something. Twan knew where the fuck I was at. Where that nigga at? Put his ass on the phone."

"Twan! Victor want you," she said steaming. Twan walked back over to the car and took the phone.

"What up nigga?"

"Man get Erica, the fuck outta here."

"Aight Victor, I'm a handle that."

"And then you send Black stuttering ass up here. That nigga took 20 minutes to tell me she was outside," Victor said laughing.

"Aight man, bet I got that," Twan said laughing as well, as he pictured Black trying to tell Victor what was up. "You wanna speak back to Erica?"

"Nah, just tell her I'll call her soon as I get back. See what she want and hit her off with some paper for me man, so she can calm her ass down."

"Aight my nigga," Twan said, as he closed Erica's cell phone.

"Why you hanging up? What he say?" Erica asked fuming.

"He kind of busy right now E. You know how that nigga is when it comes to his money," Twan said digging in his pocket. "If you need something let me know. You know I got you. He told me to hit you off." Twan pulled out ten one-hundred dollar bills and handed them to Erica.

"Nah Twan, I can't take your money.

"Come on Erica, you know he's gonna give it back to me. Here man, stop playing."

"Hey Twan, you can't speak," Crystal said.

"Hey Crystal what's up! I'm sorry baby, my mind was somewhere else," Twan said, reaching past Erica to shake Crystal's hand.

"Yeah trying to save your man's ass," Erica said.

"Go ahead with that shit, girl."

"Yeah whatever," Erica said as she sped off into oncoming traffic.

"Yo E, slow the hell down! What the hell is wrong with you?"

"I'm sorry girl. That nigga just fucked my head up. Who the fuck he think he playing with? He need to start playing lotto 'cause he'll have a better chance of winning, 'cause I ain't the one," Erica said fuming. She was getting tired of Victor's shit.

"Calm down E, why you buggin'? Didn't he say he was with Tony?"

"Bitch, don't tell me you believe that bullshit! I thought you was the one in college?"

"What the fuck is that supposed to mean?" Crystal said getting upset.

"Nothing Crystal, don't mind me. I'm just pissed right now."

"Well what's wrong? Talk to me Erica, I'm ya best friend."

"Crystal it's just that I know Victor, and I know when he's lying to me. I mean I gave this nigga my virginity and now he's playing games with me. And why you always taking up for him?"

"I'm not taking up for him Erica damn. All I'm saying is don't jump to conclusions before you know what's up. You know he's in the game and he's probably out making money, so let him do him."

"Yeah aight. I'm a let him do what he got to do, 'cause I know I'm definitely going to do me.

Chapter 12

Months had gone by and the girls were making it big. They had each established a steady clientele and were continuing to expand. Erica found herself going to work less and less and was contemplating quitting. She had never thought that in three months, she wouldn't have to work anymore. Although she was making great steps for herself financially, her life with Victor was becoming more and more strained as they got closer to their wedding date. She sometimes wondered to herself if it was even worth going down the aisle with him. Deep down she knew that she loved Victor, but she wasn't sure that she loved who he was becoming.

Just like she had been coming up in her hustle, Victor was making moves as well. They had recently purchased a house in Long Island and the money was just rolling in. Victor was out of the house so much, that he hadn't even noticed that Erica wasn't asking him for money, nor was she going to work every day. Victor just wasn't attentive anymore. And even when he was at home they were constantly arguing and in most cases he would brush her off and leave out the house again, sometimes for more than one night. Erica pushed his bullshit aside and dove deeper into her own business. She had already gotten 15 clients, which meant that she was making an additional $6,000 per month. The girls each had also gotten about 10 to 15 steady customers. If they continued like this, they'd be rich in no time. With so much extra money and cards in her possession, Erica thought it best to get a small safe. She had it installed in the attic while Victor was away on business.

Although Victor was acting like an asshole, Erica still played her role. She cooked and cleaned for him and still helped him with his own business affairs on the rare occasion that he'd he ask her. Victor had a feeling that shit was too good to be true but he felt like hey, "why look a gift horse in the mouth?" Instead of questioning Erica's niceness, he just enjoyed it for what it was worth.

Erica, however, was building her own empire. She felt like it was time for the girls to meet up again. She made a call to both Crystal and Kim and told them to make a trip to New York to catch up and see what everyone was doing. She also wanted to brainstorm about ways to make their business even bigger.

One warm Sunday night in June, the girls sat at Justin's, catching up and having a drink.

"Crystal, there go that nigga Dezo."

"Where?" Crystal asked, looking around.

"Over there by the bar. You been sweating him for years, you ain't gonna go holla at him?"

"Nah fuck that nigga. I ain't got a rap for him."

"You did a few months ago, when he followed you to my house to drop off the truck," Erica said.

"Man that nigga is full of shit. He ain't ready to settle down. I'm tired of playing that back and forth shit. We've been messing around for too long for this not to be going anywhere. And when I started beefing about that shit, he basically told me to kick rocks! Fuck that nigga."

"Well you need to say something, because here he comes."

"Oh shit," Crystal said, trying to prepare herself.

"What's going on ladies?" Dezo said, as he approached their table.

"Nothin'," they said in unison.

"What ya'll sippin' on? Can I buy ya'll some drinks?"

"Nah, we straight," Crystal said rolling her eyes.

"Shit, speak for yourself," Erica said. "I'll have a Tom Collins."

"Make that two," Tracy said, holding up her half-empty glass.

"Hoe, you make me sick," Crystal said.

"What?" Tracy asked, looking puzzled.

"Fuck him! We don't need him buying us shit!" Dezo looked at Crystal and shook his head.

"I see you still beefing, so let me bounce."

"Yeah, you do that!"

"Take care ladies," Dezo said, walking away from the table.

"Bitch what is your problem? You should have made his ass buy out the fucking bar!" Erica said with an attitude.

"E, I don't need anything from him."

"Yeah, but you should want it all. Make that nigga pay for dumping you like that. Anyway where's that nigga Ty? That nigga said he'd be here by now," Erica said, looking down at her diamond embezzled Rolex. Erica new venture afforded her more luxuries than Victor's allowance had ever gotten her.

"Man, his ass is always late," Tracy said. "Why don't you hit him on his cell?"

"Nah, that nigga know where I'm at. I ain't gonna press him. If he don't come, fuck em!" Erica said, getting up from the table. "Yo order me another Tom Collins since Crystal chased Dezo and his generosity away. I'm going to the ladies room." As Erica walked into the bathroom, there was a tall, slim, dark-skinned girl with braids blocking the doorway. Erica said excuse me several times but the girl wasn't trying to move. Erica gave the door a hard push, bumping the girl out of the way, allowing her to enter the bathroom.

"Excuse you!" the girl yelled at Erica, with much attitude.

"You're excused bitch!" Erica shot back, going into the stall. These bitches are always faking, she thought as she was relieving herself of the three drinks she had earlier. As she was exiting the bathroom heading back to the table, she felt somebody coming up behind her. I swear if this bitch knows what's really good she won't fuck with me, 'cause I'm about ready to whoop somebody's ass anyway. Just as she stopped to look back, a soft voice whispered behind her, sending chills up her spine.

"Mmm, there goes my MVP," Ty said hugging her from behind.

"Yeah well I was about to switch teams," Erica said trying to contain her childlike smile.

"Come on Ma, let's talk! You got me curious," he said, breaking his embrace.

"You never heard that curiosity killed the cat," Erica replied. Ty grabbed her hand pulling her through the crowd and into the VIP room. They sat down at the bar as the bartender came over.

"Hey Ty, what are you having?"

"For the lady, a cosmopolitan, and for me the regular," Ty said with confidence.

"How you know I like cosmopolitans?"

"Do you?" Ty said smiling.

"That's not the point!"

"Well sweetie, you are in my arena, so what I say goes."

"Oh, really?"

"So, Erica what's up with you? Everyone knows you're Victor's girl, but I'm digging you, and I ain't gonna front I want to make you mine. I love living on the wild side of life. So tell me Erica how can I make that happen?" he said, with a devilish but sincere expression. I can't believe this nigga is trying to make a play on me... he must be out of his mind. Erica was shocked.

"All I can say is that you have to work for it," she said flirting.

"That's it?"

"Unless you want it to be more... that's it."

"Well baby, all I got is time," he said smiling.

"Well let's see if it's spent on me," Erica said, returning the smile.

"OK, oK that sounds easy enough. So what's good between you and Victor? His man Black got hemmed up on my side of town, and they trying to say I did it."

Erica tried not to show the surprise on her face. "Well… did you?"

"Nah, but you know I control shit on that side of town so of course I gotta carry the weight."

"That's stupid, I don't understand why ya'll niggas be beefing over crazy shit."

"I was never beefing. Them niggas made it into a beef, so it's whatever. Fuck them!" he said getting upset.

"Anyways," Erica said rolling her eyes. "We're not here to talk about Victor. You ready to do business or what?"

"I thought we were doing business."

"We are, but if I remember a few months ago someone said that me and my team might possibly be able to come to a little conference, learn the other side of the business, you know something along those lines."

"Damn! OK I see you. Getting straight to business huh?"

"A closed mouth never gets fed."

"Aight well the event is next month. I'll keep you posted, but more than likely I definitely want you there." Erica raised a brow. "And your team too," Ty quickly added. "By the way that new shipment is ready for you. Just let me know when you're ready and we can meet at the spot so that you can pick them up. Your girls are here from out of town, so I know you're gonna want to pick up the work before they bounce."

"Cool… so when are we going to get down to the real nitty-gritty of this thing?"

"What do you mean?" Ty said looking confused as he picked up his drink.

"I mean like what's the next step? In three months me and my girls are netting over $100,000. Give us another three months and I'm sure it will be double that. So I'm sure by now I've proven that we're about our shit, so what's next?"

"In due time baby, in due time. You'll learn all of that on the cruise," Ty smiled crookedly.

"Hmm," Erica said pouting. "Whatever."

"You sound unsure baby. Never doubt me. Haven't you learned by now I'm a man of my word?"

"Yeah we'll see. No offense but I don't have much faith in men when it comes to trust. What can I say?" Erica said with a distant look in her eye. For a second she got a glimpse of her past with her father and of what her life was becoming with Victor. A sudden sadness washed over her, but she quickly took control over her thoughts.

"You oK?" Ty asked.

"Yeah, why do you ask?"

"I don't know it seemed like you went somewhere for a second. You want to talk about it?"

Erica looked down at her drink and wondered if she should share that part of her with him. Although she and Ty had become cool over the past couple of months, they had kept things at strictly business... Allowing him into her life would make things a little more personal and she wasn't sure if she was ready for that. But then it hit her. Maybe if she were to tell him her sob story, he would feel sorry for her. With him pitying her, perhaps he'd be more willing to share every part of the game. He'd think he was some type of confidant or savior or something. Men always think some woman wanna be saved, so this may not be a bad idea. Ty may be the ghetto's prince charming, Erica thought to herself with amusement. Here goes.

For the next 20 minutes Erica gave Ty a mini-version of what her life was like with her self-destructive father, Gregory "Big G" Payne. She ended with her vow to pay him back and how he had gotten arrested before she had the chance to get at him.

"Damn Ma. I never understood how people could have fucking kids and then treat them like shit!" He pounded his fist into the table as he said the words. At first Erica was flattered that he cared so much, but something in his reaction lead her to believe that her story had hit close to home. Maybe Ty had also been a victim of domestic violence? Or maybe worse! Erica shuttered to think that a man so fine could have been abused sexually or otherwise. She started to ask, but instead chose to leave it alone. She had to stay focused. He had to be feeling sorry for her, not the other way around.

"You know, I can take care of that for you."

"What?" Erica asked. She'd heard what he said, but she wanted him to repeat his statement just in case she hadn't hear correctly.

"I said I can handle that for you. I have some peoples upstate that I can work something out with. All you have to do is say the word."

Erica thought long and hard about his statement. She'd been thinking of a way to get Gregory back for all the horrible things he had done to her and her family. Revenge sat deep in her heart and she wasn't quite sure how to kill those feelings... She'd always pictured doing it herself and having the luxury of watching him die at her hands, but that wasn't the case now. This was the next best thing. It didn't take her long to come to a conclusion.

"So you really can handle this for me?"

"Just say that word, Ma."

"Do it," Erica said with a cold look in her eyes.

"Done."

"But… can you do something for me?"

"What's good?"

"Right before it's done, can you make sure to give him this message." Erica pulled out a pen and jotted a few words on a napkin and handed it to Ty. He read it and laughed.

"What's so funny?"

"You're crazy you know that? But like I told you before, I'm digging your style. Your wish is my command sexy," Ty smiled, placing the napkin in his pocket and ordering another round of drinks. On some real shit, Erica I'm telling you Victor better stay on his job 'cause if that nigga slip, I'm gonna slide right into place."

"Is that a threat?" Erica said, as she felt herself getting aroused at his assertiveness.

"Nah, that's a promise."

"Well since we're getting a little personal I have a question. A little off topic but what the hell? What are your relationships like with the girls you meet? At least the ones you're really interested in. Are they friends, lovers, fantasy fulfillers, what?"

"That depends."

"On?" Ty started laughing hysterically, trying to hide his blushing cheeks.

"Well for starters lovers and friends you can find anywhere, but they just don't mix, because someone's always going to want more. But for fantasy fulfillers, they come one in a million and it has to be with someone special, otherwise there's no real passion in it. The meaning of a fantasy is the most inner part of you that's shown in a sexual experience. You can't share that with some chicken head off the streets, feel me? But if that person shares something special with you, whether or not she goes home to her man, you know shit will never be forgotten. It's kind of like when you lose your virginity to somebody. Sometimes the relationship lasts, and sometimes it don't, but the memories live forever," he said as he stared deep into her eyes. His eyes were so beautiful. When he stared at her, it was almost like he was looking through her. She felt awkward but at the same time, she couldn't help but stare back at him.

"So what's your fantasy? I mean the most erotic dirty one of all time," she asked him.

"I can't say but I will tell you that it has to be with someone special. Is that you?" She wasn't sure how to answer his question, and took a sigh of relief when her phone started ringing. She looked down at the caller ID and saw that it was Tracy.

"What's good?"

"Where you at?"

"I'm on my way give me 15 minutes and I'll meet you at the bar."

"Aight cool." Just as they were about to resume their conversation Ty's cell phone rang. From Ty's side of the conversation, Erica assumed he was talking to a female and she had to admit to herself that she felt a twinge of jealousy.

"I'm in the city… but you told me to meet you at Jimmy's uptown," pause. "I don't see your whip nowhere in sight. I'm coming up two-fifth from the west side right now. Yo… yo…hello? Hello? You breaking up!" Click.

"Oh, you are so fucked up, you know that right?" Erica said laughing as Ty gave her a big Kool-Aid smile.

"Sweetheart, it ain't nothing. Just know that everything I do is for a reason. So don't doubt me aight," he said, lifting her chin up to look at him.

"Ty you are a very confident man," Erica said finishing her drink and looking at him with want in her eyes.

"I have to go, but I'll catch up with you later." Ty got up and threw a one hundred dollar bill on the table and kissed Erica on the forehead. "This kiss will bring you good love," he said and disappeared from her sight. Erica looked at her watch and hurried out of the VIP room to meet up with Tracy.

"So what happened, Erica? I take it you found Ty?" Tracy asked, standing at the bar.

"Everything is all good." Erica looked around and noticed that no one was around. "Where did everyone go?"

"Well while you were on your rendezvous, Dezo came back to the table and him and Crystal started talking and then they left. Then Kim left with some kid she knew, so I just sat here and waited for you to finish. I didn't just want to leave you before I knew what you were doing."

"Thanks girl. So what are you about to get into? I was thinking about heading home."

"I'm meeting Twan up here, so go ahead I'll call you in the morning."

"Alright girl," she said as she gave Tracy a hug.

On the drive back, all she could think about was her conversation with Ty. As much as she enjoyed their flirting, she couldn't help but feel a little guilty, so she decided to call Victor to try and ease her mind. After seven rings with no answer, she tried and tried again. After about the fifth call with no answer, she started to worry because Victor always answered her calls. She then tried him on his sidekick and still no answer. Her mind began to wander and she started getting the feeling that her intuition might be right. Victor had to be cheating on her. That was the only thing that made sense. She didn't want to believe it, but the changes in his behavior lead her to think otherwise.

Just as she turned onto her block, her phone rang. She looked down and began to smile. It was Ty. She wasn't sure why she was so happy that it was him calling instead of Victor, but at this point she didn't care.

"Hello," she said with the sexiest voice she could possibly muster.

"Hi. Am I interrupting anything? I could always call you later."

"Oh nah, nah it's cool. What's up?"

"I was just calling to make sure you were alright. I mean that's the least I could do. You know being the gentleman that I am," he chuckled. "But on the real, I'm sorry for running out on you like that, but money talks. Not saying that I didn't enjoy every minute that I spent with you, but you know."

"Yeah, yeah Ty. I've been around you long enough to know you mean what you say. But anyway, thanks for being considerate."

"You must not be home yet."

"Yeah I'm here, I just pulled up."

"You don't sound too happy."

"Nah it's not that, I just I have a lot on my mind."

"Anything I can do to help?"

"I can handle it, I'm a big girl."

"Shit, big girls need help too."

"I know. I didn't mean it that way. It's nice to know you are just a phone call away Ty."

"Always for you!"

"OK Ty I'll call you later. I'm about to go inside and get some sleep," she said as she exited the car, heading for the house.

"Sleep tight Shorty. One."

Erica walked inside the house, and suddenly felt lonely. She realized that she needed someone she could talk to and share her feelings with. She was feeling overwhelmed by her thoughts and emotions and wasn't sure what to do about it. It would be just a matter of time and Gregory would be out of her life forever. Erica was questioning if she could really go through with this. Yes Ty offered his services, but she wasn't quite sure that she could trust him, especially with all the shit going down between him and Victor, which she was determined to find out sooner or later.

She walked upstairs to their bedroom and began to undress. Her mind felt heavy and she wondered what her girls were doing. She started to pick up the phone and call one of them but realized that they were all out with their significant others. Everyone always seemed to envy her and Victor's relationship, yet here she sat the only one out of them alone bubbling with her own emotions. Erica curled up into her bed as her eyes welled up with tears. Fuck that nigga. I ain't gonna cry. That nigga ain't worth it, she thought as she closed her eyes tight and drifted off to sleep, which didn't last long... She was up about an hour later wondering where Victor was. She had chirped him over and over and text him on his Sidekick and he had yet to answer. After trying to hit him on the walkie-talkie, she tried calling his phone, but it went straight to voicemail. He had turned it off.

What the fuck is going on V? she thought out loud to herself. She had now been trying to reach Victor for the past two hours and still nothing. Her mind was flooded with all kinds of thoughts. Maybe Victor got arrested with that nigga Black? Or maybe worse, the nigga got killed. Or maybe he's off somewhere getting his dick sucked by some chicken head hoe and lost track of time. Erica paced the living room back and forth trying to figure out what else she could do to find Victor. She was so worried that she felt a headache coming on. Since she knew it was no use trying to get some sleep, she decided to take some Tylenol and camp out on the couch to watch a movie until his ass came in. She grabbed her favorite DVD, Heat, and lay down on the couch. Maybe I should just chill out and enjoy this time that I have to myself, Erica thought.

But just as quickly as that thought went through her mind, she laughed to herself. Men were not to be trusted. Victor was God only knows where and Ty thought that with his little two-bit game, he was going to take her away from Victor. If things didn't last with Victor, Erica was going to fly solo. She realized she had never truly been by herself. Victor was always there for her. He had been her first and her only. As much as she wanted to remain faithful, she couldn't help but wonder what sex would be like with Ty. Would he do all of the things that Victor had done to her body? Would he be better? Would it be worse? Who the hell knew? At this point maybe it wouldn't be such a bad idea to find out. Victor had been lying and keeping a secret life behind Erica's back and had the nerve to try to play her out like she was some dumb bitch that wouldn't catch on.

"I know it's another woman, but I have a plan for both of them," Erica said to no one in particular. Just then she heard a car pull up into the driveway. She ran to the bathroom quickly to make sure she looked her best, and returned to the couch. She wasn't sure why really it just seemed like the right thing to do.

She heard his keys in the door.

"Erica! Baby are you home?" Victor's voice echoed through the house.

"I'm in the living room!" she yelled out. Victor approached the living room and saw Erica on the couch with a drink in hand, watching her favorite movie. Damn, I know some shit is about to pop off, Victor thought to himself as he looked at her sitting calmly watching her movie. He thought that she would have been asleep when he arrived home, but saw the living room light and knew otherwise. He decided to choose his words wisely, as not to start a fight with her.

"How was your day baby?"

"Fine," Erica said coolly, sipping on her drink.

"So, what are you drinking on?" Erica looked at him out the corner of her eye and almost choked trying not to laugh at his attempt to be concerned with what was in her cup.

"I made me a dark and stormy," she said not even turning her attention away from the TV.

"What are you doing up so late?"

"Well let me see. I have a fiancé who wasn't home that I haven't heard from since we woke up this morning. I'm calling his phone over and over and the shit is just going to voicemail, for what reason I don't know. When I try to chirp him not too long ago, his chirps are connecting, but he's just not answering me back. And I know you got them because it says on my phone that they had been sent successfully. So that leads me to believe that something bad may have happened to my man. Yet low and behold," Erica stopped and looked down at her Rolex, "my man comes walking in healthy as fuck with no visible injuries at 3:13am in the fucking morning on a weeknight. And you ask, darling, why I'm up so late? Perhaps I was just waiting to ask you if you wanted a drink when you came in. Or maybe I could interest you in a session of Sex and the City?" Victor just stood there looking at Erica as if she were speaking another language.

"Look, I'm not feeling your shit tonight Erica. It's after three in the morning and you want to start. So no I don't want a drink. I just want to go to sleep."

"Oh I guess you had too much excitement for one fucking day. Fine boo, goodnight!"

"What the fuck are you trying to say Erica? Why must we go through this insecure shit all the time? You know I be out making moves and yet you still be on my ass!"

"Oh please, that's always your answer! Come with something better!"

"That's why my phone was off, but my chirp was in the truck while I was in the house cooking up. When I got to the truck, I saw the messages but I thought you would be asleep, so I just came home."

"You know what Victor? Your story sounds lovely, but something in my gut is telling me your punk ass is lying. So fuck that shit, I don't believe you. Come with something else; the truth perhaps. You know what? Fuck it! Don't tell me anything else; I'm sick of this shit!" Erica said, as she jumped off the couch and began pacing the room, with drink in hand.

"Every time I walk in this house, you accusing me of something. You sick? Well I'm sick of your insecurity. I'm out here making money for your unappreciative ass, but do you care? No. Do I say anything when you asking me to buy this or buy that? No! Do I ask you for money to pay for the cars out front or for the mortgage or any other fucking bill in this house? No! I do what the fuck I want, when I want. I run this show. If my phone is off, call back. You should know the drill by now."

With rage in her eyes, Erica threw her drink in Victor's face. Shocked, Victor slapped her so hard that she would have fell if he had not grabbed her by the throat and held her up against the wall.

"Have you lost your fucking mind?" he screamed, slamming her as hard he could on the polished hard wood floor. She struggled to get her feet, but was met with hard kick to her stomach that knocked all the air out of her. Adding insult to injury, Victor straddled her helpless frame and turned her head so she faced him as he summoned as much phlegm and saliva he could and spat in her face. "Bitch don't you ever throw anything in my face. Next time I'll fucking kill you." he said standing over her as she curled up in a fetal position on the couch.

I know this nigga didn't just spit in my face, she thought as the rage built up inside of her. Never before had she felt so disrespected aside from the things that happened between Gregory and her years before. *I can't believe him. Out of all our disagreements, he has never disrespected me to this point. Does he really think I'm going to let him get away with this shit? Oh hell no!* Erica pulled herself together, but remained in the living room. She had already been dealing with a whirlwind of emotions, and now to have Victor pull this shit? She only had one thing on her mind. Payback would be a bitch and her name was Erica Payne.

Chapter 13

Erica jumped up to the sound of the ringing phone. She looked up and realized that it was morning and the blue screen of the television had been watching her throughout the night. Sitting up trying to get herself together, she cleared her throat and reached over to answer the phone.

"Hello," she said in a deep groggy voice.

"Damn was it a rough night?" Tracy spoke through the phone laughing.

"What's up Tracy?"

"Well I didn't expect you to pick up the phone. I called your job and they said you wasn't there, what's up? Is everything oK?"

"Everything is fine. What's up?" Erica said trying not to sound annoyed. As Tracy spoke, last night's events replayed in her mind and she felt herself getting fired up again.

"Nothing really, I just started to worry when you weren't at work, you didn't answer your cell phone, and now I see you're grumpy at home. Where is Victor?"

"Is this Jeopardy or some shit? What's with all the damn questions?"

"Well... look, evidently you don't want me to know what your problem is so are we going to look for bathing suits today for the trip or not?" Erica thought for a second and remembered that they were supposed to be going to Atlanta in a couple of weeks, if Ty didn't come through on his promise for the cruise. Erica always had to have a back-up plan.

"Oh shit, sorry girl I forgot. Let me hit you back in a couple of hours, aight?" and before Tracy had a chance to answer, Erica hung up. She sat at the edge of the couch with her head in her hands trying to figure out what the fuck had happened in the last twenty-four hours. How was she going to face Victor after that shit he pulled? She stood up and had to hold on to the couch. Her head was pounding. As she slowly walked through the house, towards her bedroom, she realized that Victor was gone. Erica smiled to herself and snatched the phone off the receiver.

* * *

"What? You did what, Victor? Man you got to be shittin' me. I know you ain't do that shit to Erica? That's some true gangsta shit son. What did she do man? I know she ain't just take that shit. Did she fight back?" Twan asked as he chuckled to himself in disbelief.

"What do you mean, what did she do? Man she didn't do shit. What was she going to do? Knock me out?"

"What's up with you man, you losing mad cool points. What the hell could she have done for you to flip out like that? I mean, I ain't trying to get all up in your business, but you think she deserved that?" Black asked. He had been released from jail earlier that morning. It was typical in their life of crime.

"Come on Black, the bitch threw her drink in my face."

"So why you ain't grab her up man?" Black stuttered, looking confused.

"I did that shit too," Victor said with an uneasy laugh. After the words left his mouth, he didn't feel so good about what he did.

"What? Aww shit this nigga trippin'. Yo is your truck outside?"

"Yeah why?"

"You better hope it's not leaning," Twan said laughing.

"Come on now. Stop playing and stop with the jokes. Twan man, you think she's going to speak to me again?" Victor said, with a look of concern on his face.

"Shit, the Erica I know? There's no telling what that broad will do. I say call her man and apologize or go buy her some shit."

"Yo call her for me."

"Fuck no! The last time I spoke to her, you had me caught up in your bullshit with Toya's stupid ass. Poor Black standing around stuttering and shit. Erica knew my ass was lying. Why the fuck you think she is going to believe anything I say?"

"So you think I should call her?" Victor asked.

"I would. That's the only way you're really going to know what's up with her, instead of you sitting here worrying us half to fucking death!" Victor reached for his cell phone and started dialing the number.

"No man!" Black yelled out, almost slapping the phone out of Victor's hand.

"What! Shit. You almost knocked the damn thing out my hand you black motherfucker."

"Yo, ca-ca-call from my house phone. Y-y-you you calling her on your cell phone means you c-c-could be calling from anywhere. You want to make peace don't you?"

"Good looking out man," Victor responded. Twan passed him the phone and everyone sat in silence as Victor dialed Erica's job number.

He was shocked to hear her voice mail come on. He hung up and dialed her cell phone. Her voice mail picked up automatically, meaning her phone was turned off. Victor slammed the phone down on the receiver with a strained and puzzled look on his face. He wasn't sure what to do now.

"Ma-ma-maybe it's good that you don't talk to her right now."

"Yeah man," Twan agreed, "let the day play out and try again later. You know how Erica is. Maybe she just needs to cool down."

"That's the thing Twan, I do know how she is and that's what worries me. I don't think this thing should sit too long without being resolved. Ya'll know how much I love her, but I can't allow her to keep questioning me. I know I was wrong for making that kind of move, but I had to show her who was boss."

"I know what you mean V, but damn you knew how she was from jump. Ya'll been together for how many years now? If you love her you gotta take all that bullshit man. She ain't gonna change. She's been that way since the 6th grade!"

Victor sat back and thought for a moment. Twan was right. Erica was who she was and that wasn't going to change for anyone, least of all him. He had promised her a long time ago that he would love and protect her after the fucked up childhood she had, and here he was doing the same shit her punk ass daddy used to do.

"Fuck! I fucked up big time! Man let's finish bagging up. I gotta go make this shit right."

Across town, Erica had pulled into a parking space on Bedford Avenue. She glanced at her cell phone for the millionth time that day, willing it to ring. And just as she looked away, her phone started ringing and she saw that it was Victor again. What the fuck could he possibly want? Hasn't he done enough? She pushed the ignore button on the phone, which would send him right into her voice mail. She had been hoping it would have been Ty. I guess he couldn't want much since he ain't leaving any voice mail. She placed her phone on vibrate and tossed it into her Fendi bag. She hopped out of the car and hit the alarm. She walked in slow motion through the black-iron gate and up the gray steps to a four-story brownstone. Before she could lift her hand to ring the bell, the door opened.

"Oh, hey Aunt Kat. You scared me," Erica said happy to see her aunt.

"Sorry baby, but I heard the gate open and I came to see who it was." Kat noticed the solemn look on Erica's face, one she hadn't seen for a while, but knew too well. "Come on in. What's wrong baby? Is everything alright? You sounded so upset on the phone and now here you are looking all depressed and sad." Following Erica into the dining room, Kat offered her a drink. She declined.

"Well take a seat and tell aunty what's wrong."

"Aunt Kat I don't know what to do. It's Victor. He has so many unaccounted for disappearing acts. I think he is cheating on me, but I can't prove it. Then last night we had an argument about him coming in so late and not answering my phone calls. One thing lead to another and I threw my drink in his face."

"You did what Erica? Why would you do that?"

"Because I was pissed Aunt Kat and he was acting like it was no big deal coming in at 3:13 in the morning after not answering his phone all day. Then he had the nerve to make it seem like I was beefing for no reason, when he knows that if it was me, he would have been tripping! I don't know, after he started talking all this crap about me being insecure, I just lost it. But that didn't give him the right to slap me and spit in my face."

"Wait a minute," Kat interrupted trying to get things straight. "You throw your drink and Victor kicks your tail then spits in your face? Is that what you are telling me?" Kat asked with a shocked expression.

"Yes aunty. He spit me right in my face and then walked out," Erica said trying to hold back tears of anger and frustration. She hated to cry because she thought it displayed weakness and vulnerability. Kat sat there at a loss for words. She wasn't sure what to say. She took a deep breath before she spoke.

"Look Erica. You know your mother's life right? Do you remember going through things like this? Just don't make it a habit. You guys fighting and carrying on is not normal and you know that shit first hand. You better nip it in the butt before it gets out of control. You guys have to come to some sort of an agreement because you can't continue on like this. You don't want things to get too out of control."

"But Aunty, I think he is messing around. What am I supposed to do about that?"

"Well now darling you can't go around accusing the man. Either find out, or leave it alone. But throwing something in his face that you aren't even sure of, isn't going to help anything. It might even push him away. You are supposed to trust the man you are going to marry. If there's no trust, then there's no point in continuing this thing. You'd both be wasting your time."

"Aunty I don't think I can forgive him for what he did to me. I felt so low. I don't even think I felt that low with Gregory's bullshit because I always knew what to expect from his ass. This shit caught me so off-guard. Yeah I know I was out of line for throwing my drink at him, but he had no right to hit me in my face like that. How am I to know that shit won't happen again? And I can't front, I wanted revenge. A part of me still does. But when I woke up this morning, he was gone. He didn't even say sorry aunty."

"Well I don't know, maybe he's going through something. Did you ever stop to ask him what was going on before you jumped down his throat? You should hear the man out before you jump to conclusions Erica. You know what they say about people who assume," Kat said, with a slight smile on her face. "I think you should call him baby and try to work this thing out. You guys have been together too long to let something like this break you up. But like I said you have to trust him or let it be." Kat sat back for a moment to let her words sink in.

"Did you tell your mother?"

"No," Erica answered quickly. "She can't know. I don't want to paint a negative picture of Victor to her, because she only knows him as being nothing but nice. Plus all she'll do is worry herself to death and she has enough to think about. Did you know that bastard father of mine is still calling her? I was over the other day and his ass was calling collect, but you know I blocked that shit. Why won't he just leave her alone? That's my only fear aunty. I don't want to end up like them."

"Communication is the key Erica. That's what's missing. Call him. I can see it in your face that you want to."

"No I can't," Erica said, raising her voice with much attitude.

"OK fine. Go home. I bet you that he's sitting there ready and waiting to talk things out. I know that Victor loves you Erica, and I know that he is sorry."

"That's not good enough for me aunty."

"Well what do you want to do Erica? Do you want to call everything off? If so, you better do it now before you go through with this. The wedding is just around the corner. And that's 'til death do you part."

Erica sat back listening to her aunt, thinking about her wedding. Her marriage was just a few months away and here she was thinking about getting a quick fuck from someone else to help ease her mind. Erica's thoughts blocked out Kat's words and soon she started sounding like the adults in the Charlie Brown cartoon, blah, blah, blah, blah. The only thought that continued to run through her mind was that she had to get Victor back and he was going to pay royally for disrespecting her. I got to hit him below the belt. What if I fuck Black? Eww nah that's degrading, but I know I could get Black if I wanted him. But Victor would kill him ... do I want that? Nah. Maybe ... what if I just take the safe and bounce? Nah Victor would have the mob looking for me. What if I go to his stash house and switch out the cocaine for baking soda and boric acid and sell the real stuff to his competition? Nah I ain't no damn drug dealer. What if I pour lye on his truck, nah fuck that I'll pour that shit in his face! What the fuck am I talking about? What if I just disappear like he did? Hmm that's a thought. Maybe I'll—

"Erica, are you listening to me? I said go home and talk to Victor. Call him, don't call him. I don't know, just do something!"

"Huh? Oh, yes I'm listening. I'm going to go aunty. You're right," she said, getting up from the table. She gave her aunt a kiss on the cheek and a short hug before practically running out of the house. Kat just stared at Erica while shaking her head with confusion written all over her face. She just hoped that her niece would do the right thing.

Erica got back in the car not feeling much better, but she was tired of stressing. She decided to hit Tracy back and see what was good for the rest of the day.

"What's up girl?"

"Oh you decided to call me back?" Tracy said amused.

"Yeah I just had to go to my aunt's for a minute. Meet me in Tribeca."

"Where exactly?"

"On West Broadway and Thomas Street, right on the corner. You are still at work right?"

"Yeah, Tracy said.

"OK, so just walk up a few blocks. I'll be parked right on the corner in an hour." "Alrighty. I'll see you then."

* * *

"Victor you want me to break this down or give it to Toya like this?" Twan asked. He was mad that he even had to deal with the broad to begin with, but Victor decided to keep the shit at her house.

"Tell Toya to meet you and pick it up. Once it gets to her house I'll see! And don't forget that nigga owes me from the first package aight?"

"Yeah. Well what else are you going to do today?"

"I don't know. But you need to help me think of something Twan. You know I'm in the dog house." Just as Twan was about to make a suggestion, Victor's cell started ringing. The number was blocked and he contemplated answering it. He hated blocked calls.

"I hate this blocked number bullshit when it comes up on the screen."

"Nigga you better answer it. It might be Erica fool."

"Yeah you right yo," he opened his phone. "Hello."

"Hey Vic what are you doing," a female voice asked.

"Damn I knew I should have let this shit ring," Victor whispered to Twan. "I'm busy. Why what's up?"

"I want to see you. I miss you, boo," Alexis cooed.

"I'm taking care of business right now. Maybe I'll pass through later, we'll see. What are you wearing?"

"Umm daddy, I'm waiting for you, so what do you think I'm wearing?"

"Hmm let me guess. A thong?" Victor asked smiling, knowing exactly what she was really wearing.

"Wrong answer daddy. Now you know I'm sitting here wearing nothing, waiting for that big fat thing to come make me purr. I'm just getting out of the tub wet and horny and I'm thinking about you. I need you right now daddy, your pussy is pulsating. Mmmm, I'm lying in your favorite position daddy. Come get this pussy."

"Damn boo," Victor said with a sigh of guilt. Twan was looking him dead in his eyes motioning his hands from ear to ear telling Victor he was going to slit his throat. Victor cut his conversation short.

"Look baby girl, I'm gonna hit you back when I finish aight?"

"Aww come on Vic? My kitty cat is dripping wet. Come over here real quick and handle this shit. Then you can go back to whatever it is you was doin'. You know you want this."

"What I say? I'll hit you back!" Victor said, disconnecting the call. Twan just shook his head.

"Victor man, what the fuck is wrong with you? You've been sitting in this motherfucker all morning bitching about what to do with Erica.

Talking 'bout how you going to start doing her right and all that since ya'll are getting married soon. Then just now you was about to go get some pussy from the next bitch. You need to get your head right my dude, 'cause you all fucked up." Victor just stood there looking and feeling stupid.

"You have a fiancé, soon-to-be wife, who is pissed as hell at you and capable of anything and you over here acting stupid. You haven't spoken to her all day! She's not at work, at home, shit at this point you don't know where the fuck she at. That should tell you something bruh. You know she plottin'. I should slap the shit out of you man. What the fuck?" Twan said, getting frustrated with Victor.

"Vic, remember back in high school when E caught you with that broad from uptown? You remember what the fuck she did? How she beat that bitch to a pulp? She don't give a fuck when she snaps, and I don't feel like fixing shit or getting you out of the 81st precinct or dodging bullets. You know that chick is nice with the Glock. You showed her that shit. That's why my ass will never take Tracy to the range. I don't need to be dodging bullets from two crazy ass chicks. Now go home nigga and fix that shit! When wifey is upset, it fucks up everything. You not focused and shit, and then we gotta watch out for her crazy ass as well as the enemy. It's just too much man. Handle that!" Twan said practically throwing Victor out.

"Aight man damn, stop whining. I got this!"

"How?" Black questioned. "Where is she? You can't even find her. Yo your ph-ph-phone hasn't rang not once today. Fill me in on th-that shit. Obviously she ain't looking for you. You here in my face stuck on st-st-stupid. She ain't even blow my phone up like she usually do."

"Twan, Black, cool out! Let me call her mother. I'll show you who's in control," Victor smiled. Victor dialed Dorothy, determined to prove to his boys and to himself that he had the situation handled.

"Hey Ma," Victor smiled, "where's Erica?"

"I don't know. I haven't seen her all day. Victor is everything oK?"

"Oh yeah. I'll try her again Ma," he said hanging up quickly.

"Yeah you definitely slipping. Spitting on a black woman? That shit is lethal. We went to the Madea play remember? She gonna whip yo ass bruh," Black said laughing.

"Damn Victor, what the fuck man? Yo you need to just go back to the crib and wait for her ass. Fill her phone up with voice mails or some shit. You better kiss ass, or do something to make E re-appear. Once you know where she at, that's when you got control."

"Man shut the hell up. Call Tracy and see if she know where she at."

"Aight," he said dialing Tracy. "Shit man, I got her voice mail. Great!" Twan said, pushing the end button on his phone looking at Victor with concern.

"This is not good man. Now my bitch is missing too! What the fuck is going on? Don't be fucking shit up for me! I don't need this in my life. You bullshitting!!! You should have been apologized to Erica before your punk ass left the house this morning! And then you gonna sit here jonesing on the phone with some trick, when you should have been trying to figure out where the fuck your girl is. I don't have no beef with my bitch and I better not when I see her. Now stop looking stupid and do something."

"What man?"

"Get the fuck out of here! Hit the pavement and start looking for her ass. A missing Black woman is dangerous, but an angry missing Black woman is fatal."

"Where are we going to look?"

"We? We ain't going to look for shit. You are going to look for her. She's mad at you, not me. You ain't dragging my ass in some shit, especially if her ass is with Tracy. Shit is smooth in my house and it's going to stay that way! I ain't losing my life 'cause your dumb ass wanna spit on somebody like a bitch-ass. I don't need to go. That's why we got cells. Hit me up when you find her. I'll keep my eyes open and if I catch up to her, I'll hit you up."

"Aight," Victor said sighing. "I'll check you later. Don't forget to see Toya and that nigga Troy with the product and my damn paper."

"Don't worry, I got that. You go find Erica." Victor jumped in his truck and sped off the block. All he could think about was his dilemma with Erica. He felt bad for what he had done and now she was missing. All he could think was that something bad had happened to her or worse. Victor rubbed his temples and threw in his Jodeci CD to try and ease his mind. He flipped through to track five as their remake "Lately" blared through his speakers. He immediately thought back to Erica.

"Damn I fucked up," he said to himself. "I just need to talk to her. Once I talk to her everything will be oK. This can't be happening." He picked up both his Nextel and his cell phone and began chirping her. When the page was sent unsuccessfully, he tried calling, only to be sent straight to voicemail again. "Shit!"

Chapter 14

Erica drove around the city refusing to go home. She didn't feel like facing what might have been there waiting for her. Remembering some business she had with Juju, she decided to call his cell phone. She had a delivery to make. She wanted to see where they would be meeting so that he could pick up cards.

"What's up E?"

"Yo what's up Ju? I want to drop these things off. Where are you at?"

"In front of Willoughby Walk. Meet me in front on the Myrtle Avenue side, just before Kum Kau."

"Aight when?"

"In 20 minutes."

"Aight cool, I'm coming down Atlantic Avenue now," said Erica.

"OK, bet I'll be in the front. One." Erica couldn't escape the thoughts that flowed through her mind. Although she was about to make a sale, she couldn't help but be plagued by the day's events. Well at least this dumb nigga is calling, she thought, although that didn't ease her mind. They still had a problem. A big problem and she wasn't so sure how she was going to handle things. Aunt Kat's words stung her ears. She knew her aunt was right and she couldn't let things get as bad as her parents'. Erica vowed to never stand for the things that Dorothy had put up with, but she wasn't sure what to do. Would Victor ever flip out on her like that again? Would he continue to do her dirty? And if he wasn't, could she trust him? Her woman's intuition was hitting hard and she knew deep down inside that he was cheating on her, but how could she prove it? She knew that she wanted to holla at Ty, but what if Victor wasn't cheating on her? Then that guilt would ride her down forever. Erica shook her head vigorously trying to shake the thoughts out of her mind, but it didn't help.

Her thoughts were interrupted by the ringing of her cell phone. She glanced down at her phone and didn't know whether to be upset or happy. It was Ty. She answered the phone sounding irritated anyway.

"Hello!"

"Hey lady. Are you oK? Did I interrupt something?" Ty asked in a concerned manner.

"No, I'm good. I'm just finishing up some business. What's up with you?"

"Oh I have to have a reason to call you now?" Ty flirted.

"No I just didn't hear from you all day and now you calling at eight in the evening? I thought that there might be a reason."

"Well there is," Ty said smiling to himself. He had her right where he wanted.

"What Ty?"

"I want you and your girls to come on the trip. I've already discussed it with some of my business partners and they've been impressed thus far with your work. I was thinking that maybe we could link up tonight so that I could give you the itinerary for the trip and discuss travel arrangements and what not. I know this is kind of short notice, but the trip is in a few weeks, so it would be best to get your flights as soon as possible. Especially since you're all coming from different spots." A big smile grew on Erica's face. This was the best news that she had heard all day.

"OK that sounds good. What time were you thinking? I'm tying up some loose ends right now. I was supposed to meet Tracy in Tribeca, but I called her and told her to meet me at Bloomingdales instead."

"Well what time will you be available?" Ty asked, not giving up so easily.

"Oh you not taking no for an answer huh?"

"Thus far haven't I proven that I don't give up on what I want?" Erica thought for a moment.

"Sounds intriguing. Maybe I should investigate this more."

"Now that's what I want to hear. So let me try this question again. When will you be available?"

"Like I told you before, I'm handling business," she said with a slight attitude.

"Well I know that you are worth the wait. And I trust my phone should ring within the hour," Ty stated confidently and then hung up. Erica looked at her phone and laughed. This nigga is trippin', she thought to herself as she pressed the end button on her Blue Tooth. As she pulled up in front of the building, she spotted Juju. She got herself together and returned back to business mode. She couldn't let things get in the way of making money.

Juju spotted her and after finishing up with a dude from around the way, he walked towards her car. Erica unlocked the doors and Juju entered on the passenger's side.

"What's up baby girl? How is life treating you?"

"I can't complain."

"You seem a little aloof E. Is everything oK? What's up?"

"Nah I'm good. I'm just not feeling good that's all. You need ten cards right?" Erica asked trying to change the subject. She just wanted to get this over with so that she could continue with her plans for the evening.

"Yeah baby girl. Can I get a break though?"

"Ju where is my money?" Erica asked getting upset.

"I got it right here E damn, I was just asking. You can't knock a brother for trying," he said breathing heavily for affect.

"No I can't, but you can pass over my five G's!" Juju blew out a breath of air and passed Erica the envelope of money, as she passed him the manila envelope full of credit cards. "Now come with an order of twenty-five or better, and I'll give you four for yourself."

"Bet," Juju said shaking his head. "That sounds good. So we straight?" he asked, as Erica finished counting the money.

"Yeah I got it."

"Aight E. See you later. Be safe baby girl," he said opening the car door.

"You too. Nice doin' business wit' cha!" Erica said smiling. She tucked the envelope in her purse and pulled away from the building. Making a u-turn on Myrtle Avenue, Erica changed the CD. She needed some power music. She popped in her Kelis album and skipped to her favorite track. "I'm Bossy" blared out of her Bose speakers as she sang along to the words.

"I'm bossy!" Erica yelled out, as she let the music take control of her. She was tired of stressing and needed something to clear her mind. "Fuck it," she said as she stuck her Blue Tooth in her ear and turned the volume down from her steering wheel.

"Hey Boo," Ty answered.

"Hey. I'm still taking care of business, but I'll be finished at about eleven," she lied. "I'll meet you at the W, in the lounge area. Is that okay with you?"

"Yeah that's fine with me."

"OK see you later." Erica said hanging up the phone. Shit what the fuck am I gonna do now? She stared at the clock and saw that it was only 6:30. Fuck it I'll find something to do. Victor wants to act up, then fine. His ass will act up by his damn self. Let his ass worry for once. Coming in at all hours of the fucking night, knowing that my stupid ass will just be there waiting for him. That nigga knows every move I make, but when it comes to him, everything is hush ... hush. Well not tonight! I'm doing me boo! Erica thought to herself as she replayed her song and sang along. She was determined to make Victor pay for what he had done to her.

Victor dialed Erica's phone for what must have been the three hundredth time that day. And each time, just like the time before, his call went to voicemail.

"Shit!" Victor yelled out exasperated. He had done everything and checked with everyone that he thought would know where she was. He had called her mother and Aunt Kat, and he even reached out to Tracy who told him that Erica had canceled on their plans to go out for the night. Victor didn't know what to think and Crystal and Kim had already left town, so he knew she wasn't with one of them. Unless… maybe she decided to take a drive to see her friends after what happened. Yeah! That was it.

Victor picked up his phone to call Crystal.

"Hello."

"Hey Crystal. It's Victor. Sorry to bother you, but I was wondering if you spoke to Erica? You know, maybe she had decided to head your way."

"Umm no. Last time I spoke to Erica was yesterday. I haven't spoken to her since I've been back. Is everything oK Victor?" Crystal asked worried. She knew something was wrong if Victor was calling. They were tight, but that's the only time that Victor ever called her without Erica being present.

"Oh nah. Well not really. We just got into a little argument that's all, and I thought maybe she might have been heading your way to clear her head. But don't worry it's cool. She probably went to Kat's house," Victor said.

"OK, you sure?"

"Yeah. It's cool."

"Aight Victor. Hit me up when you reach her oK?"

"Yeah aight," Victor said hanging up. "Fuck!" he screamed out. He didn't know what else to do. He was completely assed out and had gone down every avenue he could think of. Erica was missing. Victor pulled into their driveway and just stared at their house. Erica's car wasn't in the driveway, so that meant that she was still gone. He sat in his car, leaning his head back on the headrest. He thought back to when he first took her virginity. Erica was scared shitless, but she tried to act like she wasn't. Victor could feel her shaking like a leaf underneath him, and he stopped asking her if she was oK.

"Yea Victor. I'm oK," she answered staring into his eyes.

"You know I'll take care of you Erica. You're mine and I'll take care of you," he said kissing her forehead. They shared a kiss and Erica stopped shaking. Victor promised to be gentle with her and not do anything to hurt her and up until this point he had kept his promise. Yet now, after a stupid fight things might be over. They were supposed to have their wedding in a couple of months and now he didn't know if that was going to happen.

Victor had always dabbled with other women every now and then, but he made sure that they all knew their positions. Erica was number one and the rest of the hoes were just that…hoes. He was always careful and always used protection. He never wanted to bring anything home to Erica, whether it be an STD or a baby by another woman. And out of all his infidelities, he knew that Erica had been true and never slept around on him. He had been her one and only and now he had fucked that all up.

Erica made him feel like a man. He was her lover, her provider and her protector. She was there for him before the music and drug game, so he knew her love was true. All those other hoes were just after his money or the power that he had. They weren't real and they weren't for him like Erica had been through the years. She even stuck by him when he got locked up for that short amount of time. Erica had been the only woman that he allowed himself to fall for in every sense of the word. He loved her. She was his earth. She was his life. Victor feeling low dragged himself out of his truck and walked towards the house. Walking in, he headed straight to their bedroom. He noticed that everything was just the same as it was from the morning. Overwhelmed with sadness Victor sat on the bed and placed his head in his hands.

Suddenly his phone rang and he almost killed himself trying to answer it in time. But it was only Twan checking to see if he had found Erica. When he told him no, Twan felt his pain. They went back and forth with possible places he could have missed, but when nothing turned up Twan told Victor to relax and call it a night. He suggested that he call the police if she hadn't turned up by the next morning.

Victor agreed, but knew he couldn't get any sleep without knowing where his angel was. He lay down on his bed and placed his two phones on the pillow above his head just in case he fell asleep. All Victor could think of was somebody hurting his precious Erica. He cracked at the thought, and a single tear fell from his eye.

Chapter 15

Erica had already made the call to her girls telling them to prepare for a cruise with Ty and his crew. They were all excited and felt like they were definitely coming up. Erica thought that this was a good way to network and maybe get some ideas on how to expand her business without getting caught. There was too much money in this game for Erica to fuck up so her crew had to be on point at all times. Erica looked at the time on her dashboard and realized she had to go to meet Tracy. They had decided to hit up Bloomingdales for gear once Tracy got off of work.

Erica was already near Bloomingdales, so she pulled her car into a parking lot and walked the block and a half back to Bloomingdales to wait for Tracy. When Tracy appeared, she had a worried look on her face.

"I knew something was up with you when we spoke this morning," Tracy said, giving Erica a hug. "So tell me what's up." Erica looked at her friend, but suddenly became embarrassed by what had happened.

"Come on E. We're best friends right?" Erica took a deep breath and repeated the story that she had been telling all day. Tracy just stood there in shock with her mouth hanging open.

"So what are you going to do?"

"At first I was going to make his ass pay for disrespecting me, but deep down Tracy I love him and I don't know if I can live without him.

Besides we're getting married soon and I'm thinking that maybe I'm just a little nervous about the wedding and I'm just finding a reason to pick a fight. But I will tell you one thing; I'm not going home tonight. I think I'm going to stay at the W. I need to just have some time to myself ya know? And besides… I want him to suffer a little bit," Erica said with a devilish grin on her face.

"I hear that. So tell me more about this trip. I know you not telling Victor, so that means we all got to get on point with our stories."

"True that. I have to call Crystal and Kim back later after I meet with this nigga Ty tonight to get the details. Until then the story stays as it was. We all going to ATL. Since it was planned at the same time anyways, no one will think any different. So that's the story that you tell Twan and I'll tell Victor the same. In the meantime don't tell Victor or Twan where I'm at. I already know they trying to find me. I'll just go home and settle shit in the morning."

"Aight girl. Oh shit look at the time! We're not going to have any time to look for anything really. And now that we're going on this cruise, I'm sure we'll need a lot more than bathing suits. How long is it anyways?"

"I'm not sure, he didn't really say. Five days I think. But look do me a quick favor? Go get my car it's in the lot around the corner. Here's the ticket. Double park right here outside the store. I'm going to run in and get four gift cards so we can shop later. I need to use up this American Express card before it goes dead."

"Aight E."

Erica looked around and spotted her victim. There was an amateur looking sales clerk standing at the Vera Wang counter. Erica walked over to her.

"Hello. Would you like to try our new fragrance?" The young clerk asked.

"No, I know what it smells like. Actually I need a bottle, I ran out. Can I also have four gift cards, with $1000 on each?"

"Sure, no problem ma'am? How will you be paying?"

"My platinum card, thanks," Erica said with a Kool-Aid smile. Erica handed her the card. "Here you go."

"Thanks," said the clerk as she swiped Erica's card through the register. As the register printed up the receipt, the clerk placed Erica's perfume and gift cards in a small bag. "Thank you Ms. Colbert," she said handing Erica the bag and receipt to sign. "OK, Ms. Colbert. Here's your card. Have a good night!"

"Thanks you too," Erica said smiling as she turned to exit the store. When Erica got onto the street, she saw Tracy sitting out front as planned.

"Here, there's a thousand dollars on each of them," Erica said handing Tracy two gift cards.

"Thanks," Tracy said. As Tracy looked for a place to pull over so they could switch, her phone started to ring. It was Twan.

"Oh shit it's Twan," Tracy said to Erica.

"OK… don't tell Twan that we're together. I'm sure that Victor's got him looking out too. Remember what we talked about." Tracy nodded her head and went to answer her phone.

"Hey baby. What's up?" Tracy cooed into the phone. They spoke for a few minutes and Erica heard Tracy answering questions about her location. After reassuring Twan that she didn't know where Erica was, she asked him to pick her up on 34th street. He agreed and Erica dropped her off to meet him.

"Thanks for the ride E, but one quick question. What's up with you and Ty?"

Erica was caught off-guard. "What do you mean what's up with us? We doing business together, what you think?" Tracy gave Erica an "I don't believe you" look.

"Yeah right Erica. Are you planning something with Ty?" Tracy asked with a mischievous look in her eyes. Erica didn't answer. Tracy just sat there and shook her head.

"Are you going to at least get in touch with Victor or accept his calls tonight?"

"Look Tracy, right now I'm all about my paper as far as Ty is concerned. Now my fiancé, hell no! I won't be talking to or seeing him until tomorrow. He deserves to be concerned about me. He's damn lucky I didn't fuck his ass up or key up that pretty little truck of his. Tracy don't get me wrong, yes I love my soon-to-be husband, but I know he is fucking around on me. And I know that people claim that the women come with his lifestyle, but shit that don't mean I'm supposed to lie down and accept that shit. He got the wrong one. If you love me then you don't need nobody else, plain and simple. All that 'men will be men' bullshit goes right out the window. My whole thing is, if you gonna be a 'man' and do dirt, then be honest about it. Why lie if you're such a big man? He needs to have his shit together at all times. Victor will learn not to fuck with me.

"Tracy I know that Ty is wide open for me and damn I can't even lie, the man is fine. But my intentions with Ty are strictly for business purposes only. I'm not saying that I'm not tempted for a little pleasure when I'm faced with it, but right now I have to stay focused and handle mine. My mind is already fucked up over this mess with Victor. Yes

I'm going back to him, but I can't forget like it never happened."

"OK girl. So I take it you won't be coming into work tomorrow?"

"Naa, most likely no. I'm sure they'll be ready to fire me soon." Tracy laughed and waved as Erica pulled off and headed towards 34th Street to meet up with Twan. Damn I hope they work this shit out 'cause both of them are trippin', Tracy thought to herself as she hightailed it down 33rd Street.

Erica parked her car in a neighboring garage once she arrived at the W Hotel in Times Square. Upon walking up to the main entrance, she was greeted by very handsome door man. "Welcome to the W Times Square," he said.

"Thank you," Erica replied as the doorman held the glass doors open for her to enter.

She walked slowly into the lobby as she pondered her encounter with Ty. She knew that she was putting herself in a fragile position by even agreeing to meet with him knowing how weak her relationship was with Victor, but business was business. She was still in love with her fiancé and had every intention of marrying him, but she had to show him that she was no fool and that there was no one person running their relationship. It was 50/50. I'm just going to have a drink with him and talk business, Erica thought to herself as she approached the lounge area. Maybe I'll do a little flirting for my ego.

She stood at the bar and looked around for Ty. She didn't see him. Since Ty hadn't arrived, Erica walked back to the hotel lobby to secure a room for the night. She reached into her purse and pulled out her American Express Platinum card that she had used in Bloomingdales. Once her slip was signed and she received her key, she headed back to the bar. While walking, she noticed that she was getting a lot of looks from men on every side. She smiled and continued on. Damn there he goes; Erica thought to herself, trying to stay composed. Having Ty in her view made her strut even more.

Ty watched her every step. As soon as she reached the table he stood up and greeted her with a hug and kiss on the cheek. Erica looked at him and smiled.

"Damn Ty. You're looking good," she said as she sat down at the table. Ty made sure that she was seated comfortably before taking his own seat. He was being the perfect gentlemen. Erica started to feel a little vulnerable, but brushed away the feeling.

"So what are you having to drink?"

"Oh my you don't know? I thought you were all knowing," she said with a smile. "I'll have a cosmopolitan please."

"Sure," Ty said, mesmerized by her smile. "Here's all the information that you'll need for the trip. It has the dates and times for everything. The only cost that you and your crew will be responsible for is your flights. Just make sure that everyone is on time, because we leave promptly. Read through that packet tonight and if you have any questions, give me a call and I'll explain whatever you need to know." As Ty spoke, Erica skimmed through the cruise packet contents. She was excited about this trip even more after viewing the itinerary. She made a mental note of the things she needed to buy. The girls had two suites on the upper deck, and there were all kinds of parties and shows to attend. Erica was excited and figured that she needed this mini-vacation that couldn't have come at a more perfect time.

"Wonderful. I'll take a look at it and make the reservations. So far things look good."

"Great. So now that that's all out of the way, let's talk about what had you so bothered earlier."

"Nothing I'm just having a little argument with my husband."

"Oh he's your husband now? Hmm… OK. Not about me I hope," he said, pretending to be upset.

"Well he's my fiancé but he's going to be my husband soon enough, so I might as well start referring to him as such. And trust our fight was not about you. Don't flatter yourself. It's personal."

"Well I know you can handle it."

"Yes, very much so. Thanks for being so concerned," Erica said sarcastically, as she stared intensely into Ty's hazel eyes. For the next hour they shared drinks and food and spoke about both their business endeavors and personal lives. At this point they were both beyond drunk. Suddenly Ty started getting sentimental and telling Erica everything he thought she wanted to hear. Erica wanted to puke. Here this nigga go trying to get some ass with this soap opera crap

"I know you have my best interest at heart Ty, and trust me when I say I truly appreciate your kind words. You are very … very tempting, but you will never handle me like a slut or any of those women you are used to dealing with who dress scantily and allow lust to control their lives. Why, because I never had a problem in self-control. See if I choose to sleep with you, I would be fully aware of why I'm there. I'm not trying to be your girlfriend or your wife or even your chick on the side. I'd be there to get some dick and that's that. If I didn't know the deal, I wouldn't be there. I've never had a problem with sex Ty, so be straight with me. All this game that you're spitting is unnecessary. I mean yes, your words are very flattering but that's all they are to me, words. I've always been a woman of action myself, and action my dear speaks louder," she said finishing her drink, and signaling to the waiter to bring her another.

"Erica trust me, I can see that you're a no-nonsense kind of lady and I respect that in you. But please believe that I have been nothing but honest with you. And be careful what you request and be ready to handle it."

"I'm ready now."

"Are you?"

"Yes," she answered slightly above a whisper. Ty stood up and gave her a once over, not missing one curve of her body.

"I have a room here. Would you like to come up for a little while? You know to sober up before you take the drive home?"

"With or without Victor's approval?"

"That doesn't deserve an answer Ty," she replied slightly offended and upset that he was bringing up Victor again, a name that she'd rather forget at the moment.

"Do you want to come up or not? Either way leave Victor out of this. Every time I see you, you manage to mention Victor's name. The shit is turning me off," Erica remarked in a somewhat slurred speech.

"I'm just saying, a woman like you sleeping away from your man? Hey I just don't want to see the brother get hurt, you feel me?"

"Aren't you two enemies? Victor is a big boy. He doesn't need me to tuck him in tonight."

"Yes ma'am lead the way," Ty responded. The two of them approached the elevator bank with Erica leading the way as Ty watched her ass switch back and forth. Entering, the room, Erica placed her purse on the sofa. Ty walked to the bedroom to click on the TV to see what movies were featured.

"Who said I was in the mood for TV?" Erica asked abruptly. Before she could say another word Ty jumped like a pubescent seventeen year old and started tonguing her down. Erica did not resist as the passion raced through her during their kiss. After a few moments of kissing, she slid out of his embrace. "Ty we can't do this," she whispered, breathing heavily and feeling moist between the legs.

"Erica, you know I'm attracted to you and you know it's not just about sex."

"I know… and trust me when I say, I'm attracted to you too," Erica said with her heart beating rapidly. Damn what woman wouldn't be? But I don't want to mix business with pleasure right now. I don't know what I was thinking."

"Erica make no mistake, I'm not requesting sex from you. But I'm not going to lie, in this position I do want to touch you, but if you're not down that's fine. I just need you to understand that I don't have any expectations for anything further," he said trying to reassure her.

"That sounds nice, but I think we've already overstepped our boundaries. I think you should leave."

"OK that's fine, but I'm just going to take it that you can't trust yourself around me and that's why you're cutting this evening short."

Ty looked away from her for a moment and then approached her at the mini-bar. His shirt was unbuttoned at the collar and un-tucked from his pants, but he still looked sexy as hell. He stood close enough for Erica to smell a slight hint of the Hennessy he was drinking earlier with a twist of cinnamon. He reached up to her ever so gently and started to caress her face, forcing her to look into his eyes.

"Ty are you not listening to me?" Ty leaned forward and began kissing her passionately. Erica allowed him to hold her, as their tongues got reacquainted. Ty ran his hands along her back and started to lift her Ellen Tracy cashmere off her shoulders. She tried to stop him with her weak voice.

"Ty…wait. I don't think I'm ready for this," she said trying to break from his hold.

"I promise Erica. I won't hurt you. Just let me have you, baby," he said as his lips met hers again. He clasped her breasts with his hands and played with her nipples until they sprang alive. He reached down and placed them one by one into his mouth sucking them softly at first and then increasing the pressure, causing Erica to squirm under his touch. The more he sucked on her nipples, the wetter her panties became. It was hard for her to contain herself. She knew she needed to stop, but he was feeling too good and she couldn't will herself to stop him. This was the kind of attention she had been missing and it felt damn good...even if it wasn't from her fiancé.

"Let me taste you," Ty whispered. "Please Erica. I need to taste you."

"I hope you like vanilla," Erica teased in a heavy breathy voice.

"That's my favorite flavor," Ty said in his own sexy tone as he began running his hand along the inner part of her thigh, laying her down on the bed. Erica lay there ready and waiting. He pulled down her skin-tight jeans and lace La Perla panties and ran his tongue from her ankles, up to her thighs and to her love. As Erica felt his tongue working its magic, she thought of Victor and wished that it were him making her moan. She spread her legs giving him more access to her clit and let him engulf himself in her juices. Erica tried to hold back her scream of ecstasy as she felt herself coming to a climax. Ty, noticing that she was getting ready to come, placed his middle finger inside of her wet pussy and started making circles. Erica screamed out in pleasure and let her orgasm take control of her body. When it was all said and done, the two of them sat in silence as Erica tried to gain control of her breathing. Shit, what the fuck have, I gotten myself into, Erica thought to herself, as Ty got up and walked out of her hotel room.

* * *

Erica opened her eyes and looked around. The sun was peaking its way through the curtains and for a moment she had to remember where she was. She sat up slowly and grabbed her head as she felt a rush of a headache coming on. She thought back to her eventful night of drinking, business planning, and foreplay with Ty. Erica lay back down on the plush king-sized bed and thought about the day ahead of her. She had to face Victor. Well I might as well get this shit over with.

She got up and took a long hot shower. She put back on the clothes she had on from the night before and put her underwear in her purse. She walked into the hotel gift shop and bought a travel deodorant and checked out. She headed to Macy's and picked up something cute including a new pair of La Perla's and tossed the old clothes in the trash. Afterward she would head back to Brooklyn. She still had a lot of preparing to do for her trip and wasn't sure if seeing Victor would further push her closer to Ty. Crossing the Manhattan Bridge she knew she had to play her position, whatever that would be after spending the night out.

When Erica pulled into the driveway, she noticed Victor's truck. Here goes, she thought as she walked into the house. She looked all over for Victor on the first floor but couldn't find him. She figured he must have been asleep. As she entered their bedroom, she saw him sprawled out on the bed snoring. Erica smiled at how peaceful he looked and couldn't deny that even when she was angry at him, he still turned her on with his adorable sleeping habits.

"Victor," she said softly while shaking him awake. When he woke up he smiled at first, but then reality kicked in and his smile was replaced by a frown.

"Where have you been Erica?"

"I just thought it was best to clear my head before I came home. I knew you were angry, and I was angry. I just didn't want to fight again." Victor sat up and the two of them had a long heart-to-heart. Erica laid everything out on the table. She told him of her suspicions and that he needed to be sure that he really wanted to marry her. If so, he had to slow down his hustle to be with her and perhaps even start a family. Victor wanted to argue at first, but took note of how much he had been spending time away from home and agreed that it was time to start planning for the future. He had to stop cheating on Erica and be the man that he knew he could be. Marriage was something sacred and he didn't want to go into it already cheating on his wife. After their talk, the two of them felt so much better. Erica had high hopes for her future with Victor and knew that if he slipped up again, she would get rid of him for sure.

The two of them embraced and made passionate love, or so Victor thought, yet in the back of Erica's mind all she could think of was him sexing another woman and his ultimate disrespect that he showed her and their relationship. Am I really going to be able to deal with this? She thought to herself as she lay next to him. The seeds of insecurity had already been planted and it would take a mini-miracle for Erica to fully trust her man again. After a few hours of quality time, Victor had to leave to handle some business, promising to return shortly.

Erica was sitting on the couch watching television when the phone rang. She reached over and picked up the cordless headset from the end table.

"Hello."

"Erica it's your father! Oh God!"

Mommy what's wrong?" Erica asked.

"He's been... he's been. Erica, he was killed last night in the prison. They say he got stabbed multiple times in the mid-section and back. He's dead baby," Dorothy said, crying hysterically into the phone.

Ty's connect in the prison had bribed a guard to leave Gregory's cell door slightly ajar. Shortly after midnight, a small team of inmates attacked him while he slept. The man who had terrorized his wife and children for several years was now an victim. As things started to fade to black, Gregory thought of the way he treated his family and his heart was full of regret. He realized that he should have been better man. It was when thoughts of the way he treated his youngest child came to his mind, he heard a whisper … "Erica sends her love." Darkness started fall over him as he bled out, covering the floor in red. "That little bitch" he thought with slight smile and died.

For a quick moment Erica was surprised and then she felt a sense of relief. Ty had come through for her and Big G was no longer an issue in her life.It took everything in Erica's soul not to jump up and holler for joy. Erica put on her best act for her mother's sake.

"Oh Mommy that's terrible. Who would do such a thing? I can't believe this. Does the warden have any information on who did this to him? Mommy, I'm so sorry, do you need me to come over?" Erica asked, pretending to be shaken up.

"Yes baby. Please come over. I need both my girls with me." Erica hung up with her mother and got herself together. Damn the nigga wasn't playing, Erica thought in the shower. Not only could she take pleasure that she was giving Victor a taste of his own medicine, but her other man had killed the only person she had ever truly feared. *I must thank him for his good deed*, she thought smiling to herself. After this bit of news, it would be a good day after all.

Chapter 16

Erica spent the next week helping her mother get everything together for Gregory's funeral and her trip. She helped her find the perfect suit, church, funeral home and even helped make the arrangements for the meal and refreshments that would take place after the ceremony at Dorothy's home in Fort Greene. Gregory's funeral would take place one week and the next week Erica was off to an exotic business cruise with her girlfriends to make some major business moves with Ty's connects. July was starting out great for Erica. With her father dead and business booming she was ready to make some changes. The first was to get out of her 9-to-5 for good.

After the funeral was over with, Erica was offered a position to work as a freelance publicist. Because she had proven to be such a hard worker in her years at the firm before she began her credit card business, her boss didn't question her sob story about her father being the reason that she had been so out of focus the past couple of months. She fed him a full-length lie about Gregory being ill for a while and it taking a toll on her emotionally. Her boss agreed to hire her for freelance projects and had even pooled money together to show their condolences.

Once that was out of the way, Erica made her last minute preparations for her trip. All the girls had their stories straight and would meet up in Florida where they were to board the ship. They all decided to arrive one night early so that they could get their heads together. The night before the trip, as Erica sat packing her last suitcase, she overheard Victor on the phone. For some reason Erica couldn't help but listen to his conversation because it seemed like he was whispering. Erica threw her last bra into the suitcase and tip-toed down the hallway and stood outside the door to Victor's office and listened closely.

"I was wondering what you were doing tomorrow night. I'm going to be alone. The wife is leaving. I know I told you we couldn't see each other anymore because I was getting married, but I thought that maybe we could have one last time for the road." Erica's heart dropped. She knew he was cheating on her before but she thought he had stopped. How stupid could she have been? She had to take control of her emotions, as she felt a strong passion of rage come over her. Erica's racing heart made her body feel like she was going into cardiac arrest. She held her hand up to her chest and continued to listen as her eyes began to turn red and fill with water.

"Come on Alexis, you knew the rules from jump so don't start that crying shit oK? Oh so you missing me boo? I miss you too. That's why we should spend this time together." Erica wanted to bust through the door and knock him upside the head, but instead she would get him back Erica-style. She wanted so badly to walk away but she had to hear what else he was saying to this broad.

"Pull the dildo out Alexis. Slide it in. Pretend like it's my thick hard dick in your pussy." Erica figured that the girl must have been doing what Victor asked because he kept going. "Alexis, harder baby. Do you love me? That's my girl… Put your thumb in your mouth and suck on it likes it's my dick and go to sleep. I'll call you later," he whispered. Erica took flight down the hallway and back into the room. She was furious. She wiped her eyes and took a deep breath. Suddenly she got an image of Gregory. She wondered what his face must have looked like after he got her message, right before he was killed. A smile crept across her face as she thought of those few words that she had scribbled across the napkin. "Payback is a motherfucker daddy, and may the baddest bitch win." Victor didn't know who he was fucking with.

The flight to Miami was short and the girls met up at the posh Delano hotel. As they sat at the bar, they discussed some last minute things that they would handle on the trip.

"OK so remember ladies. Be cool, professional and collected. Make conversation, but don't say too much. We're there to learn and network, not share our secrets. While we're there, let's try to stay together as much as possible, that way we'll never be caught off-guard. Each of us has a goal and we have to stick to that if we wanna get this big money. Are there any questions? Tomorrow's the big day."

"Nope I'm cool," Crystal said. "Actually I'm better than that. This shit is going to be a piece of cake. I can't wait to get up on that big ole boat and have me some fun."

"Damn you sound country as hell," Tracy laughed. All the girls started laughing as well.

"But seriously girls, we're on our way. Just think, in a year we'll all be set. I think after the wedding, I'm going to move my mom out of the projects. With my so- called freelance work and Victor's money, no one is going to question it. I think I'm going to try and look for something near my aunt. I saw a house for sale down Bedford

Avenue, not too far from Brooklyn College."

"Oh oK. It's nice over there," Tracy commented.

"Hey, I don't mean to go off subject, but since we're supposed to be professional does that mean we can't fuck anybody?" Kim asked. Everyone looked at each other and started laughing.

"Hell no that's not what it means. Girl, do you! Just make sure it doesn't get all over the ship. I say take your pick and just roll with that one for the entire stay."

"Cool," Kim said, sounding relieved.

"Well it's already after midnight. I think we should get a good night's rest. We board tomorrow morning at 8:00am sharp." The girls said their goodnights and headed for their respective rooms, each with thoughts of excitement about the day ahead.

By 6:15 the next morning the girls were already in a cab heading to the pier. Tracy and Erica had already contracted the services of a company called Alibi Network, which specializes in establishing alibis and excused absences for any type of occasion. You never could be too careful.

The ladies were in line by 7am and were dying in the blazing 96 degree Miami sun. A woman up ahead was having trouble locating her ticket and was holding up the line.

"Damn I wish they would hurry this shit up! It's hot as hell out this bitch," Crystal complained, as a few people grumbled in agreement with her on line.

"Well, look at it this way, at least you'll sweat off some pounds," Kim said, cracking a joke about Crystal's weight.

"Oh please bitch, I'm beautiful. You just hating 'cause you wish you had all these titties and ass, instead of bone and marrow." The girls started cracking up.

"OK, oK you got me on that one. Did anyone ever tell you that you look like Tocarra?"

"Bitch shut the hell up, I look like Crystal. You lucky it's so damn hot out here otherwise I'd knock your ass out."

After snapping on each other and complaining about the heat they were finally checked in and on their way to their rooms. The girls traveled through the cruise ship in amazement. The scenery was beautiful and the craft was set up like a beach resort.

The girls reached their rooms and decided to unpack and take cat naps. Erica wondered if Ty had already boarded the ship since they hadn't seen him on line. She lay down and gave him a call before taking her nap. Tracy was already in the bed snoring.

"Hello."

"Hey Ty it's Erica."

"I know who this is. Where are you?"

"In my room, laying down thinking of you."

"Word? Come to my room. I'm on the 5th deck, room 5103."

"Now?"

"Yeah why not? Where are your girls at?"

"Asleep I think. Well, at least Tracy is."

"So then what's the problem? Why stay in the room awake by yourself, when you could come check me?"

"OK fine! I'm on my way." Ty finished up his conversation with Erica and closed his phone. He had a lot of planning to do if this whole thing was going to go right. So far he had Erica right where he wanted her and he knew if he stayed patient and worked it the right way, he'd be able to get at Victor in no time. Ty sat in the living room area with his laptop downloading numbers and putting them in numeric order. Suddenly he heard a light tap on his room door. He moved his laptop onto his desk and went to answer the door. When he opened it, Erica stood there looking sexy as hell in a string bikini with a sheer sarong tied around her tiny waist. She stepped into his state room with a naughty look on her face. He kissed her on her forehead and gave her a big hug.

"You missed me?" he asked kissing her lips.

"Of course I did. What are you doing?"

"Come look." He sat her down on the bed and placed his laptop in her lap. "This is how you organize your numbers when you get them. I'm going to give you a copy of the program to use on your computer." Erica started looking at all the numbers on the computer screen. She was completely confused.

"What is all this Ty?" She asked full of intrigue. Could this have been the moment she had been waiting for?

As Erica looked at the screen of the laptop Ty went to a certain icon afterward he began to show Erica.

"OK Erica, I'll give you a quick crash course. This is the underground web site. What you do is download the account numbers from the web site into the program. This will generate the number you see on the front of the cards. The program will then write the code that corresponds to the account number to the strip on the back of the card. Then you're good to go. Once I set you up with the program, I'll show you how to make sure the codes go together. After you get the codes in order, you need one of these," Ty said pointing to a machine on his desk. "This is called a MRS206 as we like to call them in the hood a reader/writer. You then run the card through the machine and the codes are placed on the strip on the back of the card, along with any name that you want to place on the card and run it through. Then take the card and run it through the emboss machine and it prints up the front of the cards and they look like this," Ty said holding up a card that he had already printed. It looked exactly like the platinum card she had used in Bloomingdales.

"Once you print them up, you can start distributing them. Now I usually sell mine by cases of 100 cards at a rate of five cases a week. Once you start expanding your business a little bit more, I will hook you up with a machine of your own, the computer software and the plastic for you to print the cards on. All for a price of course," Ty said smiling. "Then, we could work together and start shipping them out all over the country. Just think, if you sell 100 cards at $500 a piece, you make $50,000 off the top. And 100 cards can go quickly if you have clients buying more than one at a time." Ty's words were falling on deaf ears at this point. All Erica could think about was all the money she and her crew were about to make once she got her equipment. Now that she had the information that she needed, she wouldn't need Ty much longer. But how would she get him out the picture? Tracy was right. Ty wouldn't let her bank all the money for herself. He was already talking about teaming up and sharing a piece of her pie. That wasn't going to happen. But for right now she still needed him, at least until she got her machine, software and found out where to get plastic from to make the cards. Shit what if I put Victor down? With his connections I could be making triple what I stand to make alone. This is getting better than I thought, she thought to herself with a smile.

"So do you understand everything that I have told you?" Ty asked seeing the smile on her face.

"No doubt. I'm ready to make this money," she said placing a juicy kiss on his lips.

"Damn what was that for?"

"For being you and for helping me with my little problem. You don't know how much I appreciate that shit. That bastard deserved everything he got!" Erica said with venom in her voice.

"It's cool Ma. Come here," he said as he kissed her lips. "Me and you are going to do the damn thing girl." He pushed her down on the bed and propped her up on all fours like a cat.

"Do you know my favorite number?"

"No," Erica whispered, feeling herself getting wet.

"Sixty-nine," Ty said as he slid underneath her.

"How about 68 and I owe you one"

Ty had started in on her clit with a vengeance and she couldn't focus on what she was doing. All she could manage to do was jerk his dick back and forth in her hands.

"Damn baby, what are you doing to me down there?" Erica shuttered. Ty licked his middle finger and placed it in her tunnel of love. Ty flipped Erica over onto the bed and continued eating her pussy like it was his last meal. Erica grabbed her ankles and let Ty sink his head deep inside. She looked down at him with lust in her eyes. As he put another finger into her pussy, Erica grabbed her titties and began sucking on her own nipples as Ty pleased her down below.

"Oh baby I'm coming!"

"Come on baby," Ty said between slurps. "Come for daddy!" Erica gyrated her hips to Ty's beat until her legs started to shake and the feeling of an orgasm took over her. Ty got up and pulled out his big hard dick and started to tease Erica's swollen and sensitive clit.

"Oh shit Ty. Damn Boo," she said as he eased his way inside. Ty spread her legs as far as they could go and went deep inside Erica. His dick touched her back walls and within moments she was ready to climax again. With each stroke, Erica met Ty pump for pump. She pushed him off of her and jumped on the dick, riding him like a professional horse jockey. Right before Ty got ready to come, Erica jumped off as his splashed his love juice all over the himself.

As they lay cuddled together, Erica couldn't help but think of all the things she had been missing wasting her time on Victor. While she was being the faithful girlfriend, he was out having his fun with who knows how many women. Men ain't shit, Erica thought to herself as she lay in Ty's arms. They're just to be used and let go. Can't take these niggas seriously. As Erica's mind was coming down from her sex high with thoughts of payback, Ty drifted off to sleep.

Erica got up slowly out of his bed, as not to wake him, and began dressing herself. Once her bikini and sandals were back on, she walked as lightly as possible through his suite towards the front door. Beep, beep. Beep, beep. Ty's cell was sounding off. Erica reached for the door knob, but couldn't help but be enticed by the phone's flashing lights. She peaked inside the bedroom and saw that Ty was still fast asleep. She picked up the phone and read the message that was on the screen. "Hope shit is going as planned. We've been watching that nigga Victor. All you got to do is get that bitch set that nigga Victor up and he's dead. We're waiting for your call."

* * *

Speechless, Erica looked at the message in outrage. In less than a week she had been played by both the men in her life. Although she had never taken Ty seriously, she thought that they had established a good business relationship. Now she felt crushed by knowing that his trust only came with the hopes that she would lead him straight to Victor.

Erica marked the message as unread and let herself out of the suite. She had a lot of shit to do when she returned to New York and it wasn't going to be pretty, but for now she had to keep her act together for the rest of the trip.

Chapter 17

The rest of the trip proved to be a success for Erica and her crew with regards to business ventures and networking. Outside of finding out Ty's plans of using her as a pawn Erica appreciated the trip. She was livid at the audacity the nigga had planning to use her to get back at Victor for some local beef. Erica opted not to tell anyone not even Tracey about what she had read on Ty's text message she would just continue with her plans to get all the information and connections she could, after all it was a business trip. The cruise itinerary consisted of workshops on Identity Theft, Exports and Imports, New retail sales technology, and poolside parties, comedy shows and several activities including a poker game, and old school dance contest. Erica had learned so many different avenues to expand her operation and had gained a very impressive list of prospects that she couldn't wait to approach when she returned to Brooklyn. Her crew had established the same and were all quite excited about their plans to take over the entire east coast and keep moving right over to the west coast.

Erica would have to decide what she was going to do about Ty not that she surely couldn't trust him. She would search for a way to delete him from the equation as soon as possible.

When Erica arrived home, things were the same as when she had left. Victor was being nicer than usual, which for Erica only confirmed that he had carried out his secret sexual plans with the woman that he had been on the phone with. Erica wanted to scream and choke the shit out of him, but instead she was receptive of his attention and affection at least until she could figure out what she wanted to do about his infidelity.

Believing in her heart that if her and Victor could make it to the wedding that he would absolutely, positively be faithful to his wife, Erica continued planning the arrangements.

It was a wedding beyond the wildest dreams of most. The ceiling of the chapel was draped in long ribbons of silk that flowed from wall to wall. Erica wore a gown that would rival even the most well off bride to be as she made her way down aisle. As act of independence, she gave herself away. Victor waited at the altar with Twan standing by his side in sheer amazement. He could not believe that she would forgive him for what he had done, much less marry him. At that very moment, he came to realize that he was the luckiest man on earth.

Erica took her time as everyone stared in awe even smiling at a few haters on the way. Shit, this nigga don't know what he's getting himself into, she thought. Suddenly, she recalled her lying helplessly on the floor, her face covered with his spit. For a second she thought of leaving him standing, looking stupid, at the altar. But, this was one of those long games, like the ones she watched her father run throughout her life. Just when the marks thought they were ahead of the game, they found they were being played all of long. Sometimes it took years, but when her father revealed his hand, they had lost everything and never saw it coming. At last, her father taught her something good after all.

After the wedding Erica was working fervently on her business expansion. Once the honeymoon was over, Erica dove headfirst into her business with such a zeal and great anticipation as if she knew this was her official hour for success. Over the next few months Erica became very hard and callous within. Her moves were all premeditated and strategic in lining her up where she desired to be in her operation. In due time she would be sitting on a gold mind and would find the opportune moment to put both Victor in Ty in their places. Erica stayed in touch with Ty, and he never had a clue that she was on to him. They had their occasion sex to satisfy her own lustful desires and for her to pick up more card shipments. As business picked up they met more often and Erica stayed hopeful that he wouldn't get to Victor to soon.

A year had gone by before Erica knew it and she had established 175 clients. With her booming business, Ty practically broke his neck to get her set up with the materials she needed. The tables were finally turning. Erica and her team had a combined total of 617 clients, meaning they were pulling in over $300,000 a month and that was just calculating one card per client. Since they're clientele was so large, Erica no longer did hand to hand transactions. Instead, she did shipments. She would print out 100 cards and ship them to her buyers. She usually did two shipments a day, which meant that she was banking $500,000 a day.

Each shipment took Erica about four hours to print, so she would start early in the morning when Victor left out and was usually done by the time he came back in. He was pathetically clueless as to what was going on right under his nose. Being married hadn't made Victor more attentive, so Erica just considered him more of a roommate and focused on her own money making.

Erica had established a high level clientele. These weren't just your local street hustlers or average crooks. These were CEOs of large corporations and construction companies, doctors, lawyers and well-known musicians and rappers. How else could they afford to buy out the bar at every release party and All-star weekend? Perpetrating niggas were using fraudulent cards that's how. Nothing is ever as it seems in this country. Those who seemingly had money of their own were Erica's biggest clients. Some men even purchased cards for their mistresses so that their wives couldn't trace their real card transactions back to infidelity. CEOs would use the cards to get expensive hotel rooms and take trips with high price prostitutes. Musicians and rappers tricked on video hoes to get some ass. For Erica and the girls this level of deceit was great for business.

Not only did Erica have her credit operation running strong she had sex out of convenience with Victor one too many times and wound up with a new baby girl, Sariyah to look after. Her daughter was her pride and joy and Erica now spent most of her time catering to the needs of her baby. She had hired a live-in nanny to help her with the Sariyah, especially during times when she had to travel for work. And Erica was no fool. The nanny she hired could have been a double for Mrs. Doubtfire. She didn't need a live in hoe caring for her baby and fucking her man.

Erica had also kept her promise and moved her mother into a nice three-bedroom home in the Flatbush section of Brooklyn, and with her father gone she didn't have to worry about her mother's safety. Victor nor her mother questioned Erica about her finances; they believed that her freelancing PR gig was paying off well. She told her mom she had several companies paying her $10,000 to $15,000 retainers a month to work on special events which is why she had to travel ever so often.

Kim was also holdin it down in North Carolina. Most of her clients were businessmen. She had done so well with them that she had picked up and moved to the west coast to expand. Hollywood was the perfect place to set up shop. All the fake boob jobs and wanna be actresses and the folks who would scam on those who came to make it L.A. was prime real estate for Kim. She started going for movie stars, producers, club owners, and other entrepreneurial types. She even hit up some of the sales people working on Hollywood Blvd shops and the Beverly Center. There were always premieres and stuff and the average working girl had to keep up with the likes of Paris Hilton, Lindsey Lohan and the rest of the superstar spoiled bitches.

Crystal was able to transfer schools and was attending Spellman. She had purchased her own home in Atlanta which was fully loaded with five bedrooms, four baths, 2-car garage, mini basketball and tennis court along with a heated pool and hot tub. Her preferred customers consisted of college students, small business owners and most of all drag queens. Tracy, who had remained at the public relations firm full-time, had discreetly hipped a few of her clients to the game and they, in turn, introduced her to more a wider market. She branched out into realtors, developers, car dealers, bankers, and even people in her own neighborhood. No stone was left unturned and because of the authenticity of their cards, the clients kept coming. Each one of the girls were truly living it up thanks to Erica plan of expansion. The information they got from the cruise was priceless to their ventures.

In the midst of success Erica had grown tired of Ty demanding a percentage of her funds and thought that it was time to make her move.

She was surprised that she had been able to hold him off for a year on his strike against Victor, and since Ty had been laying low for some other foolishness he was involved in she was able to keep him away from Victor. One afternoon after she had put Sariyah down for a nap she approached Victor, who had been working on some paperwork for the record label.

"Hey baby," Victor said, as he held his arms out for Erica to take a seat on his lap. "What's on your mind?"

"I wanted to talk to you about something, but I don't want you to get mad 'cause it wasn't my fault." Victor took his reading glasses off and looked into her eyes trying to figure out the truth behind her statement.

"OK. I'm listening."

"So, yesterday me and Tracy was at Green Acres mall getting a few things for Sariyah when that dude from Queens spotted us. Remember him? That guy who came to my birthday party at 40/40? What was his name? Tay? Tee?"

"Ty," Victor said raising his voice.

"Ty," Erica said slapping her forehead like it had suddenly come to her. "That's right. So anyways he comes to us talking about how I'm looking good and I'm filling out just right from the baby and how he would love to get a taste of this. Then he looked in the stroller and started cooing at Riyah. So I pushed him back and told him to back off and leave us alone. So then he's like naa he can't do that 'cause I'm just too sexy and he knows your punk ass ain't hitting it right." Erica paused for effect. "So I told him to mind his damn business and he said to tell you that ya'll had some unfinished business to handle. You never did tell me what happened between the two of you," Erica said coyly. She could see the wheels turning in Victor's head.

"Basically to make a long story short, that motherfucker tried to rob one of my spots with his crew and his little brother got killed in the process. That's what happens when you play dirty and he took that shit to heart and blamed me for it."

"Did you kill his brother?" Erica couldn't help but ask.

"That's not important. What is important is that you did the right thing by telling me. Don't worry baby. I'll take care of it. You know I love you right?" Victor asked as he kissed her lips.

"Yes. And I love you too. I love you so bad it hurts," Erica said, getting choked up on her words. She held Victor tight around the neck as they shared a passionate kiss and made love right there in his office. Once they were finished, Erica got dressed and headed out the door towards the kitchen to fix the baby's bottle. Step one, Erica thought as she heard Sariyah's cries through the baby monitor.

The following month, Crystal had come to New York for a visit. She missed her friends and wanted to be close to the people she loved. Although Dezo had moved to Atlanta with her, she still needed her girls around her. They tried to get Kim to come too, but she had business to handle out in Cali that was a little more important than a girl's night out. After all business was business.

"So Ms. Erica what's new in your world," Crystal asked as she took a sip of her watermelon martini as the girl ordered food from the menu at Ruth Chris.

"Not much. Not really doing that much freelancing work for the firm anymore because I'm trying so hard to build and maintain my clientele but Victor and my mom think otherwise. Plus with all these damn shipments that I have to print up, it takes a lot of time out of my day. Then there's the baby, Victor's shit—"

"Damn for somebody who ain't doing much, you sure got a lot of shit going on." They both laughed. Erica noticed that Tracy was being rather quiet and wanted to know what was on her mind.

"I'm having some problems with Twan. It's getting harder and harder to hide this cash flow. Now that we living together, he notices a lot more and I don't want this to come between us, but shit, my money comes first. What am I going to do?"

"Don't worry Tracey, I have everything under control. I have a plan that I've already set in motion and pretty soon, we all will be able to come clean. Well not exactly, but you know what I mean. Just give me a little more time and stand strong and the secret will come out soon."

"OK E. I trust you. You haven't steered us wrong so far, so I'm with you. Just try to speed this up oK?" Tracy said smiling at her friend. They all looked at each other in amazement and couldn't believe how successful they had become in the past year and they only had one direction to go, and that was up.

The girls finished their meals and headed home. Erica jumped in her brand new Lexus truck with thoughts on her mind. Her empire was growing and she had finally put in motion a plan that she had been working on for a year. Erica had one more thing that needed to be finalized before she would be able to sit back and watch her money roll in, and that was to start her own legal business. She had thoughts of this before but decided that she didn't want to pursue a career in publicity.

After researching the market, she decided that it would be best to start a restaurant. She wasn't sure what kind of restaurant or where just yet, but knew that this was the direction she would go in. Of course she had the money to buy property, but decided against that. Buying the property straight out would cause too many red flags.

Instead, she would take out a business loan and make monthly payments just like any other "struggling" business owner. She had to play this smart to stay in the game. A smile crossed her face at the thought of the business she would soon start. She snapped out of her thoughts when her cell rang. Her smile was suddenly replaced by a frown when she saw that it was Ty.

"Hey Ty," she answered unenthusiastically.

"What's up baby girl? Did you send out that last shipment to those Mexicans down in Florida?"

Why is he always asking me questions about my shit? Erica asked herself. She blew out a breath of air before answering. "Not yet, why?"

"No reason. I just wanted to know. You know I like to stay on top of things."

"Yeah oK. Listen I'm kind of in the middle of something, can I call you back?"

"No doubt. Actually I will just hit you up tomorrow. I'm on my way out myself. There's something poppin' off tonight at this club uptown, so I'll be there."

"OK have fun and be safe," Erica said before hanging up. She cringed at the thought of Ty. That was his usual. He was always up in her business affairs but never cared to share the details of his. He was no better than Victor with all his damn secrets. Erica pulled into the gated parking lot. She checked the address again on the piece of paper sitting on her passenger seat and saw that she had the right place. She glanced at the clock and noticed that she was running a little late. She decided to call to make sure he was still there.

"I'm outside," she said.

"Good. We're waiting for you. Come inside and just tell the secretary you're here to see me."

"OK. I'm on my way inside," Erica said, closing her cell phone. She took a deep breath as she stepped out of her car and hit the alarm. Step two.

Chapter 18

"Victor!" Erica screamed out. "Victor, answer the damn phone!" Erica opened her eyes when she noticed that the phone was still ringing. "Shit!" she called out. She hadn't gotten much sleep the night before, since her appointment had run over. She rolled over on her side and snatched the phone off the hook

"What!"

"Girl you won't believe this shit, hurry up and turn to channel 5!"

"Tracy? I know you didn't wake me up at," she looked over at the clock, "7:15 in the damn morning to ask me to watch some shit."

"Bitch, shut the fuck up and turn the shit on. Hurry up!" Erica searched through her sheets for the remote and quickly turned on the TV.

"Police don't quite know what caused the shooting and so far have no suspects. Once again for all those who have just joined us, we are taping live in front of Sunsplash night club in Harlem. It seems that at about 5:15 this morning there was some sort of altercation, which started inside the club and then continued as the patrons were leaving. Just a few feet away from the club's entrance, a car filled with an unknown amount of assailants drove by spraying bullets at a group of men exiting the club right here on this sidewalk. Police believe that the argument started inside the club between the men and an unknown suspect, who then called for help, thus stemming the shootout shortly thereafter.

Four men were hit in the attack. Three have been confirmed dead and one is fighting for his life at Mount Sinai Hospital. Wait," she paused. "This just in. The police have released the names of the three victims. Tyquan Carolton, 26, Phillip Watkins 24, and Troy Alexander, 26 were the three victims that were tragically killed in this blood bath. It is said that they all resided in Queens. The fourth name is not being released for the victim's protection. We will have more on this story as it unfolds. Back to you in the studio."

Tracy couldn't believe it when she heard the name Tyquan Carolton. Ty was dead.

"I just spoke to him last night and he told me he was going to some club uptown. Damn who the fuck thought this shit would happen?"

"I can't fucking believe this shit. I was up about to do my laundry and I saw this. What are we going to do?"

"What do you mean, what are we going to do? We gonna do what we been doing! Ty ain't done shit for us in almost a year besides take a cut of our money. I mean, I'm sorry he had to go, but him being gone ain't gonna hurt our business. Sad to say, but he might have helped it. Shit his clients are going to need plates from somewhere. I still have some business cards from the cruise two months ago. I should hope you still have yours and I'll call Kim and Crystal. We give this shit a week, and then we make our move. Feel me?"

"No doubt. Hey, he was a cool dude, but shit that's life in the game."

"Exactly. Go do your laundry. I'm going back to sleep. I'll call you when I get up."

"Aight. Later." Erica placed the phone back into the cradle. Now with Ty gone she had some moves to make if she was going to get Victor and his crew on her team. Although her body was telling her to lie back down, her mind was working overtime. She had some calls to make and some planning to do. She threw the covers off her legs and went to the bathroom to brush her teeth and splash some cold water on her face. She dug through her walk-in closet to find her lock box. Wait a damn minute. Where the fuck is Victor? Oh shit! Could he have… naa it couldn't have been. But then again. Damn that nigga wasn't playing, Erica thought laughing to herself. Her plan was working out nicely. She lifted up a small piece of carpet under her wall-to-wall shoe rack and picked up a small key that opened the box. There she found her mini-binder that held all of her business cards and contact information. She pulled out Jordon Diaz's card and smiled. As she moved to lock the box and place the key back under the mat, she heard Victor's music before his car pulled into the driveway. She stuffed the card into her Juicy Couture bag that was sitting on her shelf, closed the closet and jumped back into bed, shutting her eyes as if asleep.

Erica heard Victor's voice in the hallway downstairs as he greeted the nanny, Mrs. Frances and a cooing Sariyah. About ten minutes later he was on his way up to their bedroom. Erica heard him enter their room and walk straight into his closet to get undressed. Shortly after, she felt his body lying next to her. Victor snuggled up behind Erica and held her tight. It wasn't even five minutes before she heard him snoring. Unable to sleep, Erica waited just a little while longer before she was able to wiggle her way out of his grasp. She snatched the card out of her purse and headed upstairs to her office in the attic. Shit! I forgot my cell phone. Erica paced back and forth in front of her desk wondering if she should go back downstairs and retrieve it or if it was safe to make the call on her office line. Convinced that Victor was still asleep, she decided to make the call from her office.

"Good morning, Diaz and Associates, how may I assist you?"

"Hi, this is Mrs. Kane, is he in?" Erica said. When calling her clients she usually used the last name Kane as in Erica Kane from All My Children. She wasn't sure why really; it just seemed like a fun thing to do since she was a diva in control with lots of money.

"Hola, mi amor. Como está?"

"I need you to do me a favor. I know this might sound a little strange but I was wondering if you would be able to make a trip up to New York. Don't worry I will cover your travel expenses and it will only be for a couple of days. Can you do it?"

"Sure. But what is this for?" Jordon said in his thick Cuban accent. Erica went on to explain her reasoning and she could hear him smiling through the phone. "OK, sounds easy enough. Besides, after all the fun we had on that cruise, I would do anything for you."

"Thank you, baby. You're always so good to me," Erica said smiling from ear to ear. She also had fond memories of their time together on the trip. Victor had been falling off big time and Erica made good use of the time she spent alone. "OK, so I will make the reservations and send you your itinerary at some point today."

"OK Mamita."

"See you in two weeks!" Erica said smiling.

"I can't wait."

Erica hung up the phone and was excited with anticipation. Step three, she thought and smiled. Suddenly her mind wandered back to her time on the cruise. This had only been the second cruise she and the girls had attended, but because of their quick success, they were treated like movie stars. One evening while sailing to St. Thomas, Erica had wandered away from a party and stood quietly on deck to watch the gorgeous clear, blue ocean and star filled sky.

"Beautiful isn't it?" came a sexy Latino voice from behind her. Erica jumped slightly, startled since she hadn't heard him approaching. When she turned around, all she could do was stare. Standing in front of her had to be the most beautiful man she had ever seen. Jordon was about five-foot-ten, and 190 pounds of pure muscle. He was a beautiful golden complexion from spending hours in the sun both on the cruise and at his home in Miami. Jordon had wavy jet black hair and eyes that were a mixture of green and hazel. He stood about five feet away from her in a white linen suite, with his shirt unbuttoned, looking like a GQ model.

"Yes it is," Erica finally managed, right before she finished off her Sex on the Beach in one gulp. The two of them spent the rest of the evening conversing under the stars and ended the night buck wild and naked in Jordon's suite. They spent the rest of the trip almost attached at the hip, behind Ty's back of course. Erica didn't want to mess up anything just in case Ty had actually started catching feelings, but she couldn't deny her interest in Jordon who was just as successful, if not more, than Ty.

Jordon had a very lucrative textile business in Miami and Los Angeles and used the credit card hustle to get it. He had come to America only five years prior and had gotten introduced to the game six months after that. With the money he was making, he was not only able to get his citizenship in a hurry, but he made a good life for himself.

Victor walked through the house in only sweat pants and socks. He had just come upstairs from working out in their weight room and needed a bottle of water quickly. After getting the water from the fridge, he headed upstairs to take a shower so that he could head over to the studio to get some work done. It had already been two weeks since Ty's murder and he felt that things had died down enough to continue on as normal. He had been laying low since the shooting. As Victor entered his bedroom, he threw his towel into the dirty clothes basket and walked into Erica's closet to get her lotion. Although he had his own, he always liked to use hers when his was getting low. As he grabbed the bottle something shiny caught his eye sticking out of her purse hanging on the hook next to the shelf that held her toiletries.

Victor picked up the card and took a look.

"Tameeka Pearson?" Victor said to himself. "Who the fuck is that?" Victor studied the card for a few minutes before he decided to look through Erica's bag and see what else she had inside. He almost fell out at the bag's contents. Inside he found about four credit cards, all from different companies and with different names and signatures on them. "Jazmine, Michele, Regina, Barbara? What the hell?" Victor was confused. He didn't know what to think about what he had found in his wife's purse. All he knew was that when she came home, she had some serious explaining to do. He grabbed the cards and headed over to their bed. He looked at the clock on the night table. 10:42. He knew that Erica was probably out jogging, so he thought he'd give her some time before he called her cell phone. Victor tossed the cards in his drawer and jumped in the shower. He wanted to be fully prepared when she returned.

Erica jogged into the house at about twenty minutes after eleven. She had had a nice refreshing jog and was counting down the minutes for Jordon's arrival. She took the steps two at a time and almost jumped out of her skin when she saw Victor sitting on the bed, fully dressed with a crazed look on his face.

"Why the hell are you sitting there looking crazy?" Erica asked, getting her things together for a shower.

"Oh nothing, Tameeka. I mean Regina, or is it Barbara?" Erica's expression changed. Instead of confronting Victor, she acted as if he was no longer talking and continued getting her things together. As she stepped into her closet, Victor was close behind.

"Hellllo! I know you hear me. What the fuck is going on E?" Victor yelled.

"OK calm down. Listen, I'm sweaty as hell and funky. Can I at least jump in the shower and when I come out I promise you I'll tell you everything. OK?"

"Whatever. Hurry your ass up!" Victor fumed as he resumed his spot on the bed while Erica got herself together.

After Erica's shower, she got Sariyah and the three of them sat out on the deck.

"OK. I'm listening. What's up?"

Erica took a deep breath and laid it on him thick. She was actually quite honest with Victor and told him the entire story from start to finish of how she got into the game. The only difference between her story and the truth was that she replaced all of Ty's involvement with Jordon. Victor sat wide-eyed with his mouth open. Erica wasn't sure if he was more surprised at how she was able to do all of this behind his back, or because she was bringing in a half a million dollars with every shipment.

"Look Victor, I didn't want to have to do this behind your back, but I knew you would give me shit if you had known what I was doing. I know how you are and you always feel like you have to protect me. That's one of the things I love most about you. But I saw this as a once in a lifetime opportunity. In all honesty I think you should join my hustle. You, Twan, Jerod and a bunch of your other trusted peoples. The game is too dangerous and there's only but so long that you can stay on top before shit goes downhill. I need you V. We need you," she said holding the baby close to her chest. "If you get in this with me, we could be pulling even more money a month. We could get a bigger and better studio and you could help me start my restaurant. Or you could start your own for all I care. This is a great thing Victor and it's much safer than the drug game. Cops aren't always hanging over your shoulders, corner boys ain't trying to get at you. You hearing me V?" Erica asked, as she grabbed his chin and forced him to look into her eyes. She pulled him in for a kiss on the lips.

"I want to meet this cat," Victor said.

"OK, when?"

"As soon as possible. After we sit down and talk, I'll decide what I want to do."

"OK. I'll set it up. He's very busy, so I'm sure it won't be until tomorrow. Plus you remember I have that thing to go to tonight with one of my clients in the city, so I'll probably just get a room out there so I won't have to travel home so late."

"Yeah aight. Just make sure you set that up," Victor said calmly. She knew Victor wanted in. She could tell by the expression on his face as he sat there deep in thought. Step four, Erica thought as she smiled and bounced Sariyah around on her lap.

Erica was on her way to Manhattan by 7:00pm. Jordon's flight had come in around 3, so she knew that he was probably settled and waiting for her when she arrived. She got to the Waldorf at about 7:45 and checked her make-up before she grabbed her overnight bag and stepped out of her new automotive upgrade, the BMW X5. The bellhop took her bags and led her up to her suite, right down the hall from Jordon. She knew that she probably wouldn't be sleeping there at all, but she had to get the room just in case Victor decided to check on her. She freshened up and unpacked her Simone Perele negligee and some six inch stiletto heels that matched perfectly with her outfit. She swooped her hair into a tight bun and got dressed.

Erica called Victor to let him know that she had arrived safely and that she would give him a call the next day. She put on her long black trench coat, and sashayed down the hallway to Jordon's room. She tapped lightly on his door and within seconds, she stood eye to eye with him. He didn't say anything. Instead, he pulled her into his room and shut the door. This was what Erica had been waiting for since July and now she'd have him for two weeks.

The meeting went well between Victor, Jordon and Erica. Victor hung on to Jordon's every word and it took everything in Erica to keep from leaping across the table and into her Latin God's arms. Jordon was so convincing that even she had started to believe what he was saying. It hadn't even been a month after the meeting before Victor had rallied up his men to get down with Erica's hustle. She purposefully left her girls out of the picture, just to keep things smooth with Twan and Tracy. She knew he would have been more upset about it than Victor had been and didn't want to cause any static for her girl.

Once it was confirmed that Victor's crew would be joining the game, Erica called a meeting to get everyone on the same page. Kim and Crystal flew in to attend the function.

The meeting was held in a hotel room at the Hotel Pennsylvania and Erica laid down her hustle. Of course she didn't tell them that she was making the plates, but she did sell herself as the distributor. She spoke about the people that she targeted and told them to make lists and do the same. She had to make sure that they understood what her hustle was all about and how easy it was to make money as long as they proceeded with caution. The meeting ended well and Victor had to admit his girl was very smart. He couldn't wait to get started and anticipated all the money that he and his team could make.

Erica was in heaven. She finally had control of the situation.

Chapter 19

Three years had passed and the Davis Family were millionaires. They had started a restaurant and a clothing store, and Victor's label had picked up distribution with Sony Music Group. They had bought another house in Florida and in Los Angeles and had more cars than Funkmaster Flex. Erica had also given birth to another little girl named Mia and she felt that her family was now complete.

Victor was loving his new hustle and had to agree that Erica's game was a lot safer than his. He never imagined having this much money and was finally happy at how much his life had changed. Because of all the money they had acquired, Victor thought that it would be best to install an extravagant security system around their home. He had purchased four state of the art security cameras for the house and had them stashed away in the basement. The only thing left to do was call the people to have them installed and set up the monitors and other equipment in the house. Victor thought he had made a good investment, but didn't realize that this new purchase would be the end of life as he knew it.

It was an Easter Sunday. Victor and Erica had planned to have an Easter egg hunt for the girls .It was a sunny day; spring was coming into full form. Erica strolled outside on the front porch to get some air, taking notice and admiring the grounds of her fabulous three story Mediterranean style home. It was just perfect. Everything in the home was state of the art…. that broad from the Jetson's had nothing on her. The mansion had robotic appliances, plasma flat screen televisions mounted in every room, including all six bathrooms and custom made imports from all over the globe, seven bedrooms, terrace level basement three car garage and playground out back which, would rival any park facility. It was just like or better than most homes of MTV cribs.

Although, it was a holiday, Erica could not help feeling the need to make this day extra special for the girls. She was on a mission, planting eggs all around the lawn as the kids were playing on the playground. Victor was sitting on the second story deck talking on the cell phone telling a couple of their friends to bring their kids over for the egg hunt. "Victor get your ass down here and help me. Either help me plant eggs around the house or come watch the kids on the playground. Victor yelled back, "Erica I'm coming, I coming".

* * *

At about 3:30 in the next morning on an abnormally chilly night, Erica was awakened out of her sleep. For some reason she had been twisting and turning all night and decided to get up. She opened her eyes and looked around. Victor was sleeping peacefully next to her. She remembered the lovemaking that they had made just hours before she drifted off to sleep and smiled. Suddenly she heard Mia crying through the baby monitor and knew that she was ready for a bottle.

Erica got up and grabbed her robe from the lounge chair across the room. She made her way downstairs and into the kitchen to boil some water to heat up a bottle. For some reason she had this strange feeling in her gut, but brushed it off. She looked out the window of the kitchen to see if she saw anyone. Bitch, calm the hell down, you're just being paranoid, she told herself as she walked through the house and into the living room. All the riches her and Victor had acquired made Erica slightly paranoid every now and then. She'd worked so hard for this it was normal to be mindful of those who would try to take it away. She looked out all the windows but noticed nothing out of the ordinary.

Erica went back into the kitchen and filled Mia's bottle with milk and placed it into the hot water. She grabbed a bottled-water for herself out of the refrigerator and walked up the stairs with the baby's bottle in hand. She peaked into Sariyah's room quickly and saw that her angel was sleeping peacefully. She couldn't believe how much she had grown over the years and smiled at how much she looked and acted like herself when she was a little girl. She closed Sariyah's door and walked to the other end of the hall to a wailing Mia.

"OK mommy's baby. Don't cry. Mommy's got you," she cooed, as she picked up the crying child. She rocked her back and forth as she walked back into her bedroom.

"Is my baby oK?" Victor asked, still half asleep.

"Yeah, she's just hungry. Right booka?" Erica said. She quickly popped the bottle into Mia's mouth and laid her head back on the pillow as she fed her. Erica was still tired and almost fell asleep while feeding the baby. She jumped awake when she heard Mia's little voice. When she looked down, and noticed that Mia had already finished drinking the bottle and was playing around with the nipple. Erica sat the bottle on her night stand and went to burp the baby. As soon as Mia burped, she started to fall back to sleep. Erica laid the baby down between her and Victor and fixed her pillows to return to her own slumber.

As Erica fell back to sleep, Victor got up to use the bathroom and get himself something to drink. As he entered the kitchen he heard something rustling in the bushes behind the house. He peaked out of the picture window but didn't see anything. He got a glass out of the cabinet and poured himself some orange juice. BOOM! Victor dropped his glass of juice onto the floor and ran towards the staircase. Oh shit. Tell me this isn't happening, Victor thought to himself as he ran across the house. Just as he made it to the staircase, he was tackled by two men in FBI attire.

"You're not going anywhere!" The officer screamed out. "Who else is in the house?"

"Just my wife, two daughters and the nanny," Victor said. He knew he was screwed and wondered if Erica was oK. Victor was out of his element he could not deal with these men in black shit. This type of heat is what the game brings. Erica had seen him outsmart DEA and ATF agents. Half of the shit that he had been accused to have allegedly done, could be visualized in a video game much like Grand Theft Auto. All of that Victorwas undaunted.

Upstairs, Erica jumped awake from the loud sound. She looked over and only saw her sleeping baby. Where is Victor? She thought to herself.

"Oh no!" Erica got out of the bed carefully as to not to wake the baby, and crept down the hall to the stairs. She saw Victor in handcuffs at the bottom of the steps and heard the heavy steps of the officers as they roamed the house. Erica knew she had little time before they would come upstairs. She hurried back to the room and scooped Mia into her arms. As she tried to walk to the other side of the hall towards Sariyah's room, an agent approached her from behind.

"I don't think so. Come back this way," he said in a calm voice, and led her back to her bedroom. Mia had awakened from all the noise and started crying in Erica's arms. As she tried to rock the baby back to sleep, the nanny came rushing into her bedroom and onto the bed.

"Oh my God, what's going on?" she asked in a panic. I can't believe this bitch is in here in my bed, when my daughter is in her bedroom alone. I am so firing this bitch when this shit is over, Erica thought to herself as she gave Frances the evil eye.

"Detective there's been some kind of mistake," Erica said in a calm voice. "What is the meaning of all this?"

"Clever Ms. Payne, very clever. As if you don't already know," he said smiling. Erica wanted to slap the smug look off his face.

"Sir with all due respect, I don't have time for games. It's the middle of the night and you motherfuckers come charging into my home with no warrant, waking up my chil—" The detective threw the warrant into her face before she could finish her last sentence. Erica grabbed the document out of his hand and began reading. Before she could finish looking over the document, she heard Sariyah crying in her room.

"Look, my baby is crying in the room down the hall. Can I at least go and get her?"

"Sure Ms. Payne."

"Davis. My last name is Davis, but I'm sure you knew that already."

"I'll have one of these nice officers here escort you to your child. By the way, my name is Agent Whitmore." Erica ignored him and held

Mia tight, as she walked cautiously down the hallway to get Sariyah. When she entered the room, Sariyah was sitting up in her little Barbie bed crying her eyes out.

"Come on Riyah. Come over here to mommy," Erica said, standing over her daughter's bed. The appearance of the officers scared Sariyah even more and she started crying harder, causing Mia to cry as well.

"Look can I at least call my mother and have her come to get my babies? They don't need to be around all of this craziness, it's scaring them," Erica said.

"Actually that doesn't sound like a bad idea," Agent Whitmore said. The more Erica looked at him, the more he reminded her of Agent Grisam from CSI. Erica picked up the cordless phone and dialed her mother.

"Ma, sorry to wake you but we have a bit of a problem here at the house. Do you think you could come pick up the kids? I'll have their stuff ready for you at the bottom of the stairs." Dorothy could tell by her daughter's voice what was going on. At 4:00 in the morning, with their lifestyle, she knew it could only be one thing.

"Oh dear Lord, baby I'm on my way," Dorothy said before hanging up the phone. With Erica's wealth, she had bought both her aunt and mother homes in Long Island so they could be closer to her.

"Agent Whitmore, since I'm being held hostage up here, can I just get my children ready? My mother will be here shortly to get them."

"You're reaching Ms. Payne, but I'll allow the officer to escort you while you get your children's things together. Just hurry up." As Erica packed a few things for the girls and dressed them, she wondered what was going on with Victor downstairs. Aside from the sound of the agents and officers walking through the house, things seemed pretty quiet. By the time Erica had finished with the girls, the doorbell rang. The agent contacted one of the officers downstairs about Dorothy's arrival on his walkie-talkie. Erica was escorted downstairs where she placed the baby bags on the banister, on top of a bag that held the plates for the next shipment. She did this so smoothly that none of the officers noticed what she had been doing.

"Thanks Ma for coming to get them," Erica said, giving her mother a hug. Dorothy took the girls, and threw all the bags over her shoulders.

"I hope you all know that there's a serious lawsuit coming your way for harassing my family like this!" Dorothy said to the agents as she exited the house. Once they had left, Erica was placed in handcuffs and moved to the living room where Victor was being held. He looked like he had gotten into an altercation with the police because his clothes were all twisted and he was bleeding from his forehead and lip. Erica's heart ached. She wanted to reach out for him and hold him tight and tell him that everything was going to be oK. But she knew that wasn't going to happen.

"Once again Agent, why are you people here?"

"Oh good, let's get this over with. I would like to return home to my own family. Ms. Payne—"

"Mrs. Davis!"

"My how silly of me? Mrs. Davis, we have been watching your husband's activities for years. We know all about his drug cartel and his dealings with the young man that was murdered a few years ago, but we didn't have any hard core evidence. It was more like hearsay. Although we didn't have a lot to go on, we figured that if we just waited patiently Mr. Davis here would slip up and boy were we right.

About a week ago on the day of April 19, your husband was spotted at this electronics store in Manhattan purchasing some pretty expensive security equipment." The agent pulled out some photos of Victor in the store that had been taken from a security camera.

"Now of course this purchase doesn't seem strange at first, but for some reason after the purchase was made, the clerk thought something fishy was going on with your husband. So out of a pure hunch, she called the credit card company and asked them to trace the card. When they did, she noticed that the account number had been reported stolen out in Colorado. That's when they alerted us."

"Racist bitches! Just because a Black man makes an expensive purchase, you motherfuckers thought there was something suspicious about it? You racists pricks! If that had been a white man, I bet nobody would have thought something was wrong with that!" Erica screamed out.

"You fucked up big time Victor and we were here to catch you. We found the gun used in the murders at the club," Agent Whitmore said, ignoring Erica's outburst. Victor shook his head and looked at Erica. The tears started streaming down her eyes. She knew that this was the end for them and her husband going to prison.

"Put some clothes on Ms. Payne. You're both coming with us."

Erica and Victor had spent hours at the police station, before a request for bail had been made by their lawyer. Luckily since it was a week night, Erica was able to post bail later that day. Unfortunately things weren't so lucky for Victor. The court denied his bail because they thought that he might be a flight risk.

Erica worked hard with her family and her lawyers to find any possible loop holes in the case against Victor. Her lawyer had informed her that Victor was taking sole responsibility for the business. His lawyer advised him to come clean with the feds. He could get his charges brought down and his sentence lessened. He didn't know what he was going to do without Erica. She was his everything. While Victor was being held in jail, Erica visited him frequently to give him updates from their attorney. Victor told her that he would protect her with everything he had because he didn't want his girls to grow up without their mother. They cried in each other's arms and Erica told him that she had his back and would make sure the lawyer did everything in his power to help Victor.

Their attorney, Mr. White, thought that it would be best for Victor to plead guilty to the charges. The evidence that the prosecution had against him was too strong. If Victor tried to plead not guilty, and was found guilty, he would spend almost double the amount of time in prison than he would if he were to plead guilty and take the plea. After taking a few days to make a decision, Victor opted for the plea.

Unfortunately they couldn't get in front of a judge for at least three months, and Victor had to spend this time in jail. The courts had once again denied his request to post bail. Victor almost lost his mind during the three months. Erica asked Tracy, Kim and Crystal to come and stay with her for support and to help her with her girls.

Finally the time had come for Victor's trial. Erica dropped her girls off at her aunt Kat's and headed over to the courthouse in Manhattan with Tracy, Crystal and Kim in tow. When they entered the courtroom, Erica spotted a few friendly faces. Twan was there, along with Black and a few of Victor's boys. Dorothy was also in attendance and was sitting in the second row on the defendant's side of the room. Erica took her seat next to her mother and took a deep breath. She couldn't believe that in one night her world could be changed forever.

"All rise," the bailiff said. Everyone stood to honor the judge and the trial began. Because Victor agreed to a plea, they didn't have to wait. The judge would review the evidence, consider the plea and then sentence Victor. Erica shook uncontrollably as she waited for Victor's sentence. He looked back at her to see tears in her eyes and she mouthed the words "I love you" to him before he turned around. He couldn't stand to see her cry and it was tearing him apart knowing she was scared. Erica couldn't imagine what it would be like for Victor in jail and her insides shifted as she thought of all the possible things that could happen to him in the prison system.

Dorothy noticed her daughter's discomfort and thought back to the many times she had been in the same position with Gregory. Awaiting the court's decision was one of the hardest things she ever had to endure, and she knew exactly how hurt her daughter was feeling. Pushing back her own tears, both for her son-in-law and for her late husband, Dorothy held Erica tight and braced herself for the sentence.

"After reviewing all the evidence before me and taking into consideration the plea that Mr. White, the defendant's lawyer, has presented to me, I hereby sentence you, Victor Anthony Davis, to fifteen years at the Federal Correctional Institution at Fort Dix, New Jersey for credit card fraud, murder, running a drug cartel, and racketeering. Do you have anything to say before you're taken away?"

Erica wailed and fell into her mother's arms as the judge finished his sentencing. Victor put his head down and thought for a moment. He couldn't look at Erica right now. If he did, he knew he would break down.

"Yes I would like to address the court," Victor said holding himself up with the back of his chair. "I would just like to thank my wife for always being by my side no matter what bullshit I brought her way. I love you so much baby," Victor said choking on his words as he glanced back to Erica who was in shambles. "I'd also like to ask if I can hug my wife one last time before I'm taken away."

"Very well Mr. Davis," the judge said. Erica managed to stand and was led to the front of the courtroom by an officer. As soon as she reached Victor, she fell into his arms crying hysterically.

"It's going to be OK baby. We're going to get through this OK? You have to be strong for me and for our babies. They need you now. Just remember I love you baby girl and you always have my heart." Victor took one last look at Erica and wiped her tears from her eyes and placed a soft kiss on her lips. After one last hug, Victor was taken away.

Erica left the courtroom with her girls and her mother by her side. Although she was a millionaire, what good was all that money when you had no one to share it with? Erica got into her BMW and placed her head on the steering wheel. What am I going to do now? Erica thought to herself as she started her car and thought about the new chapter being started in her life. Game over.

Epilogue

Erica woke up to the sound of the waves crashing against the shore outside her window. It had been six months since Victor's conviction and she still had trouble getting used to waking up alone. Erica sat up and looked over at her two sleeping girls and smiled. Everything she had done and will continue to do was for them and always would be. She promised herself that when she had children, she would be the best mother she knew how to be.

Erica walked down her spiral staircase and into the kitchen to brew a fresh cup of coffee. Damn I got to remember to book mommy's flight today, she thought to herself as she looked through her bills on the table. Erica picked up her steaming cup of coffee, grabbed the telephone and her bills and headed outside to handle her business on the patio. She looked at her house and smiled. She had accomplished so much for herself in the past five years and she still had so much more to do in her new life in Los Angeles, California. Erica had closed all of her businesses in New York, sold her house and all her cars except for two and cleaned out her bank account and safes and moved to California. Ring.

Erica looked at the caller ID and answered on the third ring.

"Hello."

"Ms. Davis. How are you liking the new digs?"

"I'm liking them just fine but how many times do I have to tell you that I am a married woman and to address me as such," Erica said smiling.

"Well shit, if that's the case I better watch out for my wife. I couldn't imagine if she was as cold-blooded as you."

"I'll take that as a compliment and give you a word of advice."

"Advice too? Wow you must like me, seeing as though you've helped me so much over the years."

"Eh you're OK, but Agent Whitmore, never underestimate a woman's power. Men use us and abuse us, cheat on us and disrespect us and think that we're just supposed to suck all that shit up in the name of love. But after a while, a woman gets tired and has to do what she has to do to survive, if not for herself than for her offspring. Be kind to your wife detective. Treat her with respect and never cheat on her, and please never lay a hand on her."

"No worries, Ms. Payne, she's in good hands. Now let me go get back to my detective work and you go and do whatever it is that you do with yourself these days and remember, if your mind happens to think of some more names to go along with your husband's feel free to give me a call."

"Sure thing. Have a good one and thanks for everything." Erica hung up her phone and looked out onto the ocean. She didn't feel an ounce of regret for what she had done to Victor. She never asked him for much, just to be honest and treat her with respect but instead she was cheated on, slapped around, spat on and lied to over and over again.

Not too long after she had given birth to Sariyah, she found out about Victor's affairs with some hood rat named Toya, a stripper named Alexis and his other baby's mother Chante, who have given birth to his son a year after Sariyah was born. And to make matters worse, Chante was the same girl that Erica fought in high school for messing around with Victor. Erica laughed at how stupid she had been to have fought all the girls that came Victor's way, just to have him continue to cheat on her. Erica wanted to let Victor know that she had found out about his extramarital affairs, but thought best to hit him where it would hurt most.

Erica thought about all the people who had hurt her in her life. Gregory, who had started it all, was gone. Ty, who had plotted to use her to get back at Victor, was dead courtesy of Juju and the Fort Greene crew, and Victor who had betrayed her trust and broken her heart into a thousand pieces was gone as well. Anyone who had hurt her was now out of her life.

The hit at the club went perfectly. Erica had called the club a few hours after talking to Ty and asked him to come let her in through the emergency exit. Believing that she was only trying to keep their affair a secret, Ty didn't suspect a thing. At least, not until he was met at the door by the barrel of Juju's 9mm against his forehead. What happened next could only be described as a blood bath.

Outnumbered by at least a four to one ratio, Ty and his crew didn't have time to even drawn their weapons before the VIP was redecorated with fragments of their collective brains and vital organs. JuJu even went the extra mile, firing his sawed off shotgun into most of the bodies at point blank range countless times. The fact that one of Ty's boys lived long enough to reach the hospital was an incredible feat. Erica initially thought JuJu had dropped the ball, but was relieved when the only survivor died in hours later in surgery.

Ty's bullet ridden body was beyond the need of a closed casket funeral. Follow Erica's instruction, Juju gave him far more attention the others. Even cremation would be difficult considering the majority of his body were shredded beyond recognition. All things considered he still may had gotten off easy as Victor would be behind bars for the rest of his life.

Erica's train of thought was broken when Sariyah came running out of the house to greet her mother.

"Mommy, mommy" she yelled jumping into her mother's arms.

"Yes baby."

"Mia's awake, mommy."

"OK let's go get her. I'll race you," she said as she jogged into the house with her five-year-old trotting in front of her. Suddenly her doorbell rang.

"You go upstairs and keep Mia company. Mommy will be right up," she said walking towards the door.

"Bitch, don't make me hurt you," Tracy said walking into the door, followed by Crystal, and Kim.

"What the hell are you talking about?"

"Who knows? Where's breakfast, I'm hungry. We have some shopping to do for the Halloween party and don't forget that everyone's coming out here so we got to have this place spic and span," Tracy said getting comfortable. Kim and Crystal walked downstairs to put their things in the guest room.

"Do you think he knows?" Tracy whispered to Erica.

"No. And I intend to keep it that way. Besides who would tell him? You know I don't play that shit. Anyone who crosses me will get got."

"I feel you girl. Damn I can't believe you actually got away with this. You gotta let me know how you come up with this shit."

"It's all a part of the game my dear. You just got to stay alert and stay ahead and never trust anybody."

"Speaking of trust, what's up with you and that Cuban dude?"

"That's my papi. He'll be here for the party and I can't wait," Erica said as she and Tracy slapped a high-five. Crystal and Kim came upstairs and helped her get the girls up and ready.

They had a day of shopping ahead of them and a hell of a party to plan.

Discussion Questions

1. What was the real reasoning behind Gregory discarding all of Erica's belongings?

2. Why didn't the Payne family ever move out of Fort Greene projects?

3. Why was Erica so rebellious? What would have made a difference in her life?

4. Why wasn't Monica as the older sister more crazed about her family situation?

5. Why do you think Erica moved in with Victor instead of moving in with her Aunt or Tracy?

6. Since Tracy was the one that knew Ty and already had the card connect, why wasn't she the mastermind of the operation? Do you think she was ever upset that Erica took over?

7. Why did Erica and Victor move forward with the wedding as planned when they had so much conflict and distrust in their relationship?

8. Why was Victor sleeping with Toya and other woman, when he claimed to have loved Erica so much?

9. What do you think Erica learned at the end of the book?

10. Do you think after Erica's experiences with men, she will ever fully trust another?

Credit 101

Educating our youth on credit is essential. Due to the "bling, bling" era, most people have a much distorted view regarding cost and spending. More importantly, there is growing portion of society that understands very little about credit. The general public needs to know that credit can be beneficial or misuse can greatly hinder personal financial growth. The information that I want to share will be useful to everyone. However, the youth is our posterity and they are the ones who can be the most amenable to make a difference in the future.

I did realize the importance of financial responsibility during my child because I grew up "hood rich". The term refers to the perceived status quo that is prevalent in the inner city where being fiscally responsible is secondary to following buying trends. Like most of my peers, my desires and indulgences were without regard to cost or price; notwithstanding, the discipline and sacrifice involved in maintaining credit. I have experienced financial disaster because of my ignorance of how to protect and maintain good credit, which would lead me to take advantage of the same flaws in others. The fact of the matter is that in America, all of us "Charge it to the Game", in one way or another!

I have taken on many roles in my life, but being a mother what I am most proud of. This is why I have compiled the following information, which I have shared with my 17 year old daughter. I vowed upon my release from prison to educate my children and their peers on how to grow to be smart consumers. I want them to know how credit will affect them for the rest of their lives.

The story of Erica Payne is a fictional story. However, my life experiences are very much real. I am not a credit counselor, nor do, I claim to be a fraud expert. I am a person who has regretfully, committed fraudulent offences. It is my desire to give back by the sharing the same tips about credit I give to my own friends and family. I pray that you are enlightened by the information.

This information about credit is by no means a comprehensive guide to prevent credit fraud. The truth is you can't prevent it you can only prepare yourself, in the event that you become a victim of credit card fraud or identity theft. Trust me; neither your name nor your social security number is needed for you to be a casualty of credit fraud or Identity theft.

I encourage every reader of this book to examine their own uses of credit. For instance, be proactive in evaluated your buying habits. Don't use credit as a convenience. Moreover, regularly evaluate your banking and credit card statements. You need to know if there is a mistake or mayhem regarding your account activity. Your credit and identity are too important to ignore. You can always regain control and recover from debit death, credit chaos or imposters of identify, if you are armed with the right information. I hope this information can be helpful to you. Thank you, for reading my story. For more information on author Michele Fletcher log onto www.therealmichelefletcher.com.

Debit or Death of Your Credit

For years we have been told to shred important documents as well as old and expired credit cards. However, this in addition to many other common sense prevention tips drilled into our brains is not and will never be enough. As long as we as a society continue to use not just credit cards, especially debit cards on a daily basis for minimal items like gas, food and groceries, we are subject to becoming victims. The reality is that the same technology that makes our lives easier makes us vulnerable to those that steal identities and commit credit card fraud.

THINK ABOUT IT! You never really know who is on the other end of any given credit card transaction. It doesn't end with the low level clerk who processes your sale. Every time your credit card is swiped, your information goes out into cyberspace. Although this information is usually encrypted in some form or another, the certainty is that for every level of security; there is someone with the knowledge of undermining that security.

Unfortunately, there are people who make a living deciphering this information and use it for unscrupulous purposes. Criminals insert memory chips into the keypad terminals customers use at retail counters, gas stations and restaurants to record data. The only way to stop credit card fraud or reduce it is to become less dependent on credit cards and the illusion that they make our lives easier. Aside from the benefits of increasing credit scores, you gamble with the risk of becoming a victim of credit card fraud and identity theft every time you swipe a card.

What About Fraud Protection?

Don't be lured into a false sense of security, thinking that this will protect you from getting hit. Think of fraud protection programs as an insurance policy that will decrease the amount of time that you will need to recover from fraud. Sure, you are told that your credit cards are insured and that any fraudulent purchases will be reimbursed, but many times the burden of proof is on you. In addition, you suffer the inconvenience of being without your money until any investigation is completed. Again, in the end was it worth it for a pack of gum or a soda? For this reason, I definitely advocate getting fraud protection because it will provide fraud victims with a form of advocacy and it could make the difference in whether you will be able to shop next month or next year. Statistics released Tuesday by the Federal Trade Commission show that identity theft continues to be the top fraud-related complaint, accounting for 39 percent of all complaints filed in 2004.

According to the report, titled National and State Trends in Fraud and Identity Theft, the total number of complaints grew 17 percent from 542,378 in 2003 to 635,173 in 2004. The findings also reveal that another top fraud-related complaint was Internet auctions, which made up for 16 percent of all complaints registered last year. Others include shop-at-home/catalog sales at 8 percent, Internet services and computer complaints at 6 percent, and foreign money offers with 6 percent.

Topping the list at 28 percent as the most common type of identity theft was credit card fraud, followed by phone and utility related fraud with 19 percent, bank fraud at 18 percent, and employment fraud at 13 percent. The FTC says consumers reported total fraudulent losses of $547 million last year, with the median loss http://www.crime-research.org/news/05.02.2005/943/ Astounding? Yes, but only you have the ability to curtail fraudulent activities on your accounts and theft of your identity.

Are you really reading your statement?

When you get your credit card bill each month, read the statement carefully you should:

- check the amounts of each listed transaction against your card and receipts;
- spot any charges you did not make;
- study the fees; and
- note any unjustified fees.

I know it may sound tedious but it's worth the time and efforts to make sure that you are fully aware of every charge that has been made with your card every month. If you haven't already, set up a regular place—a box on the bookshelf, a folder in the den, the kitchen draw … any place where you put your credit card receipts when you get back from traveling, shopping or going out. Then, schedule time each month when you open your credit card statements and connect each receipt to each posted item (and read the small print at the bottom or on the back of each statement). You might be amazed at how many times consumers' credit cards are charged for things they didn't authorize.

Online Accounts

Most credit accounts now have online access. With these accounts, you should check for any activity on a daily basis. Many accounts will give you real time information. In other words, if you purchase an item in a store, it will show up on the online access within minutes. This way you can be sure that any purchases listed were made by you. If you spot something that does not look familiar, investigate it as soon as possible. This way the bank or Credit Company can take action immediately.

Financial institutions

If you suspect that you are victim of identity theft or you need to report a stolen credit card, contact your creditor or bank immediately. It's best to use the phone number listed on the back of your credit card or on your account statements. In case you don't have access to those numbers, here is the identity theft contact information for some of the most common financial institutions:

Advanta 1-800-705-7255
American Express 1-800-528-4800
Bank of America 1-800-848-6090
Bank of New York 1-800-225-5269
Capital One 1-800-955-7070
Chase 1-800-648-9911
Chevron Gas Card 1-800-243-8799
Citibank 1-800-790-7206
Discover 1-800-347-2683
HSBC 1-800-975-4722
MasterCard 1-800-MC-ASSIST
Orchard Bank 1-800-283-8373
PNC Bank 1-888-762-2265
Providian 1-800-356-0011
VISA 1-800-847-2911
Wachovia 1-800-922-4684
Washington Mutual 1-800-788-7000
Wells Fargo 1-866-867-5568

Credit bureaus

Contact one of the three credit bureaus to have a 90-day fraud alert placed on all three of your credit files.

Equifax 1-800-525-6285
www.equifax.com
P.O. Box 740241 Atlanta, GA 30374

Experian 1-888-EXPERIAN
www.experian.com
P.O. Box 95323 Allen, TX 75013

TransUnion 1-800-680-7289
www.transunion.com
P.O. Box 2000 Chester, PA 19022

The following are also some interesting links and resources that you can add in your Credit 101 education:

www.credit.com
www.studentmarket.com
www.jumpstart.org
www.communitycorner.org
www.moneyinstructor.com
All information above can be found online also by doing a Google search for Credit 101.

LA'FEMME
LA' FEMME FATALE' PRODUCTIONS

DC BLOOD BROTHERS

A NOVEL BY VIYO LANCE

D.C. BLOOD BROTHERS
By Viyo Lance

"Oh Franklin, I'm so scared I can hardly breathe". "You'll be fine Millie", Franklin reassured his wife as he patted her right hand. It bothered him seeing his wife of two years go through so much pain and not be able to offer anything more than the comfort of his words. "Nurse, when will the doctor get here?" he asked growing impatient. "Dr. Wilson will be here momentarily Mr. Jenkins".

Franklin looked down at his wife, who was squeezing his left hand so tight it was becoming numb. Beads of sweat appeared on Millie's forehead out of nowhere. "Here, let me get that for you, baby". A smile came to the nurse's face, as she wiped Millie's forehead. The nurse watched the couple, both at the age of 25, go through the miracle of birth with their first child. A slight beep, constantly repeating itself could be heard along with the rain that just started tapping the window.

"Franklin, I can't believe we're about to have a child". "How do you feel, are you nervous?"

"A little, just a little," he lied, with his stomach already in the air.

Franklin hated hospitals, the cold air, the sterile smell; the obnoxious rhythm of machine's supporting or tracking life beeping over and over and the cold hard look of all these metal contraptions. The hospital was a human garage of some sort, Franklin thought.

"Well folks!" Doctor Wilson said loudly as he clapped his hands together entering the room, "Let's get this show on the road." "Nurse, how far are Millie's contractions?"

"Every 2 ½ minutes now Dr. Wilson."

"O.K. Millie relax, we've talked about this numerous times, just do you're breathing exercises, O.K.?"
Millie nodded in agreement, and then looked to her husband who was scared as hell.

"Franklin, can you say a silent prayer for our baby and me?"

Franklin closed his eyes and prayed to God with all of his heart and soul. "Lord, please give us a healthy baby and comfort my wife Lord, in the name of Jesus, Amen." When his eyes re-opened, Dr. Wilson was positioning himself between Millie's legs.

"Alright Millie, your contractions are a minute apart, I want you to begin pushing now … push, push."

"Uuughh! Uuughh! Whew, Ooooohhhh, Uuughh" Millie sounded as if she was about to have the world's largest bowel movement!

"Good Millie, keep pushing" the doctor coaxed.

"Ah, Oh, Eeeeh! Whew!" Millie gasped for air.

"Keep pushing Millie," said Doctor Wilson, you're doing great; I can see the crown of your baby's head!"

Franklin's mouth went dry and his stomach began to turn ache as he witnessed his wife's body tearing and a tiny skull coming out of her.

"Ughh, Ahhh!" cried Millie.

"I've got it, I have him" the doctor said as he realized the sex of the child. "Would you like to cut the umbilical cord, Franklin?" In complete awe Franklin took the scissors and cut the fleshy cord without even saying a word.

Smack! Whaaa, whaaaa, whaaa, the tiny baby boy cried after the doctor slapped his butt. "Here nurse", Dr. Wilson got her attention and handed the baby off to the nurse.

"Well, hate to deliver and run but I have another couple waiting. I don't know what was in the air last November, but I've broken a record this July with births."

"Thank you doctor, thank you."

"Here you are Millie, your handsome healthy son, what's his name?"

Millie looked up at Franklin. "We're naming him Jason Parcell Jenkins", Franklin stated with his chest swollen with pride. July 3, 1974 was now the happiest day of the young couple's lives.

"Hi baby Jason."

Franklin just watched as his wife spoke to their son. "Thank you God for giving us a healthy baby." Franklin silently prayed.

4 days later……

Franklin moved with a frantic pace through his apartment, picking up clothes, carrying out containers that had accumulated since Millie had given birth to Jason only a few days ago. It had been a rough four days without his wife. She didn't know that he had lost his job because he called out the day their son was born. But, he had good news for his wife. He had found a new, better job. Working for the beer company on Blair Rd. in N.E. only paid $9.50 an hour; his new job at the Washington Post was paying a dollar and fifty cents more.

He looked to his watch – 12:45pm, almost an hour until time to pick up Millie and the baby. After washing the dishes, vacuuming, and spraying Lysol all over the two bedroom apartment, he walked the garbage down the hall to the trash shoot and he was done. He grabbed his car keys and stepped out of the door.

After making it to his car he turned to his favorite radio station, Magic 102.3FM. Music filled the air with his favorite tunes. Head bopping to everyone from the Isley Brothers' "Summer Breeze", Teddy Pendergrass's "T.K.O.", to The Whispers' "Chocolate Girl" made him feel even happier than he already was, as if that was possible. He enjoyed the pleasant ride and appreciated the humidity being low as he pulled into the parking lot of Columbia Hospital for Women. After parking, Franklin rushed inside to his wife and new born son.

Millie was patting Jason's back as she held him over her shoulder.

“Hey baby and little man, ya’ll ready to go home?” Franklin asked as he poked his head through the hospital room’s slightly ajar door.

“You know I am, the food here is so bland, and it is terrible.”

“Brrrrp”! “Ooh, there we go, there’s that burp Mommy was waiting for, good boy.”

The nurse appeared in the door way with a wheel chair, “Are we ready to go?”

“Yes, we are, but what’s that contraption for?” Millie asked anxiously.

“Oh its hospital policy Millie, don’t worry, everyone gets this treatment”, replied the nurse.

“Franklin, you go get the car, we’ll meet you downstairs. We’re going home Jason, yes we are”, she cooed.

LA'FEMME

LA'FEMME FATALE PRODUCTIONS

BLACK FIST

BEHOLD THE BLACK FIST

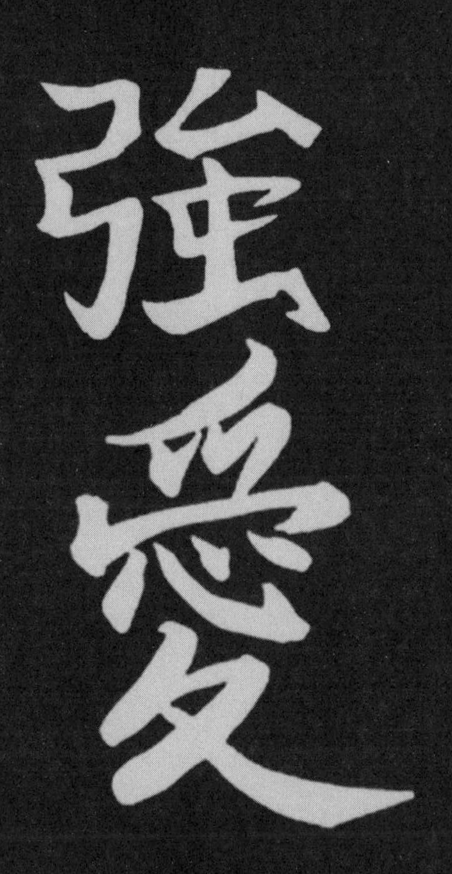

A NOVEL BY BE'N ORIGINAL

Behold The Black Fist
By BE'N ORIGINAL

12:00 PM TODAY

As I ease into position, my mind is flooded with memories of the tragic event that brought me to this isolated location that provides me with excellent concealment. And once again, rage grows within my heart with every beat. While I look through the scope of my specially modified M-16 with laser targeting and watch them enjoy what will be their last sunset, I wonder if their deaths will quench my thirst for vengeance. Maybe. Maybe not. All I know is that Aaron Jackson, William Morrison, and Michael J. Cooper Street have three things in common. They are all white men in their mid-twenties. They all took part in a crime so shameful that even the most cold-blooded convict would frown upon it and this day will be their last.

A member of the Black Fist ryu, I have killed far more than my share of men, but their deaths were simply matters of business, never personal. This, however, is as personal as it gets.

I carefully load three crossed 5.56 millimeter rounds into a magazine, blowing away any dust that might interfere with the bullets being loaded into the chamber. A crossed or starred round is when you flatten the tip of a bullet and cut two deep lines making an X in the middle. This causes the bullet to shatter into pieces upon impact with a hard object, preferably a human skull. It ensures a zero percent chance of survival, perfect for what I have in mind. These lowlifes bought themselves first class tickets on the hell express, and I'm making sure they get on board. The range finder indicates they are well within the six hundred and forty meter maximum effective range. I make my final adjustments to the weapon, aim and squeeze.

36 HOURS AGO.

Will, Mike, and Aaron were sitting at the bar of one of the city's few nightclubs drinking and talking usual shit when Will started describing the girl he had seen a few days ago in the nearby neighborhood. "Yo, she had the kinda ass Mos Def and Keith Murray were talkin' bout! She was definitely bangin'," said Will, trying way too hard to sound cool. "Did you step to her?" Mike asked. "I would have at least asked her for some head. You were probably shook, huh?" taunted Aaron laughing loudly. "Fuck you Aaron. I ain't hardly scared of no pussy. How you think you were born, stupid mutherfucker," replied Will, "in fact if I ever see that bitch again, I'm gonna do the damn thang. I think she is at the party on Catherine Street. Let's go!"

As they stumbled their drunken asses out of the club into the crowded parking lot across the street, Mike asked Will " What are you gonna do if the bitch says no?" Will replied, full of confidence with a slight grin," I ain't trying to hear no tonight. Besides, that's what you two are for. She's getting fucked she wants to or not!"

After making contingency plans for several possible and hypothetical situations, Will finally convinced them to help. They got into his car and drove to the center on the north side of town where a party was being held. Parked in a dim lit area across the street, they were easily able to observe the exit while remaining out of sight.

It was about one o'clock when the teens began to leave, and the one Will had described earlier came out. She was about 5'8", Black and Puerto Rican, with a body that was far too mature for a girl still in her teens. With full, yet firm breast and wide hips; she could very easily be mistaken for a full-grown woman, which tonight will do her more harm than good.

As she walked around the corner, she didn't notice Will's white Acura as it passed and turned into a dark alley a few houses ahead or how the driver and two passengers were staring. Surely, if she had seen the lustful glare in their eyes, she would have ran back inside the building and called the police.

But she didn't . . . until it was too late. There are no words to describe her fear when Will and Aaron grabbed her from behind as she walked pass. In spite of how hard she tried, she was easily overpowered and thrown inside the car, where Mike was prepared to gag her before she could scream. Once they managed to get her inside, they drove to an isolated location on the riverfront near Main Street, and began tearing her clothes away.

Realizing what they were about to do, she begged to be released, promising not to call the police, but her pleas were ignored by her captors who only threaten to kill her if she continued to resist. They started viciously beating her until she fully submitted to their lust, taking turns raping and sodomizing the young girl whose muffled screams for help would go unheard. She was found broken and battered eight hours later.

12:30 PM TODAY

The 5.56 millimeter round shatters as it strikes Michael forehead at over nine hundred seventy five meters per second, literally blowing most of his brain out what was once the back of his head before William or Aaron could even hear the recoil.

I fire again, this time sending a combination of lead, penile flesh, and shit flying out of a newly made six inch diameter hole in Michael's ass. He stands with his mouth wide opened as his small intestines fall to the ground while the other two marks run towards the car with hopes of escaping imminent death. But as Aaron reaches for the handle, I fire a third round about six inches below the gas cap, causing the vehicle to explode with so much force that fragments of the passenger door rip through his chest cavity, killing him instantly.

As I watch William flee the horrific scene on foot, a slight sinister smile grows across my face. You see, he doesn't know that earlier today, while he was out with his boys, I decided to stop by his apartment and left him a most unpleasant surprise. I leave nothing to chance. I only wish I could see the look on his face…

As he rushes inside, he can't help from wondering if what just took place has anything to do with what they did to the girl the other night. That's probably why he doesn't notice the once tight thin piece of fishing line that was pulled when he opened his door or the plastic spoon it was tied to, which kept two stripped wires that were wrapped around a clothespin from touching. But what does get his immediate attention is the exploding force of a well placed shaped charge that sends fire and about a hundred nails, tacks, and all the other sharp or pointed objects I could find, in his direction at over two thousand feet per second.

As he dies, smelling the scent of his burning punctured flesh, there is little doubt that he regrets ever seeing my niece…

Lá Femme Fatalé Productions
Publishing Division

Order Form

Charge it to the Game by Michele Fletcher $15.95
Shipping/handling (via U.S. Priority Mail) $4.05
Total $20.00

Purchaser Information

Name: ____

Reg #: ____

Address: ____
____

City: ____________________ State: __________________ Zip: ________

Total Number of Books Ordered: _______

For orders shipped directly to prisons Lá Femme Fatalé Productions deducts 25% off the sale price of the book. Costs are as follows:

Title of Book $11.96
Shipping/handling $4.05
Total $16.01

La' Femme Fatale' Productions
9900 Greenbelt Road
Suite E-333
Lanham , MD 20706
1-866-50-femme (33663)
www.lafemmefataleproductions.com

The Author

Located in the heart of the Baltimore-Washington corridor, just 37 miles south of the city lies Prince Georges County. A mecca for Blacks and countless African American owned businesses, it has emerged as one of the most affluent counties in the country. It is also the home of Michele A. Fletcher-- wife, mother, award winning business owner and author.

Born and raised in Brooklyn, New York, Michele had a passion for fashion, style and beauty. After graduating from high school she was determined to become part of the industry she loved so much and decided to open the first of several beauty salons she would eventually own. "I love the things that make women look and feel beautiful" she explains.

Despite being a successful business woman and upstanding member of her community, Michele lost her salons, her home and everything she owned due to her untimely arrest for fraud and was sentenced to 48 months in prison. "I have to say that it was that experience that made me a better person and gave me a stronger appreciation for life. Going to prison was the most humbling and painful process, but it transformed me into a great new person I had no idea I could be."

All this and more, particularly the lessons learned are chronicled in an action packed, street thriller, novel based on Michele's life called Charge It To The Game, under La' Femme Fatale' Publishing. With all things Michele lost, her main focus is planning a creditable new life for herself.

Michele currently lives in Prince Georges County, Maryland with her three daughters and is working on her second novel.